Santa Lucia

Santa Lucia

A Common Story

Mary Austin

Introduction by Maribel Morales

Hastings College Press | Hastings, Nebraska

Production and Proofreading
Emilie Barnes

ISBN-10: 1942885121
ISBN-13: 978-1-942885-12-2

Note on the text: This edition has been reset from the first (1908) edition. Original spelling and grammatical conventions have been maintained, except in the case of publishing errors in the first edition. The original punctuation has been maintained but updated using modern conventions (e.g., eliminating spaces around dashes).

Manufactured in the United States of America.

Text is printed on acid-free, chlorine-free paper with 30% postconsumer recycled content. Cover is printed on 100% recycled paper.

Contents

Women in America:
Marriage, Divorce, and the Emergence of the New Woman

American women have struggled for equality with men for over two centuries. In nineteenth-century America, commercial and industrial growth intensified the sexual division of labor, encouraging the separation of men's and women's spheres. White males entered the public world of business, the professions, and politics, whereas most white middle-class women remained at home, where they provided domestic, maternal, and spiritual care for their families. Barbara Welter explains that together, the attributes of "True Womanhood"—piety, purity, submissiveness, and domesticity—spelled "mother, daughter, sister, wife—woman" and complying with them was a promise of happiness and power (151). It was between 1820 and 1865 that this set of sexual stereotypes and role divisions was firmly imprinted on the American popular mind. In order to ensure its continuity the values of women's sphere were promoted in periodicals and didactic manuals on housekeeping, marriage, and child rearing, stressing the importance of domesticity. However, during the late nineteenth and early twentieth centuries, marriages in the United States began to collapse at an unprecedented rate. The divorce rate skyrocketed between 1867 and 1927 so that by the 1920s one in six marriages was being dissolved. Although marriage was considered the "greatest moment of a girl's life," the satisfactions of married life for the woman "depended largely on the adequacy of her husband, just as his happiness depended in considerable part upon his wife" (Riegel 1, 2). Many reformers and feminists advocated for divorce despite some critics who disapproved, lamenting the "collapse of America's most sacred institution, the home" (May 3). In the nineteenth century, the most common grounds for divorce were the failure of either partner to live up to conventional gender roles—to be a good provider or efficient housewife—but after 1900, suits for divorce, increasingly initiated by women, were frequently justified by the failure of marriages to live up to expectations of personal fulfillment, including the wife's craving for "excitement," "change," and "independence" (May 85).

Perhaps the most striking evidence of change among women was the emergence of the New Woman. Carroll Smith-Rosenberg describes New Women as young, college-educated women who rejected marriage and convention, and who asserted their right to a career (176). After the Civil War this first generation of such women had been formed in the world of women's colleges, where they challenged conventional wisdom about women's intellectual capacities. On graduation they were forced to choose between the traditional domesticity of marriage and a professional career. Nearly half of all college-educated women in the late nineteenth century never married. Those who married did so later than most women and had fewer children. Mary Austin was one such woman. She explains in her autobiography why possibilities for her own marriage with compatible intellectual men all fell through: "One or the other of us would have to make sacrifices; and it was always sufficiently plain that I should have to be the one" (*Earth Horizon* [*EH*] 350). Like other New Women, Austin knew that stepping out of the domestic sphere was an enormous challenge and this struggle is reflected in many of her works, including *Santa Lucia: A Common Story*.

Mary Austin and Feminism

In the autobiographical sketch "Woman Alone" Mary Austin explains how feminism emerged in her childhood experience, describing her feminism as established in her "own position in the family as an unwanted, a personally resented child" who at an early age was forced to set aside her need for affection (113). She was born Mary Hunter in Carlinville, Illinois, on September 9, 1868, to George and Susanna Savilla Graham Hunter. At the age of ten, she was devastated by the loss of the most important members of her family: her father and her beloved sister. Her mother emotionally rejected her and so Austin grew up focused inwardly on her own mental and spiritual resources. Despite expecting Mary to conform to the "passivity and selflessness of what Austin called 'true womanliness'" (Graulich 5), her mother did allow her to attend Blackburn College, from which she graduated at the age of nineteen with a major in science. Mary Austin thus belonged to the first tide of career-minded New Women to break middle-class conventions.

In the summer of 1887 her brother Jim filed a homestead claim for land in the desolate San Joaquin Valley of California and asked the rest of the family to join him. At a time when many New Women were graduating from college and heading for the cities, Mary Austin went to the frontier. During the time she spent west she recorded her studies of the natural world, the land, and the people she met. Austin had always loved botany, and she brought to her desert wanderings "curiosity and patient observation as she attempted to understand the

ecology of the region" (Graulich 7). The desert gave her a subject matter
as the new surroundings awakened her writing talent. The Hunter
family lasted nine months in the desert, however. After the drought
that cost the Hunters their homestead, Susanna Hunter moved to the
town of Bakersfield, where Mary tutored farm children and taught
school to pay her own way during these financially difficult years.
She twice failed the exam to keep her teaching position, and so she
resigned herself to marriage as her only means of economic support.
That spring, she met Stafford Wallace Austin, who was an educated
man from a prominent family that had made its fortune and then lost
it. The courtship that proceeded through the spring and summer of
1890 was far from romantic, but the couple married on May 19, 1891.
Mary had been honest about the fact that she intended to pursue a
literary career, and Wallace had agreed to cooperate. Their marriage
initially seemed happy, but financial trouble started with the failure of
Wallace's fruit farm operation. The couple moved from place to place,
job to job, but their financial problems persisted and Mary suffered
from lack of intellectual stimulation and companionship of creative
people. Though they lived in San Francisco for only two months, Mary
took full advantage of the situation and with the help of Ina Coolbrith[2]
published her first two stories. This helped to build her professional
confidence and by 1897 her stories quickly began to appear in the
Overland Monthly, Cosmopolitan, Out West, and the *Atlantic Monthly.*
However, at a personal level, her marriage was becoming "synonymous
with entrapment" (Gelfant 241).

A number of factors contributed to Austin's disappointment
with her marriage: Wallace's inability to handle the increasing
debts, their lack of agreement upon common goals and how to
make a life together, and in general their lack of understanding and
communication. While living in Lone Pine,[3] for instance, Austin was
humiliated one day when she returned from her daily walk to find

---

[2]   In San Francisco, since the 1850s, a number of illustrious magazines had
been published, among those, *The Overland Monthly.* The magazine had enjoyed
an enviable reputation when edited by Bret Harte, Charles Warren Stoddard,
and Ina Coolbrith. Ina Coolbrith was the only one still in the area and she was
known for her generosity in helping aspiring young writers.
[3]   Lone Pine is in the Owens Valley, east of the Sierra Nevada. This place was
even more desolate than the region where Mary Austin's family had originally
settled.

her belongings on the sidewalk: they had been evicted. She expected her husband to apologize, but he ignored all her attempts to discuss their financial problems or his plans for the future. As a result, Austin, pregnant at the time, started a series of temporary separations from her husband. She went to her mother's house in Bakersfield and on October 30, 1892, gave birth to a mentally retarded daughter named Ruth. As Ruth grew older, Wallace refused to provide adequate support for his family and this meant that Austin needed to work to provide money for Ruth's care. Defying the prevailing resistance of the time to allow married women to work, she got a teaching position at the Inyo Academy in Bishop (approximately sixty miles north of Lone Pine) and took Ruth with her. However, this arrangement was far from successful and Austin was criticized for abandoning her daughter and husband. Forced physically to restrain Ruth for hours each day in order to make time to write, she eventually decided to place her in an institution in Santa Clara when she was twelve. Austin never saw her daughter again and when anyone mentioned Ruth, Austin would say, "We have lost her" (*EH* 295). Ruth stayed in Santa Clara, where she died in 1914.

For Mary Austin, Wallace was a financial as well as an emotional failure. Frustrated with the family's constant financial problems, Austin moved to Los Angeles, where she met Charles F. Lummis, editor of *Out West* magazine and a writer. He became a literary model and mentor, introducing her to his artistic and literary circle, which included Charlotte Perkins Stetson (later Gilman), whose "freedom from convention" Austin admired (*EH* 293). In 1903 Austin published *The Land of Little Rain*, a collection of sketches about the west and a tribute to her beloved country. It became her first literary success and to this day is her best-known work. Austin left the desert in 1906 and built a house in Carmel, on the California coast, where she associated with a bohemian group that included writers George Sterling and Jack London. It was here that she started her new novel, *Santa Lucia* (1908).

In the summer of 1907, Austin was diagnosed with breast cancer and was told that she would probably die within nine months. Although this prediction did not come true, it nevertheless was the catalyst for further changes in her life, including a divorce. She wanted to see more of the world, for instance, so she decided to go to Europe, travelling with her friends Vernon Kellogg and Charlotte Hoffman. Austin stayed in Europe for two years visiting Italy, France,

and England, but before she left on the trip, Wallace told her he
had found a job in Death Valley and asked her to join him. In her
autobiography, Austin explains that she had said to her husband "when
you can make a place for me, a background in which I can live with
reasonable comfort and rationality, I will join you again" (*EH* 349).
But Wallace kept doing the opposite, and this time he returned to the
desert "even deeper into its desolation, at Death Valley" (*EH* 349).
Austin concludes, "He was never able to make of our marriage a Thing,
a planned, progressive arrangement" (*EH* 350). She was determined
never to subordinate her needs to a man, so she asked for a divorce, but
because of his reluctance, the proceedings were postponed. After years
of incompatibility, made tolerable by frequent separations, the couple
divorced in 1914.

In order to gain easier access to publishers and the lecture
circuit, Austin moved to New York in 1912, where she would live
for the next twelve years. She entered into literary and artistic circles,
and into a disappointing love affair with Lincoln Steffens, a recently
widowed journalist and editor. In New York City, Austin was successful,
publishing nine books, including four novels—*A Woman of Genius*
(1912), *The Lovely Lady* (1913), *The Ford* (1917) and *No. 26 Jayne
Street* (1920)—and becoming involved in both the suffrage and labor
movements. In fact, Peter Lancelot Mallios describes Austin as "one of
the most original, diversely prolific, and politically engaged authors in
American literary history" (125). In Greenwich Village she joined the
salon company of Mabel Dodge Luhan,[4] whom she would later follow
to New Mexico. In 1924 she decided to move to Santa Fe permanently,
settling into an adobe house she named "Casa Querida" ("Beloved
House"). In Santa Fe, Austin renewed her connection to the landscape
of the Southwest and during the last sixteen years of her life fought
to preserve and publicize Native American art, music, and culture,
publishing eight books, including her autobiography, *Earth Horizon*
(1932). Austin lived in Casa Querida until her death from heart disease
at the age of sixty-five on August 13, 1934.[5]

---

[4]   Mabel Dodge Luhan was a famous patroness of artists and writers in both
European centers and in New York City during the decade before she moved to
Taos in 1918.
[5]   Her ashes are encased in cement amid boulders near the summit of Mt.
Picacho, on the edge of the Sangre de Cristo Mountains, within view of Casa
Querida.

Santa Lucia

Santa Lucia is, as Esther F. Lanigan accurately describes, a "largely unread novel" (*Song of a Maverick* 96). The novel has also been largely overlooked by scholars despite its importance in the evolution of Austin's feminism. Written in the early twentieth century, it symbolizes the struggle of women living in accordance to nineteenth-century traditions of domesticity while hoping to shift to twentieth-century roles as modern individuals. As Vera Norwood points out, Mary Austin belonged to a generation of creative women who struggled to make this shift as well (918), and in her autobiography she expressed her desire for "the liberation of women for its own sake" (*EH* 279). Austin's early novel *Santa Lucia* lays the foundation for the more radical feminism of her novels in later years in which the heroine is able to break boundaries and lead an unconventional life. *A Woman of Genius* (1912) published only four years later, for instance, is considered an "overlooked classic of feminism" (Porter 297). The protagonist, Olivia Lattimore, rejects conventional marriage and succeeds in pursuing a career and promoting female self-determination. In this novel the conflicts are presented going a step beyond what the characters in *Santa Lucia* are able to accomplish. However, it is through apparent "common stories" about women that Austin introduces a critique of Victorian womanhood and conventional thinking. In real life, Austin began to write *Santa Lucia* during a time when she was unhappy with her marriage. Her thoughts about her own decisions and those of other married women created three different heroines—William Caldwell, Serena Lindley, and Julia Stairs—and they are all autobiographical characters to some extent. The novel articulates the conflicts of a generation of women who start to realize there is more to womanhood and life. Marriage is the central theme that unites the three stories, and it is through the description of Serena and Julia's marital issues that Austin criticizes the conventional values of her time.

The novel opens with a description of William Caldwell waking up to a concert of birds singing under her window. William's character has a mixture of masculine and feminine traits, which is perhaps why she is the happiest of the novel's heroines. The Caldwell family is more open to modern ideas than are other families in Santa Lucia, as seen in their decision to name their daughter William, after an uncle who died at Antietem, and supporting her love for science. Her physical descriptions also suggest that William is an atypical female character. She is described as having "heavy … long … stiff and unmanageable" hair but she is also "careless" when it comes to fixing it properly (*Santa*

Lucia [*SL*] 2, 3). The simple and careless way she dresses has her friends divided between "the opinions that she would like to dress well and couldn't, or that she knew how and didn't care" (*SL* 3). Contrary to gender stereotypes she is also courageous and physically strong, shown in an act requiring courage and strength when she rescues her future husband from attempted murder. But she is also very affectionate toward her parents with frequent displays of emotions.

Serena Lindley, however, exemplifies several of Austin's arguments about marriage and the problems that come with financial issues due to the poor management of the husband. In fact, the marriage between Serena and Evan Lindley echoes many of Mary Austin's frustrations in her own marriage. Serena is a very unhappy wife limited by the expectations of early twentieth-century society. First, the character of Serena serves to criticize how women usually are not told the truth about what marriage really is. This lack of information sets them up for a life in marriage for which they are unprepared. Serena "At twenty-one was well read, well schooled, spiritually placed though not poised, not bodily strong, clean, reasonable, and pretty; but she had never handled a baby, never been kissed by any but her own people, ... and at twenty-two and a half she was married" (*SL* 29). Like Austin, Serena also accepted the marriage proposal because she had no other options, and the courtship was as unromantic as Austin and Wallace's. For Serena "marriage was a doorway into which she had stepped in a day of rough weather—and now, suddenly, the door had swung upon the latch, and she saw the whole procession of life go by her in the street" (*SL* 49).[6]

Second, the character of Serena represents the right of women to pursue a career, one of the strongest feminist ideas to influence her works. Serena encounters the resistance of traditional values and embodies the struggle and frustrations of women who wanted to pursue a career but were not able to break free from the restrictions of the time. She attends Wellesley College, gets her degree, and wants to pursue a career. However, this idea is met with strong opposition from her aunt,

---

[6] This idea of not knowing enough about love and marriage is also reflected in the short story "Frustrate" (1912), in which Austin writes, "sometimes I think if I'd known a little more, just a very little! ... There are things nobody ever tells young girls about marriage. Sometimes I think it is because, if they knew how to estimate their experience in the beginning, there is such a lot they wouldn't go on with; and when I was married, nobody even thought of anything but that you had to go on with it ..." (467–468).

Mrs. Bixby, and her husband. Austin explains that in Mrs. Bixby's world, "not to know that marriage and the correlated callings of nursing and teaching were the only creditable employments was to evince a lapse of true womanliness" (*SL* 32). For much of the novel Serena yearns for a satisfying career and she is frustrated with the restrictive opportunities for married women and with the assumption that married women are not intellectuals. The wish to pursue a career deepens shortly after the wedding as she starts to feel oppressed in her marriage: "the sense of her married life began to go through her as something intolerably flat and stale…. The glow of the honeymoon had gone off, and nothing had succeeded it but a routine of tiring and unimportant duties" (*SL* 44–45). Serena is fond of managing money, remembering how her father used to ask her for advice when she was in her teens, and wants an outlet for "her strong bent for accomplishing things" through managing the household allowance (*SL* 45). But her husband does not understand her—"he thought it rather ridiculous; money was a man's part of life"—and tells her that "that's what husbands are for" (*SL* 45). Even when he tries to make her happy by buying her a piano so that she has something to do, he fails and disappoints her once again. Serena cries on his shoulder "tears of a sinking heart-sickness at being so misread: that he should have thought her merely the complaining wife; that she had asked for a share in his work, and he had given her a toy" (*SL* 54). Austin emphasizes that Evan's "ineptitude" and his lack of understanding result in Serena's unsatisfying marriage when he interprets her crying as tears of joy and "patted her in husbandly satisfaction" (*SL* 55). Scholars agree that Austin expressed her frustrations from her own experiences as a young wife in the novel. In addition, Augusta Fink points out that Austin also infused her male characters, Evan Lindley and Antrim Stairs, with the most "infuriating traits" that Wallace possessed (120).

Third, Serena's friendship with Antrim Stairs, the young biology professor from the east, echoes Austin's friendship with a young doctor named Woodin while living in the settlement of George's Creek, a few miles north of Lone Pine. From the first time they met, they related to each other "like two lost souls" (Fink 72–73). Coming from New York, Dr. Woodin missed the cultural stimulus of the city, but with Austin he found intellectual companionship, which she also needed. Like Austin, Serena "found the stimulus of his work and the books she read of his suggesting a relief to the definite ache of her mind" (*SL* 59–60). He finds her conversation stimulating and beneficial for his work, and she feels that what she has to say is important.

Another example taken from Austin's intimate experience reflects Serena and Evan's financial problems. Evan Lindley, like Wallace, is unable to manage money properly, and instead of coming up with a plan to pay debts "assumed new and alluring opportunities for turning his money quickly" (*SL* 122). These speculations were catastrophic for both Wallace in real life and Evan in the novel, and Serena, like Austin, is humiliated. Money problems continue for Serena and Evan, but when the health of their baby is at risk, Serena steps up and rebels against her husband in a way she had never done before. This instance together with Serena's suggestion that they move to his mother's house, the only place they can really afford, represents a turning point for the couple, whose marriage can survive only if the husband can appreciate her and see her as an equal partner. Even though Serena's attitude toward her marriage in the final chapter has been interpreted by scholars as "happy," Austin's use of words such as "colorless," "unimpassioned," "fatigues," and "sorrow" when describing Serena's thoughts about her life and the life of all women suggests that Serena fails to find equality (*SL* 223).

Julia, the third heroine of the novel, is the unhappiest of the novel's heroines, embodying Austin's most radical and controversial critique of conventional marriage within the novel. Julia is described physically as being very attractive—"full-bosomed ... slender hips, and a fine, steady color, like a La France rose"—but she "had not made so good a marriage as might have been expected with her looks" (*SL* 66, 140). Her husband, Antrim Stairs, is also described as being physically good-looking, "handsome in a formal kind of way, and cultivated and—and Eastern" (*SL* 7). Good looks attract them, but they are not enough to keep Julia happy. Julia feels bored with her life, and although her husband loves her she is unsatisfied. Julia wants "great love and abounding light and color, but the stringency of life at Santa Lucia had excluded all that" (*SL* 156). Julia is "fevered with the desire to escape into larger possibilities of living," but she is full of fear and her husband does not believe in divorce (*SL* 156). Like Austin, Julia needs some distance from her husband and leaves for days to her mother's house in the city. Away from the small town, Julia feels "the old sensuous allurement of the city ... like an exhalation, as though it were the perfume of those bright night bloomers spread abroad after the sun goes down" (*SL* 154). Julia's happiness is thus the result of moral taboo.

Esther Lanigan suggests that the emphasis in the novel is really on the misery of Julia, who is terrified of leaving her husband for her lover "because of the social stigma of adultery" (*Song of a Maverick* 100). T.M. Pearce also suggests that the gossip of her affair "destroys her reputation in the town" and this leads to her fatal ending (*Mary Hunter Austin* 92). One cannot help seeing in Julia's self-destructive escape from domesticity and marriage a parallel with Edna Pontellier in Kate Chopin's 1899 novel *The Awakening*.[7] But Austin admits that the tragic stories of Julia Stairs and Edna Pontellier were similar to her own story: "A woman whose love life has been as unhappy as mine, who had no religion, would have gone mad or bad or committed suicide. I have been very near the last many times" (qtd in Fink 1–2).

Like *The Awakening*, *Santa Lucia* was immediately controversial, even with publishing houses in New York. Century rejected the novel because it presented atypical views on marriage, but Harper agreed to publish it believing that it would place her "in the first rank of American writers" (Fink 139). Although the critical reviews of the time were mainly negative, the *New York Times* praised *Santa Lucia* for its author's "delightful art in the depiction of some of her characters" and her "exquisitely beautiful" evocations of nature ("Novel of California Life"). The *Outlook*'s review, however, damned the novel for its "painfully deficient … construction" and its "positively depressing" ending (Rev. of *Santa Lucia*). Janis Stout explains that *Santa Lucia* was unable to achieve success at the time it was published due to a "moralistic outcry" against the story of Julia, and as a result it has been little read since (*Through the Window* 43). In California, where Austin had expected to sell more copies, *Santa Lucia* "was refused by at least one public library and was pulled from bookstore shelves after a store owner reportedly said that his wife found it morally objectionable" (Stout "Mary Austin's Feminism" 82). These reactions were not uncommon in a society that firmly believed in the separation of spheres, limiting women to the domestic realm and expecting them to be submissive and passive. Mary Austin's feminist ideas make her a woman ahead of her time. In 1927 she wrote, "women should be free to make their contribution to society by any talent with which they found themselves endowed, and be paid

---

[7]   Julia and Edna share many similarities: an unhappy marriage, adultery, and suicide. Chopin makes a strong statement about a society not ready for her heroine's discoveries and ends the novel with Edna freed from social pressures to join with her natural element, the sea.

for it at rates equal to the pay of men" ("Woman Alone" 117). Her ideas resonate with readers today, and this makes *Santa Lucia,* as well as her other novels, relevant to the twenty-first century.

Works Cited

Armitage, Shelley. "Mary Austin: Writing Nature." In *Wind's Trail: The Early Life of Mary Austin.* Santa Fe: Museum of New Mexico Press, 1990.

Austin, Mary Hunter. *Earth Horizon: An Autobiography.* Boston and New York, Houghton Mifflin Company, 1932. Reprinted by Sunstone Press, Santa Fe, 2007.

———. "Frustrate." *Century* Magazine (January 1912): 467–471.

———. *Santa Lucia: A Common Story.* Hastings, Ne: Hastings College Press, 2015 [1908].

———. "Woman Alone." *Beyond Borders: The Selected Essays of Mary Austin.* Ed. Reuben J. Ellis. Carbondale & Edwardsville: Southern Illinois University Press, 1996.

Blackbird, Chelsea and Barney Nelson. *Mary Austin's Southwest: An Anthology of Her Literary Criticism.* Salt Lake City: University of Utah Press, 2005.

Canby, Henry Seidel. *A Memorial.* Ed. William Houghland. Santa Fe: Laboratory of Anthropology, 1944.

Fink, Augusta. *I-Mary: A Biography of Mary Austin.* Tucson: University of Arizona Press, 1983.

Gelfant, Blanche H. *Women Writing in America: Voices in Collage.* Hanover: University Press of New England, 1985.

Graulich, Melody. "Introduction." *Western Trails: A Collection of Short Stories.* Reno: University of Reno Press, 1987.

Graulich, Melody and Elizabeth Klimasmith. *Exploring Lost Borders: Critical Essays on Mary Austin.* Reno: University of Nevada Press, 1999.

Karell, Linda K. "Mary Hunter Austin." *American Women Prose Writers 1870–1920.* Ed. Sharon M. Harris. Detroit: Gale Group, 2000.

Lanigan, Esther F. *A Mary Austin Reader.* Tucson: University of Arizona Press, 1996.

———. *Mary Austin: Song of a Maverick.* Tucson: University of Arizona Press, 1997.

Mallios, Peter Lancelot. "Democracy of Difference: Mary Austin, Joseph Conrad, and Global Feminism." *Studia Neophilologica* 85 (2013): 125–135.

May, Elaine Tyler. *Great Expectations: Marriage and Divorce in Post-Victorian America.* Chicago: University of Chicago Press, 1980.

Norwood, Vera. "Mary Austin 1868–1934," in *Heath Anthology of American Literature,* 2nd ed. Ed. Paul Lauter et al. Lexington, Mass.: D.C. Heath, 1994.

"Novel of California Life." Rev. of *Santa Lucia,* by Mary Hunter Austin *The New York Times,* May 16, 1908: 280.

Pearce, T. M. *Mary Hunter Austin.* New York: Twayne, 1965.

Porter, Nancy. "Afterword." *A Woman of Genius* by Mary Austin. New York: The Feminist Press, 1985.

Pryse, Marjorie. "Introduction." *Stories from the Country of Lost Borders.* New Brunswick & London: Rutgers University Press, 1987.

Rev. of *Santa Lucia,* by Mary Hunter Austin. *Outlook* 89 (June 6, 1908): 314.

Riegel, Robert E. *American Feminists.* Lawrence: University of Kansas Press, 1963.

Smith-Rosenberg, Carroll. *Disorderly Conduct: Visions of Gender in Victorian America.* New York: Alfred A. Knopf, 1985.

Stout, Janis P. "Mary Austin's Feminism: A Reassessment." *Studies in the Novel* 30.1 (Spring 1998): 77–101.

———. *Through the Window, Out the Door: Women's Narrative of Departure, from Austin and Cather to Tyler, Morrison, and Didion.* Tuscaloosa and London: University of Alabama Press, 1998.

Walton, John. "Foreword." *The Ford* by Mary Austin. Los Angeles: University of California Press, 1997.

Welter, Barbara. "The Cult of True Womanhood: 1820–1860." *American Quarterly,* XVIII (1966): 151–174.

Further Reading

Ammons, Elizabeth. *Conflicting Stories: American Women Writers at the Turn into the Twentieth Century.* New York: Oxford University Press, 1992.

Church, Peggy Pond. *Wind's Trail: The Early Life of Mary Austin.* Santa Fe: Museum of New Mexico Press, 1990.

Doyle, Helen MacKnight. *Mary Austin: Woman of Genius.* New York: Gotham House, 1939.

Gabrielson, Teena. "Woman-Thought, Social Capital, and the Generative State: Mary Austin and the Integrative Civic Ideal in Progressive Thought." *American Journal of Political Science*. 50.3 (2006): 650–663.

Goodman, Susan and Carl Dawson. *Mary Austin and the American West*. Berkeley, Los Angeles, London: University of California Press, 2008.

Miller, Anna Carew, "Mary Austin's Nature: Refiguring Tradition through the Voices of Identity," in *Reading the Earth: New Directions in the Study of Literature and Environment*. Ed. Michael P. Branch et al. Moscow, Idaho: University of Idaho Press, 1998.

Pearce, T. M. *The Beloved House*. Idaho: The Caxton Printers, 1940.

———. *Literary America 1903–1934: The Mary Austin Letters*. Westport and London: Greenwood Press, 1979.

Ringler, Donald P. "Mary Austin: Kern County Days, 1888–1892." *Southern California Quarterly*, XLV.1 (March 1963).

Ryan, Mary P. *Womanhood in America: From Colonial Times to the Present*. New York: Franklin Watts, 1983.

Stout, Janis P. *Picturing a Different West: Visions, Illustrations, and the Tradition of Austin and Cather*. Lubbock: Texas Tech University Press, 2007.

Woloch, Nancy. *Women and the American Experience*. New York: Alfred A. Knopf, 1984.

....

Maribel Morales is Assistant Professor at Carthage College, Wisconsin, where she teaches courses in American Literature and Spanish. She completed her PhD in 2010 in American Literature from the University of Cádiz, Spain, where she is from. Her scholarship includes gender and ethnic studies in nineteenth and early twentieth-century American women writers. In the United States she has presented her latest research at conferences organized by the American Literature Association, the Western Literature Association, and the Willa Cather Foundation, among others. In 2015 she published an article on ecofeminism in the works of Willa Cather, Sarah Orne Jewett, Mary Austin, and Kate Chopin in the *Willa Cather Newsletter and Review,* and she wrote the introduction to the 2015 reprint of Mary Hallock Foote's 1919 novel, *The Ground-Swell,* published by Hastings College Press.

I

There had been a concert going on for an hour under the window before William awoke. The doves began it, low at first, then full and tender, as if the bluish mist had thinned from the ground and collected in soft splashes of sound among the smoky boughs. Then the blackbirds whistled warily as not being sure the day had broke, but calling it softly until the answer came from the pale storm of blossoms among the apricots. Then the meadow larks, then the vireos, then the sparrows, buntings, finches—all the feather-breasted, flute-voiced folk—piped up from the wet wheat, from the budding willows, from the trim little orchard rows that ran well into the lap of the hills, from the creek border and the blue-gums marching orderly on either side of the stiff loam of the Santa Lucia road. Under it, all sustaining and harmonizing, went the rush and babble of Toyon. Still the doves kept on until they had gathered all the dun mists of morning to their breasts, and began to flit with them among the holly and the oaks, and the sun, brightening above the mountains east, shone broadly in at her window, and William awoke. She had left the blind up the night before to watch the young moon whitening the apricot orchard, and did not draw it now that it was full morning. Jap, the Doctor's assistant, never came around to that side of the house so early, and a sombre, high-branched pine screened the window from the county road. She lay luxuriously in the cool dawning, and heard the tender, cheerful voices from the trees. A row of poplars faced the window east, but the sun overshot them, and made a patch of moving, golden water on the wall. Once she rose on elbow to look over the garden under the branches of the pine to catch the morning gleam of the brown water of Toyon, noting it with no more interruption to her musing thought than the stream made in its running as it flashed to her. Waking and sleeping, the Toyon had sung through her work and dreams for twenty years; the morning recognition was as unconscious as it was habitual. It sung to her now with the fulness of the spring.

One by one, in the house below her, she heard the accustomed noises of the day begin: Lew Sing clanking the pots in the kitchen, scolding affectionately, in his high, shrivelled, old voice, at the Doctor's cat; Jap banging the stable door, and passing the compliments of the morning to the Doctor's team; the Doctor himself calling out in his fat, comfortable voice. The smell of frying meat arose from the kitchen, and from the Doctor's study directly underneath came a deep rumbling with an occasional creaking of furniture, and between the centres of disturbance ran a pattering trail of footsteps. That was the Doctor's wife, who at fifty-seven, with a servant of sixteen years' standing, was still of the opinion that the breakfast could not be got on the table without her. When the rumble broke into staccato points of laughter, William laughed too, sat up in the bed, and began to search among the pillows for her hair-pins. When the Doctor's daughter laughed you saw at once how pleasant she was. It lightened with unguessable curves and dimples a face that was too round, too red and shining, and brought fine points of fire into eyes too palely blue and equable.

William shook down the masses of her black hair, heavy and long and inclined to be somewhat stiff and unmanageable, and stood before the glass to determine what should be done about her bangs; for when William was twenty it was still the fashion at Santa Lucia to wear the front hair cut short and curled over the forehead. But William's hair refused to curl at all without the most rigid application of curl-papers put on overnight, so that morning always found her with a row of knobby protuberances across her forehead, one-half of which were generally done in proper kid-curlers, and the rest in old play-bills, notepaper, or whatever came to William's careless hand. The disposition of her bangs was at that time the problem of William's morning hours. They certainly were not becoming in the chrysalis state, and occasions were not wanting when one wished to look one's best in the forenoon. But if they came out of their wrappers too soon, and there was company expected in the evening, or William going out, the work was all to do over again; and if no company came, and the bangs had not come down before dinner, it seemed, on the whole, a pity to undo them, only to repeat the application of curlers at bedtime; so it came about that William often spent whole days on end with her round countenance outlined with hard little bundles of hair. The rest of it lay coiled flat, covering the back of her head, from which hair-pins habitually obtruded, and little obstinate twisted tails were continually escaping on her neck.

William's figure was to match her face, round and tight, and her manner of arraying herself divided her friends between the opinions that she would like to dress well and couldn't, or that she knew how and didn't care. This morning a decision was affected in favor of the easiest toilet by her mother coming to the foot of the stairs and calling, not as if she anticipated any response (for William could be counted on to be a good quarter of an hour behind), but as a sort of preface to the acclamation that the Doctor might be expected to raise a little later. William did up her back hair with an insufficient number of hair-pins, the rest having slipped away among the mattresses, and selected a Mother-Hubbard wrapper from the closet bursting full of gay skirts like a garden-pink from its calyx. The wrapper was very full, and had a full ruffle about the hem; it was of a dove-gray tone flowered over with chubby carmine roses, not at all calculated to bring out the best points of a plump figure and a too ruddy complexion: With this and a pair of loose morning slippers tied on over very pretty feet, for her feet and hands were both pretty and small, William trailed down to breakfast.

All the doors were open to let in the morning freshness: blocks of soft, yellowing light fell through the casements into the cool, shadowy rooms; dew lay on the sills and dripped from the lilac-hedge; the grass drooped under it, and the Chinese lilies by the driveway scarcely lifted their heavy, sweet perfume above it. William stopped at the front door to look out at the Banksia rose and the great arch of the Beauty of Glazenwood coming into fullest bud, wet and twinkling in the sun.

"Hey, Billy! Breakfast!" cried the Doctor. He was already at the table and filling her plate; and when he looked up at her out of the ambush of his beard and brows, there was something of the same expression she had given to the roses and the shining water—the satisfaction of a daily habit with the freshness which twenty years of use could not dim; and there was something more: there was pride in the look, attempting to conceal itself under a quizzing humor, inordinate love, and a community of understanding.

To see that, and the way he kissed her, and the way he drew her down to his knee that she might kiss him, and the way she took his old white head in her arms and squeezed it, and the way her mother smiled at them both in apologetic delight in their behavior, and the way William went around to the end of the table to kiss her mother, and made the whole circuit in order that she might come back by her father's chair and take his head in her arm to give it another squeeze on the way to her own place, was to have a new and enlarged perception of the parental relation. William got into her seat at last, and Sing came in with the coffee, and after him Jap, the Doctor's assistant, to sit in the chair opposite, and eat his breakfast with never a word more than the usage of the meal required. Sing set up a chair for the Doctor's great brindled cat, squeaking at it in his skimpy little voice like a talking-toy that wanted winding badly, and presently, when the plates were all served, the Doctor began to laugh. He had to begin it a good while before the occasion that required it in order to bring it to the surface at the proper time. His great shoulders began to shake, and his rosy face to grow more rosy, until by the quivering of his huge frame the laugh was dislodged from the pit of his stomach, and came rumbling up, to break in a cataract of thin chuckles over his full white beard. When the Doctor laughed, William laughed, and you saw at once how alike they were. It was easy to understand why she should be short (both her parents were that), and it would be difficult to imagine how the Doctor's offspring could be anything but plump and rosy and humorous, with a strong sprinkling of good sense, for he was all that; but seeing that his daughter was to be like him in her youth, it seemed a pity not to make sure of her growing old like her mother. The Doctor's wife looked to be grandmother to a line of Dresden shepherdesses, so trim she was as to figure, so finely cut, so delicate of coloring. She had what is called an old-fashioned air, though it was not so much a matter of dress or manner as the habit of her mind, the fine reticence with which she held her thought away from the great tract of human experience which was not hers; so that if the Doctor's patients used to say of him that he kept their confidences even from his wife, they might have said of her that she kept them even from herself.

Singularly this abstemiousness got her more consideration than confidences, as many people thought her in some way deprived by being so fine. She hardly understood the Doctor's jokes, but she smiled at William's enjoyment of them, very much as if she felt that having produced a daughter who could appreciate them, was better than understanding them herself. So she looked on in a placid kind of porcelain content while the breakfast was prolonged until the golden blocks of light had reached quite across the floor and begun to climb the wall, when the one from the open door was obscured by the shadow of a small boy on a saddleless horse, gasping out that the Doctor was wanted at Thompson's, where the baby was took bad, sudden.

Jap went for the Doctor's buggy, and the Doctor himself for his medicine-bags. The Doctor's wife, trying, with the help of cold doughnuts from the breakfast-table, to extract some particulars of the Thompson baby's seizure, learned that it was playing happily on the floor of the Thompson dining-room when it let out a yell and straightened right out. It was supposed to have swallered something. No'm, it hadn't no symptoms to speak of; it just straightened right out, sudden.

The Doctor's buggy, with the Doctor in it, came down the drive by the lilac-hedge, and William walked to the gate to let him out. There was a border of Chinese lilies along the rose-garden where she went, beginning to faint with their own heavy sweetness as the sun dried off the dew. Every year, as the time of New Year in the Chinese calendar drew close, Sing presented the Doctor's wife with the bulbs to be propped up in a dish with bits of stones for blooming, and every year, when the holiday was past, she planted them along the rose-walk. There was not another place in the garden where anything could conceivably be planted without disturbing some other shrub or root. A Japanese quince burned scarlet at the end of the walk; beyond it was the *Viburnum* the Doctor's wife had brought from Back East; around the foot of it were English primroses that came from the Doctor's earliest home. The thick, wet lawn swept in the curve of the walk up to the door, and a long-leaved pine slept above the green-and-golden grass.

William opened the gate and swung upon it, watching the Doctor's buggy out of sight. It was a low and broad conveyance somewhat rakish in appearance, tumbling on behind the team, running low and light and loosely harnessed, casting up flakes of the stiff black loam. For thirty-five years the Doctor's buggy had gone like the Ark of the Convenant, with a promise of hope and security between the barley and the wheat. Long before the orchards came marching in by the Los Robles ranch at a corner of the valley, and so taken the land at last, when all the open country was put to grain, it carried the savor of neighborliness and sacrifice into the big disjointed life of the Santa Lucia. William watched it down the road, and then looked up the Eucalyptus avenue towards town, and called to her mother to bring her hat, for Serena Lindley was coming, and she would go to meet her. Mrs. Caldwell trotted out obediently with the hat, which was large and languid, and had a great many ribbons of a shade not harmonious with the roses in William's dress; but as it did not set well upon the chrysalids of her bangs and the hat-pin had fallen out, William hung it on the gate and went on without it.

"William," said her mother, "if you would wear a thick veil, and wash your face twice a day in elder-flowers steeped in buttermilk—"

"Ma," said William, coming back to kiss her, "if I washed my face in the dews of Sharon, I should never in the world have a complexion like yours. And, anyway, if I get brown I won't be quite so red, and that's one comfort."

"Have you come to spend the day?" demanded William, when Serena had kissed her.

"With all I have to do? Mercy, no! I have come to invite you to dinner, and to borrow your mother's receipt for angel-cake."

"When?" asked William, referring to the invitation.

"To-morrow. It is rather hurried all round." Then with a little pause of impressment: "We are to have Dr. Stairs."

"Oh!" said William. "Oh, Serena, the very first! And he came only Tuesday."

"Yes. But the Downings' house is quarantined, you know, and Professor King is away, and in my husband's position—"

"Serena," said William, "when you talk about Evan that way I simply adore you. Anybody would think you had been married years, and that Evan was at least the president of the college instead of the attorney."

It took a good three-quarters of an hour to settle all these points upon which a young housekeeper, on the eve of entertaining company, would wish to consult an older one, and then William, who had found a hat-pin and skewered the languid hat to her back hair, leaving the little rows of knobs standing out below it, led Mrs. Lindley away by the garden gate to the apricot orchard. Serena lifted up her skirts as they stepped gingerly along the wet borders and under the low-branched trees until they came to a sort of platform that had been used the year before in packing the dried fruit. Here Serena sat her carefully down on an overturned packing case, and William, whose ruffles were all draggled with the wet, made a "cheese" of her skirts to bring them as far from her as possible, and dropped down in the midst of them like a collapsed toy balloon. Overhead the springing boughs crossed and recrossed—delicate arches, with a mist of rosy blossoms swarming through them in the warm, sweet air. Bees hummed in it with the sharp crescendo of the morning hours falling off insensibly to the sated drone of noon. Gazing upward from the ground, the blossoming branches seemed to extend themselves infinitely into the warm sky, and uplifted the sense to the expectation of beauty on every side. They sat still until an oriole came and sang in the nearest tree and recalled them to a sense of present things.

"Now, tell me," demanded William.

"About Dr. Stairs? Well, he looks the part."

"How?" William insisted.

"Oh, handsome in a formal kind of way, and cultivated and—and Eastern." She hesitated a little over the word.

"Don't tell me," protested William, "that he is stiff at the corners, and that he has a different kind of hat for every suit of clothes."

"Probably that," admitted Mrs. Lindley, "though it wasn't what I meant. But he looks, somehow, instead of going in for Science, as our men do, as if Science had gone in for him."

"I know," nodded William. "Well, who else?"

"The Mathisens, of course, and Professor Grenning, and Julia Maybury. I invited Agnes Sterling, too, but she has an engagement."

"I do think, Serena," William reproached her, "that considering it's the very first time of asking Dr. Stairs, you might have left out Julia Maybury."

"Oh," said Mrs. Lindley, in dawning consternation, "I never thought. But the Sterlings entertained us, you know, and it seemed such a good opportunity—I am sorry—"

"You goose!" laughed William, kissing her. "But Julia does put us all out of countenance."

They walked back between the blossom-haunted trees until the rush of Toyon began to be more insistant than the droning of the bees.

"Don't turn in, dad," she cried, as the Doctor drew up by the gate, "I want the team to take Serena home!"

"But, Billy," as she dispossessed him of the reins, "my patients?"

"Oh, your patients, dad," cried William. "Your patients will get along very well. I shouldn't wonder, if I kept the team long enough, if some of them would get well." It was a favorite humor of hers, which tickled the Doctor very much, that his practice was all quackery and his medicines a pretence. "Get in, Serena."

"If you don't mind," said Serena, a little nervously, "go round by the side street, and let me out at Mrs. Mathisen's." She was not sure that her husband would be pleased to see her driving through Santa Lucia at eleven o'clock with William in curl-papers and a "Mother-Hubbard."

II

Mr. Antrim Stairs, whose arrival at Santa Lucia proved to be in advance of any preparation for it, found the occasion of the Lindley's dinner a little difficult. That he should have a certain amount of attention was properly part of his expectation; but his social sense, which had developed rather narrowly in an Eastern university town, was a little jarred at having the first advances in that direction come from the attorney for the college. Without being vain, he felt that to be called to a Professorship of Biology at his age—he was not quite thirty—was an achievement not wholly recognized by the attorney's off-hand invitation. That the president's house was shut up by diphtheria, and the head of his department away on leave, rather explained than extenuated a situation which he was withheld from giving a name to, by a doubt if it were a slight or an essentially Western unawareness of fine social distinctions. He was prepared to find such things in the West. Several times when he was dressing, a remote perception hovered upon him that he had reached a society in which a professor of biology was no better than an attorney, nor even so good, provided the attorney proved himself the better man; but it found no resting-place in his consciousness.

This confusion of his social sense, added to his natural shyness, caused the invitation so to weigh upon his mind that it brought him

to Lindley's door full a quarter of an hour before he was expected.
Lindley had been detained late at the office, and was dressing; the girl,
who was both housemaid and cook, was making herself presentable
to wait at table, and not available to answer the door. Finally, when
Stairs had rung twice, and had time for a sinking misgiving that he had
mistaken the address or forgotten the date of the engagement, Serena
was obliged to open the door, and to excuse herself almost immediately
afterwards to complete some of her arrangements, so that by the time
Lindley got down and the company began to arrive, the Assistant
Professor of Biology was more than pink-and-white colored and his
collar was beginning to wilt with a sweat of embarrassment. It seemed
to him rather the worse for being a small and informal company, for
his formality was about the only thing that did not desert him under
embarrassment, but it had quite a college flavor and the air of being able
to go on without him.

By dint of attending very closely to the conversation, he came
out of his confusion sufficiently to realize that the company waited for
a tardier guest, and covered himself with new amazement by coming
into the conversation under the natural inference that William's
name suggested, and then trying unobtrusively to correct the state
of his collar, and, being detected in it by Miss Maybury, falling into
profounder miseries.

"I'll tell you what, Serena," Lindley was saying, "when you invite
William you ought to set the time half an hour earlier."

"Why, to tell the truth, Evan, that is exactly what I did."

And suddenly the company all stood up with relief at the sound
of a horse tearing down the street, followed by a buggy that wanted
greasing.

"That's William," said Lindley, going out to meet her at the edge
of the lawn—William, with the bangs all out of their chrysalids (a
little too much of them), flowering out above a green changeable silk
of a rustling sort. That was the year when draped skirts were the only
possible mode; there had been eighteen yards in the piece, and the
dressmaker had put it all in, which gave William rather the effect of
disappearing into herself. She came out of it at the table, where Mrs.
Lindley, to make up for the lapse about Julia Maybury, had seated her
next to Antrim Stairs, with the manner that had caught his attention in

the young attorney, of being too easily at home among great thoughts and names. Not being quite free from the prevalent notion that the West was a place of unaccustomed judgments, with all his thought about it—and as early as it had been intimated to him that he might have this place at Santa Lucia, Stairs had thought a great deal about it—he was not quite prepared to fall easily into the note of Lindley's dinner-table, where biology, banking, and city improvements, lumped together under the head of a man's work, had an equally interested and informed attention. When they showed him, unobtrusively enough, that they had read his monograph on "The Meaning of Color in Sea-shells," he was not able to say if their manner of taking it as a matter of course that it should have been published by the Smithsonian was due to their rating it more or less than he esteemed it in his own mind.

He found himself going off into speculations of this kind in the intervals when direct conversation was not expected of him, and so missing a good deal of it. And then he discovered that it had taken on a note of controversy a little deeper than the usual dining-out dissension.

"Well, but what's the matter with it?" Lindley was saying. "It's as natural as life, and twice as large, and twice as much metal for the money."

"Oh, but, Vene!"—Stairs thought there was a hint in Serena's voice, as if she were not so much distressed at the opinion as at her husband's entertaining it—"but, Vene, the whole idea of it, it is so—so vulgar, and so false."

"Oh, come now! Vulgar isn't exactly the word to apply to a lady like Mrs. Bodely, and, as for falsity, well, if the Bodelys aren't the fountain-head of this college, who is? I'm sure the idea expresses the state of things admirably."

They were talking of the new fountain for the campus, it seemed. Lindley launched him a fuller explanation. The Bodelys had offered a fountain done in bronze, competitive designs by Western artists. "Good idea, too," said the young attorney; "keeps the money at home, and encourages native talent."

But it appeared that there were not a great many native artists in the West—not in the fountain line, anyway; and of the two designs submitted, the one which pleased the Bodelys seemed not to please anybody else.

"The most absurd thing," interpolated William: "Mr. and Mrs. Bodely at the Pierian spring serving out drinks in custard-cups! And the clothes: Mrs. Bodely in an overskirt and a bustle! Imagine a bronze statue in a bustle, Dr. Stairs!"

Stairs smiled as soon as he perceived he was expected to, but Lindley averred there was a story about those custard-cups which proved that the Bodelys had taken the highest possible moral attitude in the matter of the fountain. It was reported that when Mrs. Bodely sat for the model the artist had put a goblet in her hand, which Mrs. Bodely had objected to, on the ground that it resembled a wine-glass, and might suggest bibulous habits to the young people of the college. Stairs could not make out how much of Lindley's defence was mere flippancy, but his wife's disquietude was evident under it. Looking at her attentively, he thought he discovered in Serena an aptitude for finer distinctions, which he was already disposed to credit to their common derivation from the East.

"Can't you say anything, Mrs. Mathisen?" she begged.

"Oh, if he won't listen to you!" laughed the lady. "But I can tell you, Evan, what I heard those Eastern people over at the hotel say. I was there calling the day the designs were exhibited, and they laughed more than a little at the Bodelys' choice; said that was the sort of thing that made them remember that California was still on the frontier; and we can't afford that, you know."

"No, we can't," said Lindley, with some seriousness.

Stairs lost the thread of the talk when it drifted away from the college, and gave himself up chiefly to discovering which of William's surprising speeches he ought to laugh at and which take seriously. As for the rest of the party, they seemed to be rather more interested in Santa Lucia than he had expected to find them, and kept mentioning this and that to him, asking him if he had seen it, and holding it out as something he must not miss, so that without in the least intending it he found himself engaged to drive in Toyon Canon with the Mathisens and the Lindleys Saturday afternoon.

When they had gotten well outside of the house after saying good-night, Grenning asked Stairs to walk round to his room with him and have something to warm him up. It was not late, though very dark, and all the town folded in a smother of wet fog. An invisible person had been heard inquiring at the door for Miss Caldwell, and Miss Maybury had been taken home by the Mathisens. Stairs had thought that Grenning rather expected to have performed that service himself, and judged by the way she got herself out of the house that Miss Maybury thought so, too, and did not mean to let him. Miss Maybury had proved a very handsome young woman, with a high color and very little to say for herself; but when she got around behind Mrs. Mathisen, in the half-light of the veranda, she had given Stairs a look which seemed to promise that if once she got him away from these rather boring surroundings she might have a great deal to say of inestimable interest to those who understood one another. Stairs was not accustomed to think of himself as having anything to communicate to a stunning-looking girl like Julia Maybury; but now that Julia's eyes admitted it, he discovered that it was so, though as he walked away into the dark with the Professor of Chemistry he was not quite sure what it was about.

They walked rapidly, for the fog struck them with a chill; and Stairs being in train for it, and Grenning willing to accommodate him, a good deal passed between them of question and answer, set on by the wisps of table-talk that stuck in the young professor's mind.

Lindley, Grenning had told him, had come into the attorneyship by inheritance, his father having had it before him, and he, being a pet of the Bodelys, continued in it. Mathisen was a big man of the town, and a banker, and one of the trustees of the college.

"That was a good stroke of yours," said Grenning, "to get yourself asked to go driving with Mrs. Mathisen. They have the pull."

Stairs had it on the tip of his tongue to deny having intended any stroke, but he divined that Grenning saw no offence in it. The Professor of Chemistry went on to tell him that the town assumed the college as an adornment whenever it showed signs of being a credit to it, but cast it off on the least suspicion that it was not; that there was, in a social way, a little jealousy between what was known as the college set and the town set, though that, Grenning told him, was a woman's affair; that the business men of Santa Lucia were divided between the conviction that the school brought money into the town and a grudging patronage of all efforts directed towards putting money into the school. Crossing the campus, they came to the site of the proposed fountain and, very naturally, to the subject of the Bodelys. Grenning confirmed what

Lindley had said, with more detail, of how Bodely had made money
by grubstaking forlorn prospectors with the least amount of poor grub,
and, having acquired by this means a title to several tolerable claims,
had shouldered them onto the market so effectively that the original
discoverers had been quite shouldered out of sight. It was believed that
he had trifled a little with the Stock Exchange, but, finding it too busy
for him, had had the sense to follow his wife's lead into the Church,
where his millions made him a very considerable figure. Mrs. Bodely he
judged a sincere, well-meaning, ignorant woman, willing to do pretty
much as the bishop said, but with no more taste than could be expected
from a woman willing to marry Bodely. Further than that, he thought
neither of them had ever been in a college until they became the patrons
of Santa Lucia; Bodely had given the museum and the gym, and Mrs.
Bodely had enlarged and refurnished the chapel.

By this time they had come to Grenning's rooms, in which he had
the air of being very much at home. Certainly he took liberties with his
apartments that Stairs would never have thought of with his own. The
Professor of Chemistry unlocked a cupboard and took out a bottle and
glasses.

"It's only California," he said, apologetically, "but I think you'll
find it very good. This being a Church school, the social lines are rather
stringent, and the influence spreads to the town. I doubt if there are
half a dozen places where you get a glass of wine at a company dinner,
though many use it at their private tables. We school men are not
supposed to take it in public, and so nothing is ever offered."

"Don't smoke?" noticing that Stairs had not touched the cigars
which he had pushed over. "So much the better for you; there is a
prejudice against it in the school."

Grenning puffed away for a time as if he rather resented it, while
the other sipped his drink carefully, not being used to it, but not liking
to admit so much, and then Grenning asked him on the whole how
he liked the West. That, Stairs had already begun to observe, was the
burning question which the West asked of the East—what he thought
of it. And no matter how recent an acquisition the questioner might be,
or how slightingly he might be willing to speak of it in particular points,
when it came to the summing-up, always asked it with the air of laying
himself open to a compliment.

Stairs replied that he thought he should like it, on the whole, very well when he got able to make it out. He said he could hardly place the people he met. "There is Miss Caldwell," he said. "Mrs. Lindley tells me she was at Wellesley with her; I should have expected to see the mark of it somewhere. And Lindley—is he a college man at all?"

"Oh yes, he has been through the mill; only U. C., though." That was the way Easterners spoke of the University of California in the early nineties. "He's all right when he gets over being young. His wife's a great favorite of mine. Wonderful woman to talk to. I don't suppose she understands half I say when I get going about my work, but I understand it better myself afterwards."

Then the subject of each man's work came uppermost in his mind, and they drifted into the frontier of problems, where all solutions run together in a single inextricable skein. Here was a region in which Dr. Antrim Stairs was not shy, and the wine had warmed him to his best. All his life lay behind him constrained by authority—the schoolmaster, the minister, the faculty of his fresh-water college raised by his modesty and simplicity far above their deeming; his term of tutorship, it amounted to little more than that, though it had a different name in the year-book, under a man too great a scholar to be aware of his young assistant's worshipful timidity. Here he sat talking as he had never talked in his life, with a man of near his own age and acquirements, and all his life lay before him in which there was a vision of the time, very faint as yet, but drawing near through the glow of serviceable talk, when he might walk himself among the elect, and not he nor they think it strange to find him there. They sat so long that he had a sudden renewal of shyness when he got up to go at last, discovering the hour. The fog had cleared overhead, though it hung dripping in the trees; and as he saw the stars come out in the cleared space over Santa Lucia they seemed like many points in a cipher that spelled opportunity to Antrim Stairs. But as he conned them over he read in them only work, and no woman anywhere.

At the same hour the Lindleys were discussing the dinner and the guests, with frequent digressions to themselves, after the manner of the newly married; and at this time it seemed not absurd to either of them that Serena should insist on having and Lindley be perfectly serious in giving her a kiss because the salad had turned out such a success, and she had made it with her own hands.

"But what on earth, Serena," said her husband, "induced you to speak as you did of the Bodely fountain—calling it vulgar, and all that? Aren't you ever going to learn on which side your bread is buttered? And before Stairs, too, though he looks rather a softy."

"Why do you speak of him like that?" she asked, with some irritation that might refer to the first part of his remark as well as to the last.

"Well, why shouldn't I? He may be an all right professor of biology, but he isn't a sugar angel, I should hope."

"But a man who has done what he has done?"

"Why, what has he done? Oh, I know what you said at dinner— 'enlarged the boundaries of thought.' That was good; I have enlarged the boundaries of Santa Lucia, if it comes to that. But men who do particularly brainy things are likely to go as wrong as wrong about practical matters—women, or money, or something like that."

"Well, it remains to be seen whether you don't go wrong yourself in one or the other of those things," she said, smiling.

"As to money," admitted her husband—"well, perhaps; but as to women, there's simply no question about that"; and he took her in his arms.

III

The valley of Santa Lucia lies near enough to the sea for the
westerly winds that blow over it to have sometimes a tang of salt, and
proceeds so far northward that the backwater of the bay comes in by
the gap where the main-travelled roads go out. Its shape is a slow oval,
broad and shallow; it has a dozen towns scattered through it; large
estates of green pastures spreading under noble oaks; aggregations
of pretentious country residences of no particular type, accessible by
trim little stations on the local railway. One guessed well enough by
the names what they are: San this and Santa that for old towns of the
Mission foundation, with ruined adobes crumbling about their coasts,
and long-planted lines of hoary trees; musical, meaningful Spanish
names of Mexican grants long since passed to the conqueror; inapposite,
alien names filched from English country-seats and popular novels,
where *arrivés* millionaires are always just expected from the city, or just
going back to the city, or just gone; newer names of settlements that
smack strongly of their newness, that fairly glitter with the conspicuity
of California real estate.

The town of Santa Lucia—they had begun to call it city then in
the early nineties—the town where Dr. Caldwell had driven furiously
to and fro for thirty-five years, where Evan Lindley had grown up, and
Serena had come to live in her orphaned eighteenth year, where Antrim

Stairs had arrived to spell out his cipher in the skies, and spell it wrongly first and last—this town of Santa Lucia lay so near the head of the valley that now, in the pride of its prosperity, it seemed minded to run on up the hills and possess their glowing slopes. The earliest-settled part of it, where the trees were taller, where there was more conservatism among the inhabitants and more space between the houses, was Santa Lucia proper. East Santa Lucia had the brisk and consequential air which goes with the smell of new paint and ungraded streets. Queen Anne cottages, colonial cottages, miscellaneous collections of scroll-work and shingle stains had a way of springing up in cow-lots and barley-fields. Great umbrageous eucalyptus-trees, hanging like clouds above the sward, were being cut down to make room for palms that in their earliest stages were chiefly remarkable for being indistinguishable from the preserved specimens in the restaurant windows, and in maturity afforded as much relief to the landscape as telegraph-poles with feather-dusters on top.

The houses of Santa Lucia proper had a retiring habit of fencing themselves with hedges of pomegranate and breast-high shrubby geraniums, masking their entrances with great heaps of white La Marque and Lady Banksia roses. The houses of East Santa Lucia had smug little lawns, and a general effect of resembling William's bangs, from the amount of scaffolding that was either just going up or just being taken away. The business centres were perhaps two miles apart, and the college stood between them, with its grounds running back towards the orchards and the farms.

The Lindleys lived in East Santa Lucia, their house, one of the smartest of the new homes lying out on what was known as the Dolby tract, that had yet a smack of its recent status as a barley-field. Poppies and scant stools of grain defined the lawns that had their flowers and shrubbery carefully arranged to afford the greatest satisfaction to the passer-by. Antrim Stairs thought, when Serena came out of the house on the day of the drive, that it looked as little like her as anything he could imagine, though he found she fitted wonderfully well with the spirit of the day when they had come clear of the town and struck into the road winding with the windings of Toyon. It was a windless, brooding day; cloud shadows dappled the wheat; blueness swam about the bases of the hills. Single poppies, blown out like flames at the end of slender stems, sprang up widely through the grain; poppy-breasted larks piped up beside them. The apricot orchards glowed delicately pink, hints of a white wonder gathered in the prunes.

The young Professor of Biology was feeling more at ease with himself and the occasion; he had met members of the faculty in their homes, and the president's wife had sent him word that she expected him to dinner as soon as she was out of quarantine. He had met his classes, and felt that he had successfully concealed from them the extreme embarrassment he had felt on those occasions. Stairs had not lacked opportunity for discovering that he had no social initiative whatever, and now that he found himself getting on so well with Lindley's wife and Mrs. Mathisen he took a mild satisfaction in it as a personal achievement. The way they assumed him, included him in a kind of serious intimacy of allusion and half-quotation, brought things to his notice, and took for granted the ground of his own liking or misliking, was as gratifying as it was unusual. He supposed that their attitude towards him was the key to what an assistant professor of biology should be in his social relations, and was chiefly concerned to miss no hint of acceptable behavior.

They drove up along the stream-side to the mouth of the canon, and got out to walk. The Toyon was full and flooding, the long grass about its banks drooped and streamed forward with the eager force of its running. Wild hyacinths grew up under the oaks with toothwort and saxifrage; fronds of young fern uncurled all about the crevices of the rocks, where they broke through the canon wall; shrubby trees of Toyon, the native holly, clothed the slopes with shining foliage and scarlet berries of the year before. The party strolled up beside the creek. Lindley was full of a project he had for persuading the town to buy the canon and preserve it for a park, and enlarged upon it; but the women paid hardly any attention to him. They were treading daintily, with lifted skirts, about the damp grass and among the rooted rocks gathering wild flowers, conning over the names with bits of old Spanish or Indian lore hidden in a word or a phrase.

They came presently to a little widening of the canon floor, where the warmth and languor of the spring lay like a pool. Holly and oak stood up around it, sycamore in tender leaf edged with lacy shadows the open glade. Here they rested for a time, drinking in wordlessly the recrudescent beauty of the year. Lindley and Mrs. Mathisen were for going on to a spring of indubitable medicinal properties, as evinced by its nastiness; but Serena said the day was too rare to be spoiled by a bad taste in the mouth, so they two went on and left her with Antrim Stairs. It was quite still in the glade; the creek ran softly as it went through and set bright reflections to play upon the sycamore boles. Leaf shadows trembled on the sod, squirrels frisked about openly, and Stairs, leaning on his elbow, half lying on the grass, flicked at them boyishly with twigs and bits of moss. The wine of spring that quickened in his blood, the stimulus of new occasions, the ease of growing assurance in his work, tuned him towards the mood of whimsical tenderness with which Serena, sitting with her chin propped on her hand, looked out upon the green-and-golden glade. The stir of it in his understanding was like the flicker of light on boughs shaken by the wind.

"The sense of power and personality in the wild," said Stairs. "How old it is, and still how fresh! No wonder we get into the way of believing there is something in it."

"Oh," she protested, smiling, "don't be a devotee of exact science all the time. There is something in it. The whole country here is sentient with something—I hardly know what—but it cannot be shadowed forth in Greek imaginings, they are not big enough. If we had a mythology here, it would be full of tall flame-colored creatures that fill the heavens with their shining wings. Do you know, we pride ourselves in the West on our material excellences; but it seems to me that there is a hint all through of the great fancies that make the beginnings of new religions and new arts."

"Were you thinking of the Bodely fountain?" asked Stairs, pricked to audacity by the sheer delight of the day.

Serena laughed amusedly and low. "That has nothing to do with it," she said. "The thing I have in mind must come from the children born here, the children's children."

She left off as if no thought were worth going on with in the bright perfection of the afternoon. Stairs was following some dim trail in his brain, where, if he kept on long enough, he might surprise some illusive imaginings of his own; he wished that Mrs. Lindley might go on talking, not because he cared particularly for what she said, but because she pricked him forward in quest of the word his Work was to say to him. His conscious observation was that Mrs. Lindley had gray eyes rather wide apart, and her mouth, which was delicately curved, had a tendency to droop at the corners.

They were rather quiet going home, musing on the violet of the shadows and the pale golden foam of the mustard blowing on the hills. Where the road turned off from following the creek towards the town, Dr. Caldwell's buggy spun out of a cloud of dust and passed them, never, it seemed, abating one jot of speed as the team swung to one side of the road, the reins lying loosely in the Doctor's large, fair hand. William sat beside him with a hand of hers tucked under his fat arm, and even in the instant of passing and the haste of their going their satisfaction in each other's company declaring itself, and beautiful to see.

"Always going like that," said Lindley, "and always with Billy beside him whenever the time and circumstances allow. I can remember when I was a kid myself, bird-nesting about the orchards, I used to see the Doctor charging down the country roads with his face like a head-light, for he always, as I remember him, was as red and white as he is now, with William's fat little legs stuck straight out in front of her, and one hand under his arm holding on for dear life, sometimes with great tears of fatigue standing on her cheeks. But she would never let on she minded it; trust William for that; she would drive straight to blazes with the old Doctor if he had his team headed that way. And by the same token there is a serious accident about due that outfit."

"Nonsense, Evan!" exclaimed Mrs. Mathisen, who, though she had known him long enough to call him by his first name, never used the familar contraction of it. "Dr. Caldwell has been driving over these roads in just that fashion for thirty-five years, and never had an accident."

"All the more reason why it should be so near at hand. A man can't go on tempting Providence forever; something is bound to give way."

Antrim Stairs found himself in a great uplift of contentment after his drive. When dinner was over in his boarding-house he went out and walked under the oaks in the campus, and failed to think consecutively for more than two strides or three, because of a pleasant blur of excitement in his brain. He was full of a formless purpose, vague presage of power, the sense of desiring things to do and being able to do them very well. He felt that if Mrs. Lindley were here walking beside him

he would have a great deal to say to her—about what he was not quite
clear, but certainly a great deal to say. At the recollection of her light,
whimsical speech there rose up in him a cloud of his own imaginings,
not of half-human creatures in the wood, but things that come to him
about his own work: winged surmises and half shapes of thought. Truth
on his particular horizon always shaped itself out of such nebulosities
with infinite pains, now the possibility of a society where these things
might be cleared in the intimacies of speech afforded him the prospect
of exquisite relief. Still in his brain he heard the far faint trumpet blare
of triumphant things. In this mood Grenning ran upon him on his
way to find him at his rooms, and carried him off to a call at a house
where he said there were some pretty girls who wanted to meet the
distinguished Professor of Biology.

It appeared that all Santa Lucia was bent upon this same business.
Both newspapers had interviewed him, and everybody who could
by any possibility be entitled to that privilege had him to dinner.
By urgence of the college faculty and, as it was said in the *Evening
Messenger,* of many prominent citizens, he was invited to lecture in the
Assembly Hall, and got through with it much better than could have
been expected. His youthful good looks and shyness were very engaging,
his formality passed for the evidence of worth. There is, in fact, nothing
easier than pleasing a public bound to be pleased. Santa Lucia was at
that point of open felicitation upon its own advanced culture which
is a sign of not being very sure of it at heart. They and Stairs got on
better for not having had any previous experience of what the relation
of a rising and already distinguished young scientist should be to his
community. The Santa Lucians enjoyed their own appreciation of him
immensely, and Stairs was human enough to find the savor of it sweet.
But the truth was he was tuning his social behavior to the key Serena
and Mrs. Mathisen had set for him.

Stairs was of country stock, of the sort that, by dint of industry
and strenuous morality, lays in its blood the foundations of greatness.
His parents put him through college, but neither their hopes nor
imagination went beyond the fact of his initial degree. Merely to
compass that was for their way of life, as great an achievement as any
performance of his was likely to be. There they rested; of all that he
did afterwards, what he told them in his letters, what floated to them

through the press and the common report, they had an idea that it was neither more nor less than what was expected of a son who had been brought up by strict observance of the Sabbath, and put through college by prayer and self-denial. And by the same matter-of-factness that limited their understanding of his work, Serena overleaped it.

Stairs was from the East, and the East, which on the coast is the place you come from, meant to Serena just that particular mould of tastes, prejudices, and behavior to which she had been shaped by inheritance and natural aptitude, and at this time she was hungering for it as one might for the savor of fruit from old orchards. The simple largeness of life in her father's house, the simplicity of exquisite taste expressed by moderate means, and the largeness of scholarly insight, associated itself so naturally with the sort of achievement for which Stairs promised to distinguish himself, that she supposed no other atmosphere to breed it, and on such slender grounds jumped at believing him sprung from a social estate for which he was merely fit. It is probable that human intimacies are as often as not provoked by misunderstandings; to the young Professor of Biology her acceptance of him on this plane was an inconceivable spur. It pricked him forward to realizations of his work, defined him to himself.

He made his dinner-call within the week, and found Serena alone by a lamp at a low table, admitting him with a pleasant air of making room for him in her thoughts, reading a little from her book, and provoking comment by deft unconscious touches, lifting him beyond the trough of embarrassment, into which he frequently fell, from surge to surge of animated talk. It was a cool, draughty evening. The long curtains blew out from the open windows, filling the room with a sense of wings. Serena herself wore a light dress, billowy and trailing, as the fashion was, with soft, full sleeves, confined at the wrist and falling with every movement to the contour of her arms. A branch of blossoming plum was stuck in a tall vase beside her, and two or three daffodils were clasped in her belt. Somewhere at the rear of the house unobtrusive domestic noises accounted for the servant, cheerful feet of the neighborhood grew loud on the pavement and passed by, the smell of daffodils was faint and sweet. It was not until Lindley came home from the Board of Trade meeting that Stairs' stiffness returned upon him with embarrassment at finding how long a call he had made.

It had been the end of February when he came to Santa Lucia, and by the first of April the prune orchards swarmed in a white glory of bloom. All the town turned out to it as to a pageant. Whoever had an orchard paid it some observance as to a tutelary god. William gave a tea-party for hers. The orchard at Rosebank was one of the oldest plantations, and every way notable. It began on the side nearest the town, stretched out along the country road, and swept in a wide arc back of the house and up to the garden on the other side. The party was to begin, by William's express limitation, early in the afternoon and last until moonrise.

Stairs was to walk out to it with the Lindleys, or, as it turned out, with Serena, the attorney being detained at his office, to overtake them on his wheel. It had rained in the hills the night before, and wet shadows lingered about the slopes; the valley steeped in the warm languor of afternoon. Their street, which began inconsequentially among the newest of the new houses, and joined the country road at the turn of Toyon opposite Rosebank, was called Penitentia, and by tradition first trodden out by the Mission Fathers. Beyond the town open fields swept up to it, lithe poppies mellowing their borders. Here it was overhung by shaggy Eucalyptus that wagged to the wind slowly as being dull of wit; beyond them wild pastures hedged by holly and sleeping oak; here and there orchards, restrained and orderly, marching up to their confining wires. It was a day of great sufficiency, not needing the help of speech. Serena talked little, and that by way of exploiting the road. Other guests walking and riding, turned into the road; Lindley spun up beside them on his wheel. The occasion began to assume the air of a festival. William's social affairs were always a success, though curiously no one thought of crediting it to William.

The party began with a walk through the orchard, and Julia Maybury, in a white tailored-gown and a color like a La France rose, showed a becoming deference to the distinguished young professor which kept him at her side the whole of the afternoon. Serena thought it too palpably done, and that it must have bored Julia a great deal. She was feeling a little detached in her newly married estate, out of touch with the unmated and not wholly at home with the matrons, and was rather relieved to have Evan whisper to her at supper to make her excuses early. This she did almost immediately after, as the intimacy of the two families allowed, quite happy to be out on the road again with her arm tucked under her husband's, and the slow approach of the moon whitening the farther hills.

"Is anything the matter, Vene?" she wished to know.

"Oh no, only I am dog-tired and out of sorts. I quarrelled with one of my best clients to-day—Warburton. He came in to see me about that confounded Bodely fountain; he had heard I was using my influence for it, but I didn't catch what he was driving at just at first, and got off on the wrong foot. The old fogy has a notion that to accept it is to subvert all the canons of art here and now. Art!" he said, and kicked at the grass of the roadway. "It isn't a question of art, it's a matter of business. If we accept this fountain, we get the new building; if we reject it, ten to one we don't. It's a piece of ridiculous vanity, of course; but if it comes to a matter of taste, it seems to me it is about as bad for us to pick and choose from the gifts that are offered us. I had a talk with the old lady, and I know she feels hurt about it. If there is very much more of the sort of talk Warburton gave me to-day we will lose them altogether. Still, I wish I hadn't got mixed up with Warburton. I've got nothing on hand of his just now, but he brings in a good bit of business in the course of the year; besides, he is the first one of father's clients to get miffed, and I don't want to see them begin."

There was nothing in this to which Serena felt she could reply, the immediate consideration swallowed up in her mind by some vaguely terrifying sense of irreconcilable differences in their point of view. Evan scuffed at the road impatiently as they walked on in the slowly silvering dusk.

IV

In that part of Santa Lucia called "Old Town" by the inhabitants
and "Boarding-house Park" by the college students, because, though it
bore not the slightest resemblance to a park, it was largely given over to
student boarding, there was a house which was expressly of the sort that
Serena Lindley described as sketchy. It was no more pronouncedly of
that sort than many others in the same quarter, but she knew it better,
having lived in it. The building bore every evidence of having been
erected at a time when building material was hard to come by: the roof
had the smallest possible pitch, the eaves were the narrowest allowable,
the very windows looked pinched. The props of the veranda, which
from a front elevation made a good appearance of being pillars, were
merely planks. The body of the house was weather-boarded, but a later
rear addition was of up-and-down boards and battens. It was painted a
dull-green, with a profusion of dull-green shrubbery about it. The yard
was very grassy; perennial herbs established themselves along the walks
and kept the boarders ragged. There were two or three old fruit-trees
about, and over the thin roof of the veranda a heap of Banksia roses that
wanted pruning.

At that time, when there was but a single streetcar line along
College Avenue connecting the old and the new parts of the town,
Boarding-house Park had a rural aspect. People drove about there in

buggies and buckboards that would have been smarter for a little paint. It was even possible, occasionally, to see a woman in a sunbonnet on the cross-lot paths. There were broad green plats of pasture between the dwellings, and the streets were outlined with poplar rows, never unattractive even in winter, when, bare and leaning all one way before the prevailing wind, they marched through the slanting mists of rain. The streets were stiff with mud in that season, and deep with dust when the rains forebore.

It was to this house and its inmates, settled flockwise with dwellings of its own kind among the trim, planted rows of trees, that Serena had turned for a home when her father's sudden death had left her with no other shift. She was eighteen then, and entered in her first year at Wellesley, and her father's only child. Stewart Haven had died quickly, but he had seen his end before it came, and made the best provision he could for her. He had a married sister removed West years before with an ailing husband who had died there. This sister, Luella, he had visited in the year of her widowhood, and found her with a comfortable home, a cheerful outlook, and four daughters of her own. Serena, he felt, needed the companionship of women; it was some such notion had set him on in his choice of a woman's college; face to face with the end of his life and the unfolding of the scroll, he had a secret uneasiness lest he had kept her too much with himself, had enjoyed her too much, and prepared her for life too little. There was another reason why he wished his daughter to go West to her aunt; he could leave her money enough to put her through college, he intended she should go on as she had begun, but not much more. Serena, it appeared, would have to earn her own living, and at Santa Lucia, he had been keen enough to see, it could be done without the loss of social prestige by which it must be accompanied where she now stood. So it was arranged very quickly, with as much thought as they could spare from the nearing terror of final separation, that Serena should finish her college course and spend as much of the long vacations as was expedient with her aunt, and afterwards make her home there until she had won some other station for herself.

Aunt Luella Bixby had four daughters, but one was married and gone, two were teachers, and the youngest still a high-school girl with her hair in braids and her skirts to her ankles. So it came about that

Serena had no particular intimacies with her cousins, but fell in love
with and was absolutely adored by William Caldwell. There was no
question about the adoration, because William declared it—would, in
fact, have enjoyed an occasion for sealing it with some soul-scarifying
vow. William was then attending the College of Santa Lucia, but the old
Doctor, having a shrewd suspicion that the variety of scholarship offered
there was still a little raw at the edges, and a little afraid, as Stewart
Haven had been, of his own fondness, was persuaded, with no more
difficulty than his private one of parting from her, to send William back
to Wellesley with her friend.

This occurred during Serena's second visit to Santa Lucia. The
two girls roomed together for two years. But when Serena had taken her
degree, William had still another year to go, and, confronted with the
prospect of leaving both her parents and her friend, flatly refused the
occasion, got no particular urging to it from any quarter, and took what
finish to her schooling she could get nearer home. So Serena was turned
out, finished, furnished—or so she was supposed to be, and what else
but the proper furnishings for such a setting out she was getting and
paying for, heaven and the college faculty only knew—and was put to
earning her place in the social organization. At twenty-one she was well
read, well schooled, spiritually placed though not poised, not bodily
strong, clean, reasonable, and pretty; but she had never handled a baby,
never been kissed by any but her own people, was not learned in the
practice of propping the moral insufficiencies of those in whom it is
heart-break to admit the need of props; and at twenty-two and a half
she was married. Some day there will be a means discovered to weave
education and the process of life in an indistinguishable thread; then
one may come out of school without having to lap back on the path and
begin the occupation of living at a point of lower vantage. It is here the
shuttle halts and the pattern goes awry. Serena was unfortunate at this
juncture to have no other adviser than her aunt Luella, because Mrs.
Bixby had arrived at that point of satisfaction with the issue of her own
life which made it impossible for her to understand that it was not also
the best for her niece. She even thought, sometimes, confronted with
some puzzling evidence of the girl's originality, that it was a mercy the
good Lord had taken brother Stewart just when he did, or the child
might have been spoiled; for as much as she attempted anything to the

girl's betterment, it was by way of taking out of her what her father and the good Lord had put in. Mrs. Bixby had no faith whatever in the ability of Providence to prefigure what He wished women to be by the faculties with which He endowed them. The root of the matter was to be found not in the secret capacities of the individual, but in the promulgations of the W.S.A., the W.F.M.S., the W.C.T.U., and the Articles of Faith of the Church of Christian Endeavor, which name will stand as well as any other for the Protestant sect of Mrs. Bixby's allegiance.

It is a question often whether the narrowness of some extremely good people is the more exasperating, or their complacency in it. Mrs. Bixby was a good woman; whether she should be called a pietist depends on how you view her habit of putting the milk ticket for the Sunday morning's milk on the gate-post Saturday night. She was prompt in testimony and prayer, and it was not to be denied got a real spiritual uplift from the somewhat barren and inartistic ritual of her church. During the life of her husband, and while her children were still young, most of her activities were of that neighborly kind that in simple communities are transacted across the back fence. But in middle life, when Serena came to Santa Lucia, she was chiefly concerned with what she understood as the World's Work. All this was alphabetically indicated in the heads of societies before named. She was also on the pastor's relief committee, and attended mothers' meetings, together with other women like herself, whose children were grown up, and schoolteachers who, if they had taken steps legitimate to become mothers, would have immediately lost their positions. All of which activities, taken seriously, were everything of enlarged life and opportunity to Aunt Luella; and all women not directly related to these labors were curiously outside her pale. She had never approved of Serena's intimacy with Mrs. Mathisen, and that not for anything the lady was, but because she could not believe that a woman who read Balzac in the original, and liked, really liked, Shakespeare, could have any grip on the stable things of life. If there was any pride of righteousness in this, neither Mrs. Bixby nor her intimates were aware of it. They lacked imagination perhaps, and entertained a belief not uncommon, that nothing can be really practical which is not also a little dull. And if you wanted proof of the exceeding practicality of the many initialed scheme of life, Mrs. Bixby would have pointed you the issue of her own. There was one daughter comfortably married, and two self-educated as teachers in the town schools, and the little income her husband had left her, helped out by their means, until it afforded her a best black silk dress and a not too straightened hour to spend over the printed slip, on which she certified the amount of her contribution to the various exigencies of the church.

"If that wasn't practicality," Mrs. Bixby would have said, "what was it?"

Aunt Luella was a large, comfortable woman with the type of face that is called motherly; able to overlook tolerantly finicky tastes in literature and lax views on the duties of women in her neighbors, particularly if they were church members, but quite resolved not to countenance them in her brother's child. In truth, Serena was much taken with her aunt at first. The girl had a mind avid for realities, and being then at the inquiring age, found much in her aunt's conversation that interested and, since a girl must be set thinking at some time, no doubt benefited her. That happened to be the summer that Mrs. Bixby was busiest in the distribution of various printed matter, called literature in the Shibboleth of her societies, on the subject of heredity in connection with what she habitually referred to as the Liquor Question. "Enough," Roxanne used to say, "to scare you out of the notion of having children forever after." The A. B. Z's, as Roxanne nominated her mother's various affiliations, dealt in heredity, the married estate, the abolition of poverty, and, with equal seriousness, the abolition of the bustle, the induction of the Indian into the house habit, and the South Sea Islanders into Butterick-pattern clothes. And when Aunt Luella found Serena ready to go into all these with the serious ignorance of eighteen, she felt the world go forward with palpable shoves. What Serena had to learn afterwards was that when a woman in middle life takes what she is pleased to call advanced ideas, it is more than likely they are merely an occupation, and confronted with a particular instance she reverts to the judgment of the generation that shaped her. It was to be a shock to Serena to discover the purely extraneous character of her aunt's views; perhaps not less of a shock to Mrs. Bixby to come face to face with the reality of their proper outcome. Such mutual discoveries began soon enough, but it was not until it came time for Serena to choose a work and do it that they were in serious opposition.

Serena's notion was very simply, to consider with what capability the Distributor of Benefits had endowed her, which, as nearly as she could determine, was an aptitude for construction, and, having found, to follow with the directness of a wild thing following a scent. And the trail seemed to lead in the direction of one of the artistic crafts. If the girl had had a squint her aunt would have grieved over it without being ashamed, but that she should make her career a personal matter between herself and Providence gave the good woman a sense of mortified affront.

"Why, she talks like a man!" she said to her eldest daughter, in the privacy of the bedroom which they shared.

"A great many girls do," said Kate, who taught in the high-school and might be supposed to know. "Though I don't see why they shouldn't, as long as they have to live with them."

But Mrs. Bixby thought the least they could do was to keep the knowledge of Serena's aberration in the family. In Mrs. Bixby's world not to know that marriage and the correlated callings of nursing and teaching were the only creditable employments was to evince a lapse of true womanliness.

Mrs. Bixby rather thought that her niece's attitude might be the result of having had too many fairy stories read to her, but she stuck to it that Serena could not be allowed to throw away her education by getting a living by handicraft. Aunt Luella was not singular in the notion that getting a living by your education meant decanting it for a salary. She was so far successful that before the end of the summer Serena was engaged to teach school at San Marco Junction.

Serena loathed teaching. It came upon her as a confusion of urgent voices exploding questions of which she but dimly understood the purport and did not know the answers. She grew thin and fagged, and showed signs of a break-down as early as Christmas. Her aunt might have worried about it, but she was very much taken up that winter with a series of lectures directed towards limiting the population in the interests of the standard of purity, and because of Evan Lindley.

It was agreed that the Lindleys were in every way a desirable family to marry into. It was thought that if the Judge had lived a little

longer he might have been governor. He was ailing the winter Serena
taught at San Marco, and Evan, who had taken his degree and been
admitted to partnership in the same year, always contrived his business
trips so that they fell on the days when Serena would be going back
and forth from school. It was very pleasant to the girl to drop off the
puzzling, squalid labors of the week, and find him waiting with just
the touch of conscious intimacy, which Evan, who had not shirked any
occasion for rehearsing it, knew how to give.

It was on towards the end of December, one day when she had
crossed the prejudices of San Marco, and been set upon by the small
meanness which to be offended by is an offence to one's self, that she
had done the unaccustomed thing, letting her troubles slip from her in
speech, and Evan had declared that this would be the end of it. They
had the car all to themselves, and saw the wet world glide by in sheeted
mist. It was very pleasant with the cold and dreariness shut out and
Evan's arm very near her shoulder. Serena did not remember very well
what passed until they came out at Santa Lucia with the rain falling and
Evan, in a state of exhilaration that seemed all out of proportion to the
event, putting her into a hack. "I'm coming round to-night to tell them
we are engaged," he whispered. Serena put out her hand in a startled
instinct of protest, but Evan clasped it, and the impulse dropped and
died under the quick, warm contact. Riding away in the darkling rain,
even in the glow of being possessed, she wondered to feel it stir again
with the sense of something missed.

Mrs. Bixby was undisguisedly glad. Really things turned out very
well in this world if you did the best you knew and trusted Providence.
Serena had been a problem, now resolved to the fixed and stable estate
of marriage; for what has a married woman to do with questionings,
adventures, and passionate experiences—what, indeed? Mrs. Bixby felt
she had discharged well her duty to her brother's child, and gave thanks
for it.

The young people were married early in the summer, sooner
than had at first been thought advisable, but the Judge had died at
the end of February, and Mrs. Lindley determining to make her home
with a married daughter who needed her, Evan was left without one.
Mrs. Bixby would have liked to see Serena "make a little more out of
her education," as she phrased it; it hardly seemed fair to poor brother

Stewart, after he had spent so much money on it; but she reflected that the girl's health would hardly have allowed it, and the marriage was in every way desirable. The last night but one before her wedding Serena spent with William at Rosebank. When the long twilight began to dusk the orchards and the sky was saffron bright, they went out by the Toyon to be alone in the leave-taking of their girlish intimacy.

William, who dearly loved a make-believe, was for trying some childish oracle at a place where the water, rising and falling to far-off snows, gurgled out intermittently under the roots of a sycamore.

"To see if you are going to be happy or not," she laughed, but the oracle went contrarily.

"I suppose that means that you have to make your happiness yourself," she laughed.

"Oh," said Serena, "I shouldn't care for a manufactured happiness; I shouldn't suppose humans had the secret of it, anyway; Happiness is a gift of the gods."

"Well, I don't see why we should expect just being married to make one happy; it is such a common experience, almost like getting your second teeth," said William; and then: "Serena, will you promise me something?"

"Well, what?" asked Serena, leaning over to trail her hands in the water.

"Well, if the time ever comes when I have to make up my mind to be married—I suppose it will, though I've never seen the man yet that could take me away from dad—if the time comes, and I come to you, for of course you will still be my dearest friend, even though you *are* married, and if I ask you if marriage is really worth while, will you not pretend, but tell me truly what it is?"

"Why should you suppose I would tell you anything else? You know that I think a lie about life the worst kind of lie."

"But will you truly?"

"Yes," said Serena, solemnly, "I truly will."

But it was not until eight months later, when the matter of the Bodely fountain came up, that Serena discovered that two people could come together in marriage without on that account coming together in their views. It had been an amazement to discover in Evan capabilities of admitting the Bodely fountain, often more of an amazement to find him unaffected by her deprecation. She was still so secure in her traditional bridal preciousness that she did not wholly realize the nature of her husband's attitude, until, at the annual meeting of the trustees of the college, the fountain was accepted, and the newspapers conceded that "our brilliant young attorney Evan Lindley" had moved with credit in that business. In the face of the public felicitation she found no occasion to express the secret mortification the announcement caused her. About that time Warburton, who had a suit for foreclosure coming on, took it to another man.

V

The house at Rosebank was divided in the middle by a wide hall,
through which a stair went up by easy landings to the low-ceiled second
floor. East of the hall, below-stairs, was the parlor, a square, high room
with deep shelves built into the outer wall, and a tall old mantel with
an oil-portrait of the Doctor's mother and the Doctor at the cherubic
age, as round and red and white as now. There were tall old vases on the
mantel, and tall windows with soft old hangings, and tight old furniture
that gave the room the air of having been laid aside for a remembrance,
like sprigs of rosemary in a book. It was a room that made you look
for, and not be disappointed in finding, a hint of mould on the fat old
volume of Dickens and Cooper in the deep shelves, and accept it when
found as the last consummate touch in a room so unrelated to its time
that it set you wondering how it could be so successful; the sort of
room that, Mrs. Mathisen used to say, once you had sat in it an hour,
prevented you forever afterwards from thinking William ridiculous.

Back of the parlor was the long dining-room, with the Doctor's
office thrown off from that, to be easiest of access from the road; across
the hall, such other rooms as accommodate the business of living; and
directly in front of the second-story landing, one, hardly more than
a closet, really the end of the hallway cut off by a partition, called by
the Doctor "William's Heart." It opened into her bedroom, and was

probably intended for a dressing-room, but William, who changed the bent of her interests frequently without dividing them, made it the visible sign of their occupation. At one time it had accommodated a numerous family of dolls, valued in the order of their disrepair, and later became a den, choked with souvenirs, cushions, and school photographs, which gave place presently to busts of the poets, severe shelves of books, and a little table by the window which looked out under the long-leaved pine towards Toyon, where William wrote sonnets that invariably lacked a line or two. It had been athletic when William was, and domestic the summer she attended cooking-school, and in the spring of the year, when Antrim Stairs came to Santa Lucia, it had been a studio, where William, who knew nothing technically, set down her impressions in paint, or pinched them in clay, or hammered them in metal; in fact, there were so many activities that could be appropriately indulged in a studio that William's Heart appeared to have become entirely habituated to its air of accomplished disorder. Therefore, it was with surprise that Serena, going up unannounced, towards the end of June, met Jap coming down with an armful of sketches for the kitchen fire, and William with the Doctor's big microscope at the table poring over fragments of the scum of pond water, and a row of wide-mouthed bottles full of pollywogs on the window-ledge.

"You don't mind Jap and me going right on, do you?" she inquired. "I am so anxious to get the laboratory in shape before Tuesday, for I expect the class out here. Why, yes, haven't you heard? Dr. Stairs is having a class in biology. I am taking it up; I feel so much the need of mental stimulus," said William, feeding green scum to the pollywogs with a seriously experimental air.

"I remember Kate told me some of the teachers were trying to get some summer work with him, but I didn't know there was anybody else. I might have been interested in it myself."

"Well, you see, for a purely intellectual affair we didn't need a chaperon. Why, some of the teachers must be years older than Dr. Stairs; so we haven't any married women."

"I don't see why," said Serena, taking the conversational note lightly. "I don't see why married women couldn't be interested in it on their own account, and not simply to afford you the occasion of being interested with propriety?"

"Well," said William, squinting judiciously at her slides, "married women usually have interests of their own."

"They generally have, but I don't see why it should be so taken for granted that they are not intellectual." Serena put up her hands to her cheeks, which were hot with some secret indefinable mortification. Then she laughed. "I believe I am cross; it must be the weather." It was a close, suffocating day—heated air pent in the valley under a gray tent of cloud.

William went on explaining her cultures, interrupting herself to give directions to Jap about the shelves he was putting up, and interrupting that to gossip about the class and Antrim Stairs.

Was Julia Maybury in it, Serena wanted to know, and was not surprised to hear that she was. William thought Stairs had invited her out of compliment to the Sterlings, with whom she was staying. What Serena was thinking of was one of the commencement functions not so long ago when she had been talking with Antrim Stairs, interesting him, drawing him on to talk, with all the best she had, and he pleasantly aware of acquitting himself unusually well, when Julia Maybury came by, and the young man had turned to the girl and finally gone away with her, even in his formal unaccustomed manner, naturally, as if the mere fact of Julia's unappropriated state was better reason for seeking her company than Mrs. Lindley's better understanding. It is a moment to which all young matrons must come, and to a woman not accustomed to think of herself as an object of desire it comes with a shock to find herself personally cheapened by the act of entrance to a larger social estate. In Julia's manner, at least, there had been something that accused her of forgetting that a married woman and a girl of exactly the same years are not of the same age, and in the young man's unconsciousness of any claims to his social consideration in her finer attune to his key, something that left her vaguely hurt. Within the week he had been at her house with the proof-sheets of a magazine article, wanting her opinion, but with not a word of his class, as if, though she should partake of his interests, she was, being married, quite out of the pale of his activities. But the pang of it was still too quick and indefinable for speech, and William was going on light-mindedly about Julia Maybury.

"I can't think it is anything but a fad with Julia. She knows absolutely nothing about it, not even the terminology, and makes the funniest mistakes. But anybody could afford to make mistakes with such a complexion. Those San Francisco girls all have so much color. Where shall I put these tubes, Serena?"

"Not there, where you will have to move them every time you take down your slides. Let me show you."

Serena with her hat off and her mouth full of nails, William dropping breakable things on chairs and afterwards dropping hammers on them, both the girls giving orders and countermanding them, and Jap going up and down stairs three steps at a time in a very agony of helpfulness, was so much in the old manner that it quickened their intimacy to its old girlish warmth. They had hammered and contrived so often together that they fell naturally into its accompaniment of gossipy speech, not minding Jap in the least—when had they ever minded him, or who minded him, anywhere? He had not the effect of minding himself even. Serena used to say that his intelligence was merely a dynamo which could be turned on and off as required, and of late, she had added to herself, how light a touch of William's would bring it into play.

He was originally a fair, thin-skinned man, with a good deal of light, lank hair, but, by dint of running out with his hat off in great eagerness on the Doctor's affairs, had burned to a purplish-brown, and bleached his hair in a curious, streaky effect which was heightened by a white lock in the midst that had a way of becoming conspicuous under excitement. It was this which made people look twice at him when no motion or assumption of his would have betrayed him to attention. He was quick and eager when the Doctor or William spoke, or any other in their interest, and appeared to fall apart, so far as his mentality was concerned, like a mechanism, when that stimulus was removed. For ten years he had been hostler, assistant, nurse, and handy-man for the old Doctor, and gotten himself accepted as much of a neighborhood institution as the Doctor's buggy. The only capacity in which he called for comment was as a nurse. He seemed to set himself as a spring, sensitive to the least fluctuation of the patient's condition, even to such not evident to the sense. He was never tired, he never fidgeted; if he slept it was always with this extra intelligence at the point of attention. If he made alterations in the treatment, it seemed to be by a kind of divination, for he never accounted for them, and they were always found when the Doctor came to be the best possible. Mrs. Mathisen used to say that the Doctor looked at Jap when he came in before he looked at the patient. What was curious about this, though it was a long time before it became to be commented upon as anything more than a coincidence, was that he consistently avoided the actual moment of death. Gradually it had settled into one of the traditions of the Doctor's practice that when he took Jap off a case it was time to begin to think about the funeral. People who remembered when he came to Rosebank recalled that he was then recovering from a long illness, and insensibly the impression got about that he was a medical student who had broken down from overstudy, and had since been not quite right in his head. For the rest he was simply Jap, the Doctor's man. No one seemed to know whether it was his first name or his last, or whether, in fact, he had ever had any other.

To William, Jap was exactly an important adjunct to her father's comfort, and incidentally, when her father was not occupying him, to hers—a sort of easy-chair, to be pulled forward or pushed back as required. Nothing could have suited Jap better; he was as happy in effacement, supposing effacement was what the occasion suggested, as in service. He suffered no sense of slight, nor was any intended.

William had a manner towards him as kind as to her father's team, to which she fed apples and lumps of sugar, as approving as to the cushions of the big lounge in the office when she patted and plumped them for the old Doctor after a long day's ride. To William it was just as natural to have Jap putting up shelves and sawing out brackets for her laboratory as to have Serena, who, though she had not William's bent for violent readjustments of her enthusiasms, enjoyed to the full the process of them. She had been used to say that she had to go to William's to get chances to do things, for Mrs. Bixby was one of those competent housekeepers whose work has become a habit rather than an occupation—a habit which it bothered her to have disturbed by essays of inexperience. It was one of Aunt Luella's theories that housework was a holy office, expressly and infallibly ordained for women; but it was a fact that none of her own girls knew much about it.

With so much willingness brought to the work, the afternoon in William's Heart wore away rapidly enough, so that by the time the apparatus was all in place, and Jap was quite done with running downstairs with discarded plunder, and then carrying it up to see if after all it could not be used, when Sing had come up the stairs with a plate of cookies warm from the oven, and William had begun to make tea over the spirit-lamp that had been part of their college furnishings, the sky was quite overcast.

The rush of Toyon, which should have run low at this season, seemed to fill all the space between them and the sky. They could pick out the separate tones of its passing under the bridge below the house, of the fall of the head-gate half a mile away, and the whispering ripple of the curve.

"Why do you go so often to the window, William?" asked Serena. "That's the third time in the last ten minutes."

"I—I hardly know. I seem to be expecting something on the Toyon road, but I don't know what. Dad is up at McCloud's; but he will hardly get away before night, if at all." Then, as a moment later she caught herself doing the same thing, she laughed. "Sometimes I think the flicker of the water under the willows by the turn of the road has hypnotized me. I cannot keep away from it very long, but to-day it's worse than usual. There goes Jap clear out to the turn, looking and looking. It's curious to me how Jap always seems to be affected the way I am about things, but always a little later, as if he caught it from me. It's particularly so if it's about dad. Times when I am worried at night because he is late, and go up to bed without saying a word for fear of worrying ma, the first thing I know there will go Jap out with the lantern to find him on the road. Did you notice this afternoon? He was as restless about the window as I was."

This reminded Serena of something else she had noticed, which it seemed now had occurred to her a good many times before that afternoon without her being wholly aware of it. She thought it an excellent time to give the matter speech.

"Billy, did it ever occur to you that Jap might fall in love with you?"

"Se-re-na!"

"Well, why not? I am sure the way he looks at you—this afternoon for instance—"

"But Jap! Why, I should as soon suspect him of anything of the kind as suspect—the—the furniture. Poor old Jap!"

"He's only thirty-two. And now that I have got to understand men better, I can see—" William cut off her friend's speech with a suffocating squeeze.

"Now, now, don't you try any of your matronly airs on me, Mrs. Lindley, for I won't stand it! A lot you know about men!"

"Well, you must expect to be fallen in love with some time."

"Oh, I suppose so. I suppose I would be disappointed if I wasn't. But Jap! There used to be a time when I expected to see the Not Impossible riding down the Toyon road in a silver armor. I believe I used to get up early on purpose to see.

> "'Tir-a lira, by the river,
> Sang Sir Launcelot.'"

she hummed, sitting on the arm of Serena's chair. "Somehow," she went on, more soberly, "I have a feeling that nothing real and moving can come into my life that does not come down the Toyon road. It is so much a part of all that I have lived—that little bit of it between the sycamore and the turn beyond the bridge; and though I know every foot of the way it comes and the country to which it goes, it always seems to begin in mystery and to lead directly to some place where I have always wished to be."

They were reminded suddenly how late it was by Mrs. Caldwell coming up softly to ask Serena to stay to supper.

"Mercy, no—thank you! Nobody knows where I am, and Evan will be distracted. Luckily we are having dinner later these hot days, or the cook would be worse than Vene."

William went a bit of the way with her, and after she had turned alone into Penitentia Street she saw Antrim Stairs wriggling from under a barbed-wire fence at the edge of a stubble-field. He was splashed and flushed; there were seeds of evil weeds pricked into his clothes, his oldest suit; and nothing so became the formality of his manners as his best, but there was a boyish glow about him that was pleasant to see. He had been exploring the irrigating ditches, and had a case full of bottled infinitesimals, which he named over to her as quite sure of her appreciation.

"William has been telling me about her class," she said. Perhaps she had not quite succeeded in keeping a suggestion of alienation out of her voice, for the words seemed to cause him a sudden accession of embarrassment.

"Yes," he said, "I hardly liked to mention it, it is so elementary, … and I had not quite decided on it until after our talk the other night. It was what you said about the obligation of passing on the truth as soon as we became sure of its truthfulness, and not thinking too much about how it was received as how it was delivered." He was mopping his face with a handkerchief which had already been used to wipe off ditchwater that afternoon, which, when he happened to catch a glimpse of it, added considerably to his confusion.

"And as I had expected to spend the summer getting to know the possibilities of the neighborhood," he went on, "I thought a class might prove—that is, it might be an opportunity." He did not take the personal note easily, and he felt that he had accused himself of using his pupils too much to his own advantage. But that he had fallen into the way of expecting Mrs. Lindley to take his meaning at the highest point, he would not have been able to get so far with his explanation, but Serena kindled for him, glowing always a little ahead of his thought. They dropped more into commonplaces after that, and at the next turn he excused himself to her, not wishing to pass through town in the state he was in, and went swinging his specimen-case across the field.

Serena came home a little wearily; the long walk in sultry weather was too much for her strength, her husband said. The house, shut up for the afternoon, was close and stuffy with the smell of dinner. Everything in it seemed obtrusively new and smart, the dinner was not very good, and the girl sulky. Lindley's usual appetite and complacency seemed vaguely an offence. After dinner they went out and sat on what there was of porch behind the gingerbread-work. The tight little lawns, the rows of other tight little lawns, all carefully arranged to give the best possible impression from the outside, the unshaded, unpaved streets between, the compact, snug little cottages, seemed to impinge upon her soul, to narrow and shape it to their likeness. The sense of her married life began to go through her as something intolerably flat and stale. They had lived in this house now ten months less two weeks of their wedding journey, and she had yet no feeling of being at home in it. The glow of the honeymoon had gone off, and nothing had succeeded it but a routine of tiring and unimportant duties. She had leisure hours, but found no way of filling them that bore any relation to any point or purpose of their life. If she had any young wife's dreams about her entering into her husband's career, Lindley's utter unconsciousness of such expectation, or of any obligation on his part to make a place for her, would have proved a check; in fact, there were not many ways in which she could have helped him. Of his law practice she had no technical knowledge, and in those things that engaged him in what he phrased as the interests of the town, she was not particularly quick nor adaptable. Once she had planned a decorative scheme for the Chamber of Commerce when the town was entertaining a tourist party from the East, and the plan, when she had persuaded him to carry it out, had proved a great success, but the hurt she had in discovering that her husband had no immediate conviction of her helpfulness had prevented her making any further tender of services. What she perceived chiefly was that Lindley took the greatest satisfaction in his own achievements of that sort, and it had simply not occurred to him that he was not equal to them alone.

Serena had confidently looked to find some outlet of her strong bent for accomplishing things in the management of the household allowance; now, when they were well settled, she had come rather slowly to adjust herself to there not being any.

"Why, what on earth do you want with money?" said her husband. "Don't you have everything you want? Just go ahead and get what we ought to have, and I will see to the bills."

"How will I know what we ought to have if I do not know how much money there is to spend?"

"Why, just about what other people have in our circumstances. If I see that we can't afford things I'll let you know."

"But, Evan, suppose I think we can't afford it?"

Lindley stared at her in good-humored amazement. "Why, I don't see what that has to do with it. Don't you worry about affording. That's what husbands are for."

It was a view that Lindley could not be brought to—that the care of the income would be a pleasure rather than a worry. He thought it rather ridiculous; money was a man's part of life. Serena was fond of managing, and went back now in her mind to the time when even in her teens her father had used to consult her about their small enjoyments, planning to forego one that they might compass another, and felicitating themselves wonderfully on some fortunate stroke. She had looked forward to something of this sort in her husband's house, bringing her wit and experience to achieve comfort, and at the same time add something to the fund of fortune, making forward by ever so small degrees, but still forward, through the years to competency. She took her housework seriously enough, but upon the present basis she admitted to herself that it lacked zest.

Sitting there in the hot dusk of June, a little fretted by weariness, yet with the taste of the afternoon's activities pricking pleasantly in her mind, she put aside her husband's cheerful commonplaces with pointed soberness.

"Vene," she began, "there is something I want to talk to you about. Vene, I want something to do."

"Something to do?" he asked, in puzzled wonder. "Something to think about and plan for and spend myself upon."

"Well, I thought when we were married you were going to spend a lot of yourself on me," he said, loverly. She was still too newly a wife not to respond to that a little, though it did not turn her from the point.

"But, Vene, you don't seem to—to need me in your business," she protested.

"Well, I should say not. I married a wife to take care of her." He put his arm about her strongly.

"Oh, you do, Vene, beautifully, but—" She hesitated for words that should convince without accusing him.

"What's the matter, darling, can't you trust me to make you happy?" he asked, mannishly.

"Oh, happy—happy!" she broke out almost, in exasperation—"I don't know that it is so necessary to be happy. I would rather be doing something."

He was sitting still with his arms about her, and she turned her cheek to his shoulder to atone for the petulant speech, but saying nothing more, not knowing how to put to her husband the sense of imperative energies not quite absorbed in the obligation of wifeliness, and not sure she had not herself fallen short, since loving left her still with a want of occupation. Sitting so in the still dark they could hear the feet of passers a long way up the pavement, reinforced by echoes of houses they passed, or falling faint opposite the unbuilt lots. One such double trail of steps approached them now, catching the idle attention as they passed, and showed against the circle of the street-lamp farther down—a man and a woman dressed for an evening's entertainment, the woman in fluffy white that showed very plainly as they came into the circumscribed arc of the street-lamp: how the young man whipped his arm from around her waist for a more conventional proffer of it. Lindley gave his wife a squeeze, chuckling a reminder of their own courting days. Serena did not laugh. The man was a stranger to her; but as the couple passed directly beneath the lamp she had recognized the girl as Julia Maybury.

VI

During the long vacation, while William hunted pollywogs
with Dr. Stairs, and talked of primordial slime, Serena found herself
thrown back on her situation as a young matron with a new sense of
its inadequacy, though she was not in any other case than too many
women in whom the sedulous social ideal contrives to nourish only the
susceptibilities of the intelligence. Unripe for passion, she had accepted
marriage not so much as a solution as a chivalric attention. Say she had
found the way of life left to her by her father's death a shade too hard
for her nurture; marriage was a doorway into which she had stepped
in a day of rough weather—and now, suddenly, the door had swung
upon the latch, and she saw the whole procession of life go by her in the
street.

As Serena Haven she had wholly satisfied the requirements of a
thoroughly nice girl, which makes her the greater prize for marriage
in knowing the least what it means; and, not being able to find its
transports an occupation, was disposed to credit her disability to the
finer radiancy of bloom not breathed upon by desire, when, in fact,
she did not know in the least how to love. At this juncture a woman
blames marriage or the man, and finds a warrant for it in his own sense
of blameworthiness in the greater distance he has come towards a larger
appreciation, and a readiness to believe himself rather the less deserving

of its rapturous intimacies as he is the better fit for them. It is a pity, since a man knows so much, he should not know a little more, and understand that after the "I pronounce you" the precious quality of the bride's inviolateness leaves something still to be won. Commonly nothing comes of this ineptitude but the young wife's conviction that her husband does not truly love her, which she suffers for as long a time as her remoteness defeats an appreciation of the quality of his regard.

Serena, not being of the nature that imputes blame, supposed merely that she had discovered that happiness does not come by saying so, but remains to be achieved; and for immediate relief fell back on the passion of loyalty which is the peculiar genius of women. In the mean time she had, literally, nothing to do. The maid-servant was proved reasonably competent, the appointments of the house were fresh and of a completeness rendering unnecessary the contrivances that exercise ingenuity and time. Lindley had no capital when he married, but the generous loyalty of his father's clients and the percentages of a promising real-estate business which he had brought together himself, seemed to justify the expense of a family.

Santa Lucia at that time rather abounded in devises by which a man was legitimately made to anticipate frugality and enjoy his income in advance; in fact, you might say prosperity was fairly hurled upon you. City lots beguiled buyers by easy payments; houses were put up by building and loan concerns, on what was, according to the way you looked at it, exorbitant rental or liberal terms of purchase; furniture came into the house on the instalment plan—rather the furniture came in complete from attic to cellar, and money went out for it in such moderate quittances as you were supposed not to miss. There was nothing lacking from the Lindley's establishment for which a modern house might conceivably find a use, though Serena owned to herself a want of satisfaction in the result; it was all so obviously the product of the shop rather than the requirement of living, and afforded not the slightest excuse for occupation.

"I do believe," she confided to Mrs. Mathisen, when she had been married six months, "I should be glad to see a hole coming in the carpet, and it was a positive relief when Vene's underwear began to go."

Outside the house there was equally nothing to do. There were red geraniums along the east side of the house and pink geraniums

in front and a clump of callas at the hydrant on the lawn; there was
a La Marque rose at the front of the veranda, and a Gold of Ophir at
the end, a Cherokee rose on a screen at the kitchen door and a yellow
Banksia over the woodshed; there were two fan palms exactly two and
a half feet high on each side of the front walk and an ornamental iron
hitching-post in the ribbon of grass between the pavement and the
street. There was nothing to be done for any of these things; if there
had been, Lindley would have employed a man to attend to it at once.
Serena could not escape the conviction that her husband valued the
geraniums and palms as the evidence of his being up to date. He would
have as readily taken a sentimental interest in the paint on his house.

In the beginning of their plans it was a question whether it
would be better for the young people to begin their housekeeping in
the old place of the Lindley's, which the Judge's widow had a tender
unwillingness to let, yet would have wished her son to occupy; but
Evan pooh-poohed the suggestion. He thought the home place, with its
untrimmed shrubbery and wide old trees on wild lawns, a derogation
of his position as leader of the party of civic improvement in East Santa
Lucia. What he wished to stand for was the latest.

So the new house came about, though Serena had admitted, even
in her honeymoon, that it gave her rather the feeling of being done
up in glazed paper and sent home from the milliner's. And there was
obviously nothing to do about it.

"Well," Lindley wished to know, "why should she do anything?
Had she not a husband?" This being eminently the proper frame of
mind for a young husband, Serena found no fault with it. It appeared
this was a woman's problem—and Aunt Luella was a woman steeped in
problems, breathing an atmosphere of advanced solution. Aunt Luella
was not perhaps on one's own plane, but here, at least, one was sure of
her sympathy. With a tingling sense of being at least face to face with
something, Serena went out for the afternoon at Boarding-house Park.
Aunt Luella looked at her amazedly over the tops of the spectacles she
had lately begun to use.

"So you want something to do, Serena? In my time when a young
woman married she was supposed to have found enough to do."

"In your time, Aunt Luella, she probably had. Father told me that when you were first married to Uncle Bixby you kept bees, and sold the honey to buy your parlor furniture."

"And had plenty to do taking care of it."

"Aunt Luella, do you see anything wrong with my housekeeping?"

Mrs. Bixby's eyebrows expressed a conviction that there must be if the housekeeper found herself out of employment, but she had to admit the spick-and-spanness of her niece's home.

"If you were to do your own sewing—"

"Aunt Luella, what have I heard you say about the women whose whole time was occupied with personal adornment? Besides, I have stacks of clothes."

"Well, child, what do you want, then?" Serena searched in her memory for the phrases that, heard first from her aunt, had a kindling sound.

"I want," she said, slowly, "my share in the world's work." It had the effect of bringing out on Mrs. Bixby what Kate called her apostolic smile. Kate found in her mother's moral enthusiasms a fund of quiet irony and an occasional tang of bitterness which Mrs. Bixby laid to her eldest daughter never having had an offer of marriage. But since Aunt Luella had entered upon the business of setting the world to rights, the necessity of being oracular sat upon her visibly. Taken unawares, she was prone to answer you out of her natural good sense, which was great; but when the subject revealed itself as steering towards the postulates of the organizations she affected, she fell into a manner curiously like that of a very intelligent dog, who would have you to understand he has not missed the drift of your conversation; but it was a manner which, once it had grasped your question, admitted no possibility of not owning the right solution. She set her glasses on the top of her head, and dispensed sweetness and light, saying:

"What better work can a woman do to help the world onward than by being a noble wife and mother?"

"Oh!" fretted Serena; she thought of many things she might say to that, but tears choked her.

"What could you do?" asked Kate. "You are only fitted to teach, and now that you are married you couldn't do that—at least, not in Santa Lucia."

"I wasn't thinking of teaching," disclaimed Serena.

"I should hope not," interposed Aunt Luella. "A married woman's place is in her home, I think. What's the reason you don't have a baby, Serena? You've been married long enough, I should think." The question shattered Serena like a slap in the face. She got up to leave: she had forgotten to give directions for dinner, she said. All the way home she told herself that she would never have expected it of Aunt Luella, and would never feel the same towards her again. The offence lay in being expected to make an end of what was merely the perquisite of living, and rankled all the more, as it was instinctive and incoherent.

The passing of the languor of summer heat brought days of sane, inspiring weather, quickening pulse and thought. Pools of leafage caught in hollows of the country roads were whirled up by the wind, shining as they turned in air like conjurer's gold, dropping now as orchard litter, sear and brown. They turned before her as the days of her life, now colored by her dreams, now fading and tattered at the edges, her passion too virginal to gild them with romance, her purpose too aimless to keep them up and whirling. Serena's young elastic mind ached in the cushioned hollow of her environment. She was the more glad, on that account, to meet with Antrim Stairs.

The year before coming to Santa Lucia he had been intimately associated with the experiments of Professor Lehr, since become of public interest; and an Eastern magazine had asked for an account of them made intelligible to the untechnical. He brought the matter of his sketch to Mrs. Lindley as to a touchstone, and brought it twice or thrice until it was cleared of scholarly obscurities. He came again because the principal of the high-school had begged his co-operation in reshaping the laboratory work in zoology. Stairs searched for material by the creeks, by the headgates, and the pools of slack-water that came—from the sea on the north. Serena saw him often across the fields by the bright, falling weirs with the Sterling girls or Julia Maybury, or walking with William along Toyon. Social use in Santa Lucia permitted this; the savor of science made it commendable; the Professor's dip-net and specimen-case stood in lieu of a chaperone. At Santa Lucia there was a general notion that all association of the unmarried was a tentative motion towards matrimony, as such demanding the sanction of considerable freedom. Antrim Stairs might take young girls with him on his excursions up and down irrigating ditches, but a young married woman—no.

Stairs glowed over the possibilities of his nearly virgin field, and, being a man, needed some one to glow before; he did, therefore, go to discuss his finds with Mrs. Lindley, but not with perfect disingenuousness. Stairs was ambitious, and coveted the gift of communication. Mrs. Lindley drew him out. Before her, his thought shaped itself, and astonished him with its appositeness. He coveted the effect she produced upon him, the lift of her buoyant mind above the embarrassment of his own self-consciousness. He began to understand that his science had no value except in its relativity to the wants of men; but as yet the perception broke wordlessly in a thin, rainbow bubble in his brain. In his thought he had no relation to Mrs. Lindley; it was the agreeable easement of his relation to himself that appealed.

Serena saw that he tried himself against her; but the deep, indefinable hurt was not in that she was made use of, but that she was used by Antrim Stairs. She was good enough for him, it appeared, but she was not good enough for her husband; for she had no thought to hide behind that another would have answered better to Lindley's need. He had all he wanted of her, and there was still something left over for another to pick and choose from. Lindley's sense of the sufficiency of his own resources made him value her in proportion to her lack of cogency to his general scheme; the male egoism suffered in a mere hint of the wish to be of use to him. But he meant, of course, to make her happy.

Coming late from Rosebank one afternoon, she found Lindley in the parlor gloating over a piano that smirked at her from the lifted lip of its lid with all its ivory keys.

"Oh, Evan! Whose is it? When did it come?"

"Yours. I bought it."

"But—"

"Didn't you tell me you were suffering for something to do? Well, now you can put in the time practising things to play to me."

"Oh, Evan! Oh, my dear!" She was crying on his shoulder—tears of a sinking heart-sickness at being so misread: that he should have thought her merely the complaining wife; that she had asked for a share in his work, and he had given her a toy.

"There, darling, I'm glad you like it. I selected it myself." He patted her in husbandly satisfaction. "Come, let's hear a tune on it."

Serena could play a little. She had had as much money spent on her musical training as would have established her in a useful trade, and she could play a little. She tried the piano, and praised its tone, inexpressibly touched, and cloaked her hurt with affectionateness.

"But, Evan dear, could you afford it?"

"Well, Maskey made me terms on it—a mere trifle of instalments. We'll never miss it."

"I am afraid I cost you a great deal, Evan."

"Ah, well, you are worth it. That's my lookout. Besides, I stand to make a pile on the Bodely addition. You know the Bodelys have bought the Dos Palos ranch, and will cut it up in villa lots. They have taken rather a shine to me on account of the way I've stood about the fountain, and I count on getting the handling of the property. We will set up a phaeton, maybe." Lindley walked up and down, glowing with the warmth of his prospects. Serena smiled. At any rate, she believed in his capacity to make money.

VII

The date of the unveiling of the Bodely fountain was set for early in October. The fall semester would then be in full swing, and all the new students properly instructed in the college yell.

The fountain arrived, sacredly swathed in canvas, and was set in its place; the artist came; the Bodelys came. On the evening of their arrival they had dinner with the Lindleys, but the day before the *Day* they dined with the president. Excursionists came in from neighboring towns, reporters came down from San Francisco. It happened about that time, also, that Wilmot de Long came to Santa Lucia. De Long was an artist—from the East—who painted genre water-colors with such a nicety that once they were framed and on the wall they could with difficulty be distinguished from the printed reproductions of themselves that came as supplements to the art magazines. At his hotel he was recognized by a reporter for the daily *Examiner*, and was carried off for a private view of the fountain. De Long looked amazed. Then pained. And bored. Of course, if that was the sort of thing people in California wanted—pardon, if that was the sort of thing the Santa-Lucians wanted—they were fortunate in being able to get it. It was certainly very large. And excellent metal. De Long laid the tips of his fingers together and blew them apart; so he disposed of the Bodely fountain.

The reporter made a good story of the interview, but no one heard of it until the next day.

By this time Serena's vague dissatisfaction in her husband's attitude had yielded a little to wifely pride. She divined on the evening of the dinner-party, on which occasion Mrs. Bodely had called her my dear, and Cyrus J. had bubbled solemnly with hints of patronage, that their enjoyment of the situation made up to them for the shifts and slights of the ungracious years. The fountain glowed in their simple-minded satisfaction, touched by no baser thought than the mere vanity of giving. In it they saw themselves, though childless, adjusted to their generation. If you looked at it long enough as a way of being kind to the Bodelys, Mrs. Lindley admitted that it lost some of its offensiveness.

By the Santa-Lucians it was looked at as a way of adding glory to Santa Lucia. It was a great thing for the town. It was said to have cost five thousand dollars. It was an attraction; it provided Santa Lucia an amount of free advertising. It must have cost at least seven thousand dollars. None of the other towns in the valley had anything like it. And the Bodelys were sure to put up the new science building or endow the museum. It was reported that they had been willing to spend as much as ten thousand dollars on the fountain alone. Who were these people who talked about bad art? Why should one Santa-Lucian know more about art than another Santa-Lucian? Such people were knockers.

The day of the unveiling was a great day for the college. It was to be known as Fountain Day, and would probably become an institution. At the end of it Evan Lindley hugged his wife with enthusiasm.

"The school will get the new building, and I will get the Dos Palos business," he said. "You little prunes and prisms, you don't seem to care a bit!" He had worked hard to bring the event about, for there had been an amount of quiet opposition in the faculty that did not reach the public notice; in the glow of success he coveted his wife's praise. There were times when he wondered if she was really going to be interested in his lifework.

The next day after the unveiling the *Examiner* came out with the De Long interview and a sketch of the fountain, in which Mrs. Bodely's overskirt and Cyrus J.'s frock-coat were brought out particularly. The Santa-Lucians pooh-poohed at it. The *Examiner* followed up with the opinions of local artists, including the author of the neglected design.

Then the towns of the valley that had no college and no fountain began to sound. The Dos Palos *Bulletin* deplored the lowering public taste. The *Messenger*, at San Carlos, said it was such lapses that made the Pacific Coast a mock to the East. The *Times* wanted to know how long wealth was to vulgarize our institutions of learning. The Santa-Lucians stood out for it that this was envy, but Lindley suffered the writhing sensitiveness to public criticism that is the penalty of suiting one's action to the public key. As he had not spared to make himself a figure in the general eye in connection with the affair of the fountain, he came in for some sharp scourging, in which Serena suffered, but suffered the more lightly, as, not being properly a Santa-Lucian, she had no rabid pride of locality to appease. The situation had no poignancy for her, except as it concerned her relation to her husband. Evan had made a mistake which she would have saved him if he had allowed it. What she minded was not so much his not knowing about art, but his not deferring to her knowing it. Though she was hurt for his needless mortification, she would almost have welcomed the incident as providing the basis of a better understanding; but it was the bitter smart of Lindley's annoyance that his wife was of the party who tipped the board. He was not going to blame her; it might cause a serious disarrangement of his affairs, but he would not blame her. Serena perceived that he made a virtue of it, and the moment of sentimental reconciliation in which Evan was to admit his error and concede her superior fineness floated out beyond even a hail.

The young people made up their coolness after a while, as young people must; it is only the middle-aged who can excuse the indelicacies of living together on any grounds but mutual tenderness.

Serena was happier at that time, filling her days with the appearance of busyness. Though she had no talent for it, since the piano came, she had taken up the practice of music. There was a Professor Grunsky who came down from San Francisco once in a fortnight to give lessons that were said to be worth the two dollars and a half one paid for them. It was steep, but Lindley's idea was that in things of this sort it paid to have the best. And if the Bodely business should fall in fortunately, they would never miss the money.

She saw a great deal of Antrim Stairs, and found in the stimulus of his work and the books she read of his suggesting a relief to the definite ache of her mind, trained sedulously to require it. But about holiday-time she began to be made uneasy by reports that he was paying attention to Julia Maybury, though Julia was by report engaged to a J. J. Halford, of the wholesale grocery trade, who had been seen by all Santa Lucia devotedly attending her gloves and her parasol on Fountain Day. Lindley, who had known Halford at Berkeley, described him as a good fellow—"one of the kind that gets fat early, and bald early, and never gets any older. Everybody calls him Jimmy." Serena had drawn this from him on the evening of a day when Stairs had brought her one of his magazine articles to read, and the pages had opened on a torn scrap of envelope that had been used as a marker. The name on the envelope was Julia Maybury. Mrs. Lindley wondered if Julia had had the first reading, and, contemptuously, whether she had understood it.

"Of course," William had said, "nobody thinks for a moment she means to marry him."

"Why should anybody think he wants her to?" asked Serena. This was about Christmas-time, when William was experiencing the annual excitement of getting twenty-seven Christmas presents ready in half the time required to make them, and had fallen back on Mrs. Lindley, whose own list was appreciably less.

"Oh," explained William, fringing ribbons, "he is positively there all the time! Agnes Sterling told me. He even reads to her: poetry, you know, and sentimental essays. Agnes said it was Theocritus last time."

Serena thought that Julia wouldn't have cared a great deal for Theocritus, but it appeared that Julia thought she did. When her friends had commiserated her on a possible boredom she had been quite miffed; but it was not supposed that it had got beyond being a whim with her, because, as William explained, contemplating her work with her head on one side, "Julia is half engaged to Jim Halford, you know."

"No, I am sure I don't know what it means to be half engaged to anybody," said Serena, a little stiffly.

"No, of course you don't, you are so intense, Serena. It would have to be the whole thing or nothing with you. Agnes explained to me. She says it means that Jim is engaged to Julia, but Julia is not engaged to Jim." William had a great deal more to say about Jim Halford, who, from living next door to the Mayburys, and having no mother, had been, you might say, brought up with Julia, and was supposed never

to have thought of any other girl; and Julia was expected by her family
to marry him when she should make up her mind to it, and the family
thought it high time. "Agnes says she can't imagine what has got into
Julia, except that Dr. Stairs is a new man," concluded William.

That was chiefly, perhaps, why Julia Maybury did not become
bored by the conquest of Antrim Stairs; he had taken a new way with
her. All Julia's lovers had set themselves to getting her what she wanted.
For the favor of her society they had paid in opera tickets, theatre
suppers, and flowers out of season. It was a method least likely to
lead to misunderstandings, and on the whole Julia was honest in the
balancing of her accounts. If a young man brought her bonbons, she
did not neglect to smile upon him; if he sent her jonquils in December,
to sit out dances with him on the stairs. The Professor of Biology read
poetry to her and sent her books with marked passages. It was not clear
that he expected to gain anything by this. It appeared to Julia that if he
approached her on this ground it must be because he had discovered in
her aptitudes towards high thinking undistinguished by her friends.

"Ju thinks she has been greatly misunderstood," Agnes Sterling
told William at New Year's. "She has a whole collection of phrases about
the intellectual life, and she snubbed Jim horribly."

Julia's mother was a sister of Mrs. Sterling; a widow with nothing
to think about but her health, consequently she thought about it a great
deal. This year she was going about with a trained nurse trying rest
cures, and Julia, who found cures depressing, was much of the time with
her cousins, and went out with Antrim Stairs.

"Do you think it means anything in particular?" William, always
anxious to discuss a love affair, wanted to know of Agnes.

"Oh, I am sure I can't tell. He is reading Byron to her now. How
much do you suppose that means?"

Not even Julia could say what that meant, but there were other
things plainer to understand. Stairs was immeasurably moved by
her beauty. She saw that he identified in her the springs of the great
romantic passions, and played up to the part. And there were things
not so plain, for though Antrim Stairs assumed the habit of a lover
he was not in the least loverly. He had not, for instance, tried to kiss
her. Understand, Julia was a nice girl. She was not to be kissed by just
anybody, nor by the clumsiness of being asked for it; nor except on an

occasion providing a sufficient excuse, and in a manner that asured her
not being thought any the less of on account of it. But Dr. Stairs got no
further than reading Byron. Julia did not know quite what to make of
it; but being a young woman of direct methods, and quite sure of what
she wanted, it was clear she would make something of it before all was
done.

Julia was a great deal at Rosebank that winter, and William,
who lived heartily in her friend's affairs, hugged the situation to her
breast. Where Julia was, Antrim Stairs was sure to be spending much
of his time, and Jim Halford would come whenever the interests of the
wholesale grocery trade demanded his presence at Santa Lucia, on which
occasions he found himself thrown back on William for entertainment
without minding it too much. He had always managed to stand fast
through Julia's numberless flirtations, and to be taken on again without
cheapening the quality of his devotion, and William was expressly made
to afford the relief of confidences. Julia Maybury had found her equally
good to talk to about Antrim Stairs. Did William think him really as
clever as people said? What was it Mrs. Lindley had told her about
the book he was writing, and was she really a judge? Oh, of course, if
William said so. Mrs. Lindley was so serious it was difficult to make her
out. Intellectual people always were serious. Like Antrim Stairs. William
could hardly be expected to understand what it meant to Julia to have a
friendship with an intellectual man. It was so—so uplifting. Was it true
that if Dr. Baker resigned at the end of the year that his place would be
offered to Dr. Stairs, and what was the salary? All the reflected lights of
Santa Lucia's self-felicitation in Stairs's growing reputation, all Serena's
starved response to the stimulus of his mind, all William's generous
deliverance of herself to the genius of her friends, played upon Julia's
thought and hid it from herself.

Matters being in this posture, remained so on into the quiescent
period of the year when one is unwilling to say it is still winter and
cannot declare with definiteness that it is spring: while there was still
snow on the Santa Lucias and the beginning of pussy willows along the
creek borders. It was Sunday afternoon, and William, detained at the
house, was hurrying to join the others, gone ahead with Antrim Stairs
to hunt for larvae about the soddy banks where the back-water of the
Toyon made still pools among the willows. Widgeon whirred up from

the reedy edges and mallard drakes could be heard calling in the pale, equable hour between the sun and the chill of night. It was a quarter of an hour before she had a glimpse of Julia's dress across the glimmer of a pool where the willows reddened as a sign of spring. She could not at that distance, and because of the interlacing stems, make out more than the figure of the man beside her; both Stairs and Halford were in black, and of about the same stature. She could see him put back the thick branches for the girl to pass; then, as the slender figure poised for a moment in provocation, saw her swept against his breast, and felt rather than saw the long, passionate kiss that the fringing willows swung back to screen. The ache of that moment seemed to lie a long time in the heart of the quiet hour. But when William came up with them, the three were waiting for her on a fallen log, and though she lagged on the homeward road with Jim, and had an hour of confidences with Julia in her room that night, she was obliged to be satisfied with what conclusion she might draw from what Jim Halford had already told her: that he did not know whether he was engaged to Julia or not, but that he loved her with all his soul, beyond all lesser passions, being very much as other men, with all the plain, clean hunger of a man for his natural mate, beyond all reason, beyond all belief in his own constancy, and beyond all time.

VIII

That the Lindleys found their second winter rather more
comfortable than the first was due, in part, to the *Post-Darwinian
Theories of Evolution,* which Antrim Stairs read to Serena as he wrote.
The book reflected in its color and vitality the nature of his response
to the profound disturbance of Miss Maybury's bodily perfection.
Though it was based very simply on the stimulus of her long curves,
the subtle way of her throat, and the play of her fine color, Antrim
Stairs's passion emerged from him in the form of renewed activities.
Snared by the ineradicable sense of the appropriateness of beauty to
specious sentiment, he credited his performance to Miss Maybury, and
proved it to her by citations from the poets. Julia liked all this, because
it was new and interesting. She enjoyed being the fountain-head of a
world-wondering work, and became rather insufferable to her friends
on account of it, but she was satisfied to let the world wonder, and
forestalled his attempts to read it to her with the skill born of long
experience in the avoidance of being bored. In his second year Stairs
was thought rather a bore by all Julia's friends, who neither understood
his work nor thought it important to pretend to. Stairs found it very
pleasant then to share his exuberance about it with Mrs. Lindley.

All that winter the elevation of his passion inducted him into the
whole process of nature: the earth was sentient and the sky a brother

to him; clouds that rolled up blackly along the crest of Santa Lucia and spread whitely out in snow, torn gray film of the firmament and finely divided twigs of the poplars marching through the rain, had speech for him. Men began to stand for their hidden meanings, and the meanings noble. All this because Julia Maybury was full-bosomed and had slender hips, and a fine, steady color, like a La France rose. At that time Antrim Stairs was attuned to life and his proper use in it. Being so humanized he became likeable, and began to find community of interest even with the brisk and busy attorney. He was much at the Lindley's, and read chapters of his book to Serena as they came fresh from him, and found them to light up wonderfully in the radiancy of her finer mind. Lindley, affecting to laugh at it, was secretly rather proud of his wife's ability to be interested in what bored him excessively. As an appenage to the career he had cut out for himself as a prominent citizen, it was entirely satisfactory that she should be sought after by what stood for higher culture at Santa Lucia. When he came late from Board of Trade meetings to find that Antrim Stairs had been reading to his wife, attending rather hazily to their talk through the smoke of his cigar, it flattered him to think that if she wanted to amuse herself with professors of biology, he could afford them.

Often upon such occasions Mrs. Lindley suffered a vision of herself, in the lack of any more related employment, passing from one to another such extraneous interest, which should only be saved by the flavor of scholarliness from the fads and purposeless enthusiasms of other idle women, against which her vigorous youth cried out. But Serena was spared by finding herself, with the increase of the spring, beginning one of those absorbing experiences which, by merely being dwelt upon and flooded with brooding tenderness, stands competently in the place of something to do. It was an experience in which there was practically very little to be busy about, so little disturbed by imperative distractions of the attention, so well able to proceed to a competent conclusion in the absence of tender welcome, but defying all reasonableness in its power to become an occupation in the mere suffusion of its moods.

It was because of that, and for the reason that with it all Serena was not very strong that spring, that Lindley, when he told her at last that the Bodelys were not yet reconciled to the college, and that the

Dos Palos business had been given to another man, neglected to tell her that the facts had any direct relation to their manner of living, and to Serena's inexperience it did not occur to ask.

In the distraction of her condition Mrs. Lindley had seen very little of Antrim Stairs for a month or six weeks; therefore, one morning on her way to Mrs. Bixby's, she came upon him with the pleasant shock of renewal which such chance meetings had for them. Serena had come across the campus, finding walking preferable to the motion of the car; and now, turning into the long, poplar-shaded row, he turned and kept on beside her, as if his walk had had no other purpose from the beginning. He had taken her hand at meeting with a warmth unexpected in him, whose manner was more a habit than an expression of personality, and she saw that he was changed. As he talked he turned towards her with the new, indefinable warmth upon him, with a touch of friendly intimacy strange to him, and she said to herself that he was changed for the better.

She asked him of his book, and he answered, with a flush, that it stood at the point where she had last seen it. He had been very busy, but he would be taking it up within the week. He had a new way with him then, she saw, as he talked of some changes he would make, as if he had somehow come clear of the work, and was better able to handle it so disentangled from his consciousness. It was such a day as lent itself to the expression of growing competency and power: opulent, bursting foliage, crowding the sod with wild bloom that flared along the fences and the road border, that broke up riotously through the cracks of the pavement, and was with difficulty prevented from the lawns. Every tree was a tent of tremulous young leaves, the flaps of which gave upon the foothills, smouldering with burnt-out poppies, from which a faint haze went up like smoke.

As Stairs talked, Serena, perceiving what the man might become in fortunate circumstance, thought, as women do of a man who interests them, that a successful marriage might be the mordant which should fix him in the happy fitness for his work, which he showed that day. They lent themselves with eagerness to the hint of largeness in the noon hour, hearing trumpets from the hills, and warning each other with disbelieving laughter that their promises to themselves were already tinged with the truly native spirit of inflation. Being a Californian,

Serena told him, was, after all, a state of mind. They walked on after that in the airy warmth and color of leaf shadows. When the occasion offered, Mrs. Lindley had a little to say of herself, and saw in his fashion of receiving it, in the smile that he turned towards her, that he was happily changed.

Serena, when she had reached Mrs. Bixby's, and had been properly scolded for not coming to see them before, and for coming so far on a warm morning, and had been made to smell of lavender salts, and propped up on the lounge with an extra pillow, answered to Aunt Luella's question that it was Antrim Stairs who had walked out with her.

"Did he say anything?" asked Roxanne, with interest.

"About what?" Serena wanted to know.

"About his engagement." Serena sat up, a little bleak about the heart, a little tremulous, wondering at herself.

"Didn't you know?" Roxanne went on. "It isn't announced yet, but Agnes Sterling told the Blake girls, and Isabel told Mabel Stone, so it comes pretty straight. I should think he would have told you."

"I—was rather expecting it. It hardly seems—suitable. No, Aunt Luella, I am not faint. It is only that the morning is so warm, and I walked from the campus. Dr. Stairs was talking, and I suppose we walked too fast."

Aunt Luella was at the table busy about the minutes of the W. C. T. U., of which she had been lately elected secretary, and it was peculiar to Aunt Luella that the contact with any of her alphabetical activities created in her the necessity for a moral attitude. Now she shut her secretary's book, and looked at her niece judicially over the tops of her glasses.

"I don't know as it's exactly the thing for you, in your condition, to be walking in public with a young man. It doesn't seem quite womanly."

"Oh, mother!" interposed Kate, coming to the help of Serena's sick indignation, "I don't suppose Dr. Stairs knows what is the matter with Serena, and, anyway, he is engaged to be married."

"Aunt Luella," cried Serena, sitting up and holding Kate's hand, but with hot flushes of color, "Dr. Stairs is an old friend, and as for his knowing what is the matter with me, he ought to, for I told him."

The shock of this announcement almost displaced the expression of admonishing mentor on Mrs. Bixby's face. It sat there all awry as her niece went on, finally to be succeeded by something curiously tinged with the suggestion of quizzing vulgarity that passes for humor with many excellent women.

"Well," said Aunt Luella—"well, I should think he might!" And that was not the first instance of the difference between what might be called her aunt's official attitude towards the beatitude of motherhood and her practical relation to her niece's condition, which had expressed itself chiefly in a disposition to hustle her into corners when there was company. Serena was glad to lie back among the pillows and seem too tired for much comment.

The day turned out so warm that the youngest Bixby was despatched to the corner store to telephone Evan not to expect his wife home to lunch. The haze of the foothills thickened and darkened, and by the middle of the hot afternoon the sky was quite overcast, strained, and tight, with a hint of storm moving thunderously above it to take up its station on the farther ranges. Now and then the whole body of air flapped and tugged, too heavy to free itself in wind. Serena not feeling well enough to trust herself alone, Kate went with her on the car. They saw the last rain of the season break in the hills above Toyon and stream like thin veils down the canon. The gray tent of cloud above the valley quaked with thunder.

When Mrs. Lindley had gone to her room to lie down and Kate bent above her to say good-bye, she saw two clear tears slip on the pillow.

"Kate," whispered Serena, "did … did you think … "

"No, I didn't," reassured Kate, kissing her heartily; "neither did mother, nor Dr. Stairs. Mother's got a lot of left-over solemnity that she was too busy to use in her own life; but don't you let her palm it off on you."

The coming of dusk brought no relief to the stifling day. The Lindleys sat out on the veranda after dinner, and listened, through intervals of desultory talk, for the breath of the wind and the faint roar of the rain in the wide-mouthed canon. Presently the low, troubled thunder seemed to break into the beat of hoofs on the street, flying towards them with a hint of terror in the sound. It struck upon the sense like the snapping of the tense, hot dark. There was no reason why they should expect it to draw up at their door, no reason why they should be half-way down the lawn to meet it, but they were, expectant of the voice that called, "Lindley! Lindley!" mixed with panting and the thud of a horse's feet. A man cast himself out of the blackness, half dragging his horse across the lawn.

"Lindley! Lindley! For God's sake!"

"Jap!" cried Serena.

"It's the Doctor! He's hurt! Toyon road!"

Unconsciously the man fitted his words to the rhythm of the horse's gallop, as if he had been saying them over all his ride.

"Will you ... go for Lawrence, Lindley, ... and whoever else ... you can get?"

"I'll come myself. Is he at the ranch?"

"They are bringing him ... I must go back."

"Go," said Lindley, "I'll do the rest." Neither of them spoke to Serena. She heard Jap galloping through the dark and the sound of her husband's feet running in the street.

IX

At Rosebank that afternoon the indrawing day, the low, close firmament, pressed upon William's spirit. She went out by the Toyon road and walked along the creek until she found Jap sitting on the sprawled, sagging sycamore; his hair was tossed back from his sharp, vacant face, the white lock singularly whiter in the dusk. The hour should have been about sundown, but the tight, gray film of storm shut out any hint of it. There was no wind; the noise of the water rose insistent and troublous. Little clacking movements woke in the leaves of the sycamore and were stilled, broke out again in the oaks, rustled and fell off again, whispered and lurked in the holly; and yet there was no wind. Seldom large drops of rain fell from clouds shaken thunderously. Said Jap:

"It will be raining at McCloud's by now."

"Well, I hope Mrs. McCloud is sick enough to keep him all night," responded William, fervently. Whenever Jap volunteered anything by way of conversation it was always William who divined its relevancy to the Doctor. They walked towards the house, watching the gathering of the cloud mass scattering and reforming in the heavens above the mountains, and met the Doctor's cat, which, from being made much of, had acquired a trick of following. Jap took Belshazzar in his arms, and at the gate, Lew Sing, with his apron standing out stiffly like the garment of a wooden toy, and the pink tassel of his queue hanging coquettishly over one ear, was calling them to supper. As they passed him, Belshazzar leaped with light deliberation on his shoulder. Lew Sing cackled with a rusty joy.

"You see!" he squeaked—"you *see!* K'y heap smart, he savy Dlocka getum wet, he go see. You think come plitty soon? I keep suppa, huh?"

If Lew Sing had not had occasion every day to move the Doctor's kept-over meals forward and back on the top of the stove according as he wavered in his conviction as to the time of the Doctor's arrival, he would have missed the absorbing concern of his life, though he occasionally conceived himself aggrieved by the necessity. This evening they heard him sliding the saucepans about and banging the oven-door with more than the usual vacillation.

"It's the weather," said William, getting up to go to the door again. "Even Sing and the cat feel it. I wish, though, it didn't seem so like the day of destruction." Suddenly rain began to fall, sharp and quick, on the roof, running on into the sharp beats of hoofs and the jingle of broken harness on the Toyon road. They knew even before Jap was out to fling open the gate that it was the Doctor's team. As they swung, lathered and quivering, into the yard, it seemed to the Doctor's wife that all the thirty years of her married life had been keyed to the anticipation of this hour.

Afterwards, when they had time to inquire, it appeared that the shock had effected a hiatus in the old Doctor's memory. He remembered the horses starting at a blown weed by the roadside, and the snap of the parting traces, and then his own room with the lamp burning and William crying at his bed. Some farmer folk, returning late from the town, had found his insensible body where the road turned in between the fenced lands, his clothes sodden with the rain that had fallen for an hour, his white hair fouled with blood and dust. When Jap met them they had come three miles towards Rosebank, and he himself turned off by the shortest way to bring help from town.

They laid the old Doctor on the wide, leather covered couch in his office, where he had been used to sleep, not to disturb his family when, in times of much sickness, calls came unexpectedly in the night. Jap came and cleared him of the stain of his hurts and the road; his wife stood at his head, her hand touching his soft, abundant hair; William sat and sobbed with controlled breath on the floor beside him. Sing built up a roaring fire in his kitchen, which was his way of meeting an emergency, and went and squatted in the damp outside the door. Neighbors came with whispered proffers of assistance, Lindley came with the physician from town, and at last the old Doctor himself came back out of stunned disorder and looked feebly about the room. His gaze travelled slowly from his wife to William, took in the figure of Lawrence at his side, and Lindley, standing strained and still, at the foot.

"Jap!" said the Doctor.

Jap's lean face came out of the blackness beyond the shadowed circle of the light and bent to the feeble question.

"Jap," said the Doctor, his words trailing from him with heavy-breathing gasps, "am ... I ... all ... in?"

"Oh, no, no no, Doctor!" in an agony of whispered reassurance.

"Jap ... Furniss. Harry Furniss, ... he's the man."

"Yes, Doctor, yes."

"Old Furniss, Harry Furniss ... Frisco." And then, after an interval: "Mrs. McCloud ... expect crisis ... tinct ... depend ... you Jap." And the Doctor slipped back into oblivion.

"He wishes to have Dr. Furniss called," said the Doctor's assistant, quietly, straightening from the bed. Dr. Lawrence pursed his lip.

"Ah, yes, Furniss," he said. It appeared to him rather extraordinary. He was a youngish man, brisk and consequential, to whom Dr. Caldwell was merely an excellent type of the old-school, the eccentricities of whose practice were only equalled by his amazing luck in recoveries—and Furniss; Henry Furniss, whose consulting list was three weeks in advance of his time! Dr. Lawrence pinched his lip between his thumb and finger, his elbow resting on his other palm; it was a favorite professional attitude.

"I assure you," he said to the Doctor's wife, "it is not—ah, um— indispensable. Dr. Furniss is much occupied."

"They were at school together. I will be obliged to you if you will send at once," said the Doctor's wife. An hour later, when Lindley brought back word that Furniss was coming by special train, Lawrence began to shape a paragraph to appear in the local paper, in which his own name and that of the famous surgeon were to appear in the most fortunate conjunction.

The old Doctor lay breathing heavily; nothing transpired but the steady drip of the rain, until the great Furniss came in at the door a little after the turn of the night, and lifted the strained tension of all the house to his shoulders. Behind him his assistant guarded the instrument-cases from the wet. In a very little while he said:

"We are about to begin now, Mrs. Caldwell, and shall want the room." His keen attention halted at Jap, who made no motion of departure.

"I have been Dr. Caldwell's assistant for ten years," said Jap, "and I will not leave him now."

"Are you a graduate physician or a nurse?"

"I am the Doctor's assistant."

"The Doctor would want Jap," said the Doctor's wife from the doorway.

Furniss took the man in in a look as keen and incisive as a scalpel. "All right," he said. "You wait outside, Rhewold, I'll call if I want you." The surgeon's assistant went out and sat in the living room. He had a pleasant, homely countenance, open and capable and young. William had brought a stool and sat near the door of the office with her head against the wall, her small palms, curled upward, lying in her lap: her hair hung in two braids on her shoulders. Dr. Rhewold thought she would be about sixteen.

"Miss Caldwell," he said, kindly, "believe me, you had much better go and lie down."

"Oh no, no!" protested William.

"Then will you not sit over here? There's quite a draft by the door."

"I want to be as near as I can," quivered William.

They were quiet a long time, and the dawn began to lighten through the mist of rain.

"What is that smell of burning?" asked the young doctor.

"It is Sing burning punk, I think."

"Then that must have been he that I heard sing-songing a while ago."

"He was saying his prayers," said William; "he was very fond of my father." The surgeon's assistant got up and moved out to the veranda. Lew Sing squatted at the door of his own room with a semicircle of burning punk-sticks stuck about him in the ground. He had Belshazzar between his knees, and stroked him; now and then he whimpered a little like a hurt dog.

"Cheer up, old chap," said the young doctor.

"Me plenty solly," wailed Lew Sing, "sometime Dlocka he no come, I keep suppa two three hour. I plenty mad, I say damn. You fixee Dlocka all lite, I no say damn any more." He blew softly on his punk-sticks that burned feebly in the drip of the eaves.

"The old Chink seems a pretty decent sort," said the young doctor, going back to find William had moved to the deep davenport on the other side of the room. Sitting down beside her, he saw that she was rather pretty, and had been crying more than was good for her.

"Dr. Rhewold, what is the matter with my father?"

"Well, there's a slight fracture of the skull, and a compound fracture of the thigh, and some minor injuries; but unless something internal develops, nothing to be alarmed about. Furniss will pull him through. The things I've seen him do—" He beamed upon her with young enthusiasm. Suddenly terrible sharp groans broke upon them from the other room.

"Oh!" said William, quivering.

"There, that's a good sign. What we had to fear most was insensibility. Really you shouldn't allow it to distress you. See what a pulse you are getting." The surgeon's assistant took her wrist professionally between his thumb and finger. The groans came sharp and deep; William caught at his hand. He held hers frankly and smiled encouragement. He said to himself that the Doctor's daughter was a nice little thing, and behaving like a brick. Jap, coming out of the office with a basin, saw them sitting so, and hung for an instant on the threshold. Something came into his eyes that was not quite expressiveness; it was as if an emotion had arisen to look out of his face and failed. The surgeon's work was over, and the Doctor lay in his own bed. Lawrence, who had hoped to be seen driving his eminent colleague through the streets of Santa Lucia, had been obliged to depart without him. Furniss, the great Furniss, in whose anteroom millionaires waited humbly with their hats on their knees, sat still and contained beside the old Doctor's bed. Now he dropped medicine between the parted lips where the breath dragged heavily, and now he touched tenderly the hand of his friend. It was late in the morning, the house had returned to the semblance of its daily use, and the rushing of Toyon sounded murmurously in the darkened room like the mindless rush of time, when the old Doctor awoke.

"Ned," said the surgeon.

"Harry." The Doctor's hand twitched feebly, and Furniss took it in his own. After an interval:

"What ... did ... I get, Harry?"

"Well, you didn't get it." A ghost of a glimmer played in the old Doctor's eyes.

"Then you think I'll pull through?"

"Sure, Ned."

The Doctor swung back into the shadow of unconsciousness, and, rousing, seemed not to be aware of the lapse of time.

"My ... patients, Harry, ... don't let ..."— the soul, like a pendulum, swung into outer darkness and returned upon its track— "Lawrence ... get 'em."

"All right, Ned, I'll leave Rhewold here."

"Tell Jap ... " said the Doctor. "Tell Jap ... " And the pendulum swung out again. When it came back Furniss was gone from the bedside, only his wife sat with her hands folded on the covers, and the barred light from the chinks of the shutters glinted on the opposite wall. It was Jap who drove the great surgeon to the station and had his last instructions.

"And permit me to say," Furniss went on, "that you handled that bandaging extraordinarily well. I have seldom seen a lighter touch. And Caldwell's practice could hardly have afforded you occasion to become so proficient. Have you ever thought of studying?" Something like a reflected glow came on Jap's sallow face, shining from some enthusiasm gone down beyond the horizon of his life.

"I—studied—once. But—I my—health—"

Furniss cut into him with his knife like glance.

"Well, you look fit enough now. Why not think of it?"

"Oh, I—I couldn't think of leaving the Doctor now," said the Doctor's assistant, with a kind of strained eagerness of excuse.

He was no sooner at Rosebank again than he claimed the night-watch, which the weary household surrendered, Dr. Rhewold having gone to the relief of the Thompson baby, which had taken this opportune time for straightening right out, sudden. Jap sat at the foot of the bed in his customary nursing attitude of absorbed attention; his hair was tossed back, the white lock showing like a crest. About the recurrent hour of the accident the Doctor began to rouse to sensibility, to the pains and discomforts of his situation, and to wish to talk more than was good for him, his mind running on his practice as it might have been at the moment of the shock. Whenever Jap's hand came out of the dimness to smooth his bandages, or Jap's voice reassured him, he quieted for an interval, and then began again.

"Jap," he said, "where's the young doctor?"

"Looking after your patients."

"He's young, Jap—very young." He lost himself under the influence of a soothing medicine, and returned again when he heard the wheels of the buggy on the gravel of the drive. His mind ran on like troubled waters with the affairs of the Thompson baby and Mrs. McCloud.

"They won't like it, Jap, … seeing a stranger in the old Doctor's place. They will hear the team going by in the night and the rain, … they will look out of the window, Jap, and see the Doctor's buggy, … but they will miss … the old Doctor. And they aren't going to like it, Jap."

"Not for long, Doctor, not for long."

"Thirty-five years, Jap—thirty-five years, and never missed a trip … thirty … five … " And he swung away into oblivion. The young doctor stood in the driveway holding the lines of the team; one foot was on the lower step of the veranda, and William sat above him with her head against the pillar of the wistaria-vine, stroking Belshazzar's back. The earth swam in a moist dark-like mist, swallows flitted against the belated glow of the sky. Jap came with his noiseless, nurse's tread out of the inner room, and stood in the shadow beyond them in the black gap of the veranda. It was rather by sense than by sight they discovered him there.

"Now," said the young doctor, in his quick, light way, "if you will show me about the team, Jap—" At that something seemed to thrust into the quiet evening like a sting; they could feel Jap's figure stiffen to his tone.

"My name is Jasper, sir—Edward K. Jasper. I have engaged the Schallaber boy to care for the horses. You'll find him at the stable."

"All right, Mr. Jasper," said the young doctor, with the greatest cheerfulness. "It is only that I am not much used to horses, and we have never been really introduced, you know."

"My goodness!" gasped William, when the dark of the room beyond had swallowed up the Doctor's assistant. "I've known all these years that his name was Edward K. Jasper, but I never heard him say so before."

"Jap," moaned the patient, beginning querulously, and easing in response to the moistened bandages, "they won't like having a stranger. If you … had taken your degree … as I wanted you to … they … wouldn't have … to see … a stranger … in the old Doctor's place."

The shape of an emotion, which had lain there since the night before, rose now and struggled to look out of the nurse's face, and it was the shape of a poignant regret.

"You are disappointing me, Jap; … you … ain't … where I … need you most," whispered the older man.

"Oh no, no, no, Doctor, don't say that!"

"You … could 'a' … kept 'em … from having a stranger … in the old Doctor's place," went on the Doctor, with the weary iteration of the sick, falling away into the gulf of unconsciousness and returning on the wave of pain. "You could … 'a' kept 'em together, Jap." The light burned low, and the nurse moved to trim it …. "Thirty-five years and a stranger in my place … " Now the wind set the shutter a-creak, and the Doctor's assistant crossed to it with his shadow large upon the wall, and roused the sick man on the trail of his weary thought …."You've disappointed me, Jap …" So the voice from the bed fretted on, and at every recurrence of the phrase the shape of contrition struggled in the nurse's shallow face as he bent with soothing-drops above the pillow.

"Oh no, no, no, Doctor, don't say that!" And again: "No, no, not that, Doctor—never that!" with an energy of entreaty all too insistent for the flitting of the sick man's mind.

X

It was an immediate result of Dr. Caldwell's accident that
Belshazzar nearly died of overeating and William left off curl-papers for
the rest of her natural life. Under the tension of agonized days William's
bangs went straight back from her forehead to meet the flat coil of her
braids, and though in time they loosened and became a soft roll framing
the full oval of her face, they never went into the chrysalid state again.

The loose gowns went, too—the languid ruffles and flowing
sleeves that obstructed the business of nursing, the flapping slippers that
clattered on the stairs; for William had at least this trait in common
with her mother: that she would not cheapen the quality of disaster
by meeting it in dishabille. The two women, shocked suddenly into
the protracted struggle with death, tucked in the superfluity of their
garments as soldiers tighten their belt-buckles going into action.

You could have wished for no more acceptable sight in the sick-
room than William going about with smooth hair and snug little shoes,
and neat little cambric dresses, and small, cool hands that were never
fidgety nor unsure.

As for Belshazzar, the habit of luxurious eating that gave him his
name came near to finishing him. For, word of the Doctor's accident
going about among the orchards, the wide ranches, the homesteads of
the hills, the little cabins of the mountaineers, there ran with it a pang

that quickened and tugged at the submerged sentiment of country neighborhoods, and provoked it to homely, inadequate kindnesses. There was a stream of wagons and buckboards and buggies going by on the Santa Lucia road or turning in from the Toyon to read the daily bulletin which Jap found it necessary to affix to the gate, and another stream of broths and jellies and custards and dressed chickens going in on foot at the back, or handed out on horseback at the front, or arriving in the young doctor's buggy, packed in baskets or pinned in napkins that were the bane of William's days to sort and return to their proper owners. So, because Sing was too jealous of his office to furnish the family table cheaply, and because of his own greediness, Belshazzar fell into an indigestion which would have killed him had not the young doctor, to please William, given him medicine.

"It's the chicken livers," said William, "and the whipped cream; though whatever we are to do about it I don't know, for Jap won't let anybody help with the nursing, and we can't refuse the things people send if it's any comfort to them."

"Oh, it is—the greatest comfort in the world," said the young doctor, "I feel that; even when I am tucking them under the buggy seat and hoping they will lose out before I get home. They never say much, but there is a way they have of making you feel that it is not the good it will do the Doctor, but the time and labor it costs them that counts—like the candles people burn on shrines, I suppose." He laughed a little, and went on in a kind of boyish way he had, pleasant and attractive in spite of his homely countenance. "Do you know, Miss William, I wouldn't have believed I should be able to feel so much through the skimpy little things they say. It's in the air, I think. Yesterday the Macklins met me at the lower bridge—Mr. and Mrs. and a whole wagon-load of little Macklins wanting to know how the old Doctor did. Macklin never said a word but that—just: 'How's the old Doctor a'doing?' and sat there with his whip-lash dragging, looking at the horses' ears. And after awhile Mrs. Macklin said, out of her sunbonnet (you know the kind she has), like a person at the bottom of a well, 'We ain't had no doctor but the old Doctor fur nigh thirty years.' She trained her sunbonnet along the line of little Macklins, and turned it back towards me—'Fur nigh thirty year,' she said, and somehow I understood." He caught his breath and colored a little, but William covered it with quick appreciation.

"Yes, it's like that," she said, "especially among the mountaineers. I've noticed how the conversation seems to go right on without words. That's why dad didn't want them left to Dr. Lawrence. He never understands anything except what's said to him."

"Well, I can understand that, too. It is a wonder I am not like that myself. This means so much to me. Of course, I knew I should have to be a country doctor, and made up my mind to just put up with it; and when I had the chance to be with Furniss for a year, I said: "I will have something to look back to, anyway.' But there is something in this, too. It is mostly sheer science in the city, and the patients are just patients, but here they are—folks."

"I am glad, I'm glad!" said William, tears coming. "When poor dad is so sick I couldn't bear to have anybody think slightingly of his work. And Belshazzar—but perhaps I shouldn't have asked you to prescribe for a cat?" She broke off in dawning consternation.

"Oh," said the young doctor, "it might worry your father when he begins to take notice, if anything had happened to Belshazzar. He will be asking for him in a day or two."

He said things like that whenever occasion admitted, the more readily as he was the less sure in his mind that the old Doctor would ever take notice again. Week by week he lay breathing heavily, or endured great pains with wavering and broken words. He would swim up gasping from deeps of oblivion to see Jap always leaning over him at one side and his wife or William at the other, with the figure of the young doctor, contained and quiet at the foot, and the sunlight streaming through the cracks of the blinds, shining on the western wall; and when he had but dozed and stirred a little, the yellow bars had shifted to the wall on the east; or he would rouse to the morning freshness and Jap wetting his bandages, but before he had done with it and turned his pillow, it would unaccountably be night with the shade of the lamp dimming all the room. Furniss came twice from the city at intervals of a week, but to the old Doctor he had but quitted the room a moment; and waking to find the surgeon there, he returned to the first morning of his sickness and the point of professional interest in his own predicament; or he would hear the wheels of his own buggy going out

with the young doctor, and fret upon the grievance of the stranger and
the reiterated charge, to which Jap answered with the same vehemence
of protest and reassurance. It seemed as if the Doctor's mind hung upon
the mere point of his last conscious contact with life, not to be forced
from it at the risk of life itself. So for three weeks, while the Doctor's
man lent his whole thought to sustaining it at that point, stooping
at the bed, rising up and sitting down, eating and sleeping with the
soothing, unwearied readiness of the perfect nurse.

It was after three weeks that William admitted, for the first
time in her life, she had forgotten to listen for the voice of Toyon or
to look for the morning shine of its waters, and as she went out and
walked beside it again, it seemed to her that the stream had been away
for a long time of which it could give no account. That was the day
after a day on which Furniss had sat by the side of his friend for half
the round of the clock, and tried what Dr. Rhewold, who knew him,
understood to be the remedy of the last resort. By degrees the labor of
the old Doctor's breathing eased, though they could not say at first if it
was merely to grow fainter; and about the moth hour they heard him
chuckling in his bed. To William, leaning over him, he whispered that
he thought of prescribing flannel cakes for Mrs. McCloud's rheumatism,
and asked her what she thought of that for a dietary, and fell off
immediately asleep, waking into the sense of present time and ready
for going on, though he went on feebly enough, and it was a long time
before he could be moved about the house.

In the mean time dust gathered in the room which was called
William's Heart, the green scum dried in the glasses, prune-packing had
begun in the orchards, and Antrim Stairs had gotten a more important
thing to think about.

The end of that time found William pale and thinner from
confinement, so that it was fortunate the young doctor should be
driving so often about the intricate lanes to give her occasion to take
the pleasant air. The shadow brooding over Rosebank for months past
was gone up from all the world; high and wide the sky went over them;
color of pale-gold glimmered on the fields; over westward, beyond the
rifled hills where the sea was, a mild radiance reflected from it played
upon the world. Berries of Toyon began to redden, gold of pollen

dusted all the trails, the orchards had a winey smell from droppings of neglected fruit.

"I'll tell you a secret, Miss William," said the young doctor, as the wheels of the buggy clattered on the bridge, "though I do not know why it appeals to me as a secret just now, for I seem to have had an inkling once or twice before, but I have discovered that the world is a very beautiful place."

"Oh," said William, brimming with a child's irresistible laughter, "I wanted to say that myself."

"Well, I'll let you say it to-morrow—you are going with me to Macklin's to-morrow? It will be just as true then, I've a notion."

"Yes, that's the best of it," assented William; "only somehow, once the beauty seemed to hurt—you know what I mean, as if it reminded you of something sad that happened so long ago you had forgotten everything about it except the feeling. And now—"

"Now," said the young doctor, "it keeps hinting at something pleasant about to happen."

"Why, yes. I am so glad about dad getting well, I suppose, I can see gladness everywhere."

"That's good, of course. And it is digging away so long in the city—two years at Berkeley and four in the col—makes the country seem so good to me. I was born in the country, you know—on a ranch in Nappa. Nights when I wake up here at Rosebank and hear the dropping of ripe fruit in the orchards about, I'm surprised to stretch myself and find I've grown so large. Let's go home by the lower road, it's ever so much longer."

"Jap," the old Doctor was saying just about that time, himself grown pallid and shrunken, squinting along the injured leg stretched out before him—"Jap, don't you think you could manage to make things a bit pleasanter for Dr. Rhewold? You don't want to remember all the things I said when I was off my head. Of course, I have always wanted you to be in a position, if anything happened to me—but there, I won't say anything about it. It isn't many of these young chaps would give up a place with a man like Furniss to keep up the practice of an old back number like me (I suppose he thinks I'm a back number), but he takes to the work amazingly. If you weren't quite so offish with him—"

"Just as you say, Doctor, just as you say." Jap had changed, too, since the Doctor's accident. The confinement had subdued the tan; he wore his hair continually tossed back now, and it became him; distress had tightened the slack corners of his mouth. He began to look as if in time he might actually have an expression.

The old Doctor began to get about on a crutch totteringly; he was easily shaken, and weakness fretted him. Lying abed so much by day, he slept little by night; and of all his household found none so well able as the young doctor to keep him company such hours. Hot nights, when Dr. Rhewold had been driving late, he would find the old Doctor, by the glow of his cigar, stretched in a steamer-chair on the veranda; or, later, when the fogs closed in, propped on the worn office couch with the office stove chortling over fat blocks of pine, with the office lamp glowing dimly through the smoke of the old Doctor's cigars. It was the source of the greatest satisfaction to Dr. Caldwell, when the younger man had admitted an appreciation of good tobacco which his student means had not permitted him to encourage, to contrive ways of insinuating upon his assistant the acceptance of a cigar, and, looking at him through the pale reek of Havanas, began to experience the affectionateness of an older man towards a younger one whom he has made comfortable.

Such hours they fell into long professional confidences and reminiscences of Caldwell's thirty-five years of Santa Lucia. Short days shut in by mists of rain, or seldom occasions of cold returnings from late calls, the old Doctor, lying awake and listening for the din of the wheels on the bridge, followed by the accustomed creaking of the gate and the noise of putting up the team, found himself a little fretted by Jap's too ready acquiescence in Dr. Rhewold's stipulation that no one should wait up for him to attend the horses.

"It is what I pay him for, though, to tell the truth, he is several shades above the position of stable-boy. But he never seemed to mind doing it for me. By-the-way, I have noticed you call him Mr. Jasper. How did you happen to drop on to that?" Dr. Rhewold, unwinding the Doctor's comforter from his neck and shaking out the damp, answered that it was Jasper's own suggestion.

"Ah, well," said the old Doctor, "it is my belief he hasn't been called by it these ten years. He used to quiver at the sound of his name, as if I had struck him with it, so I took to calling him Jap for short. But I want to tell you that Mrs. Caldwell and myself take it kind of you that you show him so much consideration, especially as he has rather a stand-offish way with him."

"Why, as to that," said the younger man, with the simplicity of one whose sentiments are matters to live by, "I could understand how that was, seeing a stranger taking your place with him; and now that you speak of it, I have noticed he seems rather above the average run of male nurses. What professional training has he had?"

"To tell the truth, nearly as much as you have. He came within a few weeks of his diploma. It is rather an odd story. I shouldn't like to have it get about the country here, but there is no reason why you should not hear it—it's the kind that goes with a good cigar." The old Doctor settled himself in the cushions with the air of a man who approaches the time of life when talking is a sufficient occupation. The fog gathered outside on the wistaria-vine, and dripped down steadily by the windows. Belshazzar woke, and purred at the Doctor's feet; when the wind stirred towards the house they heard the louder purring of Toyon.

"It must be all of ten years," said the Doctor, "since Momson sent him to me. Yes, Momson, of Philadelphia. He was in the class above me, and we were as thick as thieves, ... and now he is president of the college .... Well, this fellow Jasper was the brainy man of his class. You know, the kind—thin skinned, blond type—that goes through his work like a streak, and gets the knack of doing things so quick he seems to have been born with it."

"Men like that in our class," said the young doctor, "and conceit is the breath of life to him."

"It was conceit that Jasper fell foul of," suppressing a groan, as he shifted his aching limb. "There was an accident in one of the wards when he happened to be there—hemorrhage, I believe; anyway, instead of calling help, Jasper undertook to handle it himself—and the man died. Maybe he'd have died anyway, but the nurse talked. Jasper was the kind that got people down on him somehow ... and the affair got into the newspapers and made considerable of a row. Somehow people got stirred up about it, and there was some talk of refusing him a diploma; but Jasper took the matter out of their hands by going into a brain-fever, what with the natural worry of it, the man's widow calling him a murderer, and the newspapers cutting into him and all. He was mortal sensitive, as all those clever, conceity people are, but the conceit was all gone out of him when he recovered, and the cleverness with it. Momson took an interest in him, and as the poor devil hadn't any folks to speak of, sent him out to me. Been here ever since." He was silent for a while, blowing rings of smoke and watching them as if each one had been the circlet of a year through which he viewed the progress of the man nurse up to that hour, and at the third one, which was about the time in Jap's history when it first began to be noticed—

"That accounts for what the farmers' wives tell me about his always quitting a case just before the end," broke in the young doctor. "I thought it just a queerness."

"Not so queer when you come to think about it. At first he was shy of patients, but the natural fitness, I suppose, was too strong for him. He just took naturally to nursing as some men take to drink."

Probably there is no thought in a man's life which he will not tell to another man at the right conjunction. Dr. Caldwell, when he had found another cigar and lighted it, returned to the thought which hung in the air, and said, with what definiteness the theme allowed, that it grew upon him in the intimacies of his country practice, there was, under all the monstrous mistakes and vagaries of medical practice, a theory of healing too tenuous to be grasped, and a gift of it, fugitive, but not less sure than the reagencies of drugs; and so returning by citations to the case of Edward Jasper.

"It is a pity, when you come to think of it. He can diagnose better with the ends of his fingers than Lawrence with all his five senses; but I doubt he will be anything more than Jap, the Doctor's assistant, and a queer stick at that. Momson, I know, thought that his balance would return once his health was re-established; that is why he sent him to California; for there was danger of melancholy madness at first, but he is well past all that. It is the dread of death mostly that unstrings him. Sometimes I have thought—I have lacked the heart to put it to the proof—but I have thought if he could be brought face to face with it, under the stress of some other emotion strong enough to override his obsession, he might pull out of it yet. However, I am glad to have had this opportunity to tell you how much we appreciate the good-nature with which you put up with his cranks and quirks. Mrs. Caldwell takes it very much to heart, his devotion to me in this sickness, and we wouldn't like to have him snubbed."

"Indeed," said Rhewold, "I should hope myself beyond that in any case; but now that I have heard his story, I shall try to have him not take my being here so hard." And being as good as his word, he laid himself open to Jap's regard with so much heartiness that to offset it the Doctor's assistant became absolutely waspish.

"I suppose it is simply a case of I do not like you, Dr. Fell," Rhewold said to the Doctor's daughter, as they walked out together after a shut-in day.

"Well, I shouldn't mind it," said William. "You can't put any more into a pint cup when it is full. Jap has his limitations. He adores my father, and you would be astonished to see how good he is to me."

"I should be astonished if anybody should want to be anything less than good to you," answered the young doctor, with so much earnestness that William laughed. I have already said that the Doctor's daughter was very pretty when she laughed; all sorts of delicious little kissey places came out around her mouth and distracting little sparkles in her eyes. They being at the end of their walk, as the young doctor swung towards her at the turn it happened that he found this out for himself, with so much pleasure in the discovery that he spent the rest of the walk in making her smile as often as possible.

XI

At the end of the spring semester Antrim Stairs was made
head of his department, so he had married Julia Maybury and gone
down the coast on his honeymoon to Monterey, Santa Barbara, and
Los Angeles—splendid names to string on the thread of a wedding
journey, tender and glowing with the color of romance. Among those
of the college set who had really cared for him, estimating him at
the possibilities of what he might become, the fact of his marriage
occasioned a distinct sense of loss.

"It is not," said Grenning, who had gone up to San Francisco
in the character of best man, "as if Julia were not a nice sort of girl,
but she isn't the sort who ought to marry into a college faculty. She is
only taking account of Stairs as a man, and if he is going to amount to
anything he has got to be a biologist most of the time."

But the Lindleys and their circle had very little thought to spare
outside of their own interests, except what went to sustaining William
and the family at Rosebank in the long turn of the Doctor's illness.
The confinement, the cessation of his lifelong activities, told on his
shaken frame; the ebb of his vitality in the summer's heat brought out
unguessed acerbities of temper and whims as thick as limpets at low
tide. William had enough to do to keep him amused, the more so as
Jap showed himself unequal to that business. It became evident that the

Doctor's accident had worked a great change in the Doctor's assistant. He sat more by himself, and watched the other more intently, smiled awry as he watched, and walked out often when he was most wanted. Dr. Rhewold was always picking him up at cross-roads, and William, if she drove to Santa Lucia, would run into him unaccountably in the shops, or if she had walked in to see Serena would be sure to be overtaken by him, walking home.

"I positively never knew anybody with such a faculty for pervading the surroundings," she complained to Serena. What William did not admit to herself was that Jap's presence never presented itself so much an intrusion as on those occasions when she and Dr. Rhewold had something to say to each other. They had a great deal to say, it appeared, and had somehow fallen into a way of being able to say it much better when they were quite alone.

Now and then, in the preoccupation of her father's illness, William was half aware that the new obtrusiveness of the silent and self-effacing man nurse was the issue of some indefinable change in the man himself, and wondered to find herself put out of countenance by it. Once when she had sat with Mrs. Lindley on into the ebb of the vivid afternoon, and found herself hurrying home through the warm twilight on the Penitentia road, to her sharp annoyance Jap rose up from under the shaggy eucalyptus and swung into a walk beside her. She knew that Dr. Rhewold was to have driven out that afternoon, and wondered that her father should have been left alone. They walked on, saying nothing, she swallowing back her vexation with studious kindness, too tired for casual talk, and habituated to his taciturnity. But there had come a change even in the character of Jap's silences. His want of speech, that had appeared mere vacuity, began to assume the oppressiveness of a preoccupation, shouldering rudely against William's musing thought in the warm earth-scented dusk. She caught herself looking at him, half wondering to see that the definiteness which seemed to grow upon the inner man, and emerge from him, wrought so little change in the effectiveness of his exterior. He was still lean and loosely built, and had a slack, uninterested face, yet as he walked he began to exhibit a kind of meaningful energy as of another man walking inside him, and the other man in a great passion and talking to himself. Certain heavings of the chest, shudderings, clinching of the hands, quick breathings went on in him without so much as altering the expression of his face or letting a word out of him; it wrought upon William like the suspicion of a devilish contrivance in the guise of some household utility. They walked on, she trying in sheer nervousness for a note of naturalness, suddenly inexpressibly relieved at the rattle of a buggy on the road behind her. Without so much as turning her head, she knew it for Dr. Rhewold driving with her father's team.

"Will you ride?" he asked, drawing up beside her. "I found I must drive through town for a prescription, and hoped to overtake you." Jap held her skirts as the doctor cramped the wheels.

"See you later, Mr. Jasper!" called the doctor, cheerfully. And then to William: "Why, you are trembling! The walk has been too much for you." He drew up the dust-robe carefully over her soft ruffles, for all the roads were thick with the powdered earth that clouded up about the wheels. He spent such care upon it, coming across one of William's small bare hands which must be stopped of its trembling, taking such a long time to it that he forgot to inquire, and William to tell him, what had occasioned it. The young doctor smiled down at William, and William smiled back, more directly perhaps because the deepening twilight screened them from each other, so directly that his gaze caught the sparkle of hers, and hung there for an instant that gave him the greatest possible satisfaction to recall, which was singular, as the chief end of his dwelling upon it was to create a desire for a repetition of the experience.

It was no longer than two days, or perhaps three, after that the Doctor's daughter went into the room at the head of the stair which was called William's Heart, and had lately served as a laboratory, and had Jap carry down all the signs of that occupancy. The little square closet had gotten quite a scientific air that winter, when Julia Maybury had been coming out to see William, and William's studies had been as good an excuse as any other for Dr. Stairs's coming out to see Julia, and Jim Halford had come without any excuse at all. William thought a great deal about Julia as she put away her father's microscope, remembering how the girl had bent above it, her dark hair sometimes quite touching Dr. Stairs's cheek as he guided her hand upon the slides. She wondered if it could be possible that two people could be unhappy together, though they loved each other. Then she thought of poor Jim Halford, and the green scum dried on the wide-mouthed bottles and the dust

over everything gave her quite a sentimental feeling. She recalled what
Agnes Sterling had told her of how Jim had looked at the wedding,
and how, as soon as Julia had gone away, he had returned to his room
in his father's house, and there the wedding guests, departing late, had
seen his shadow passing on the blind, going to and fro steadily with its
head upon its breast, passing and repassing on the block of misty light
on into the night, and the bridesmaids had shut up the windows so
that Mrs. Maybury would not see. She wondered if another man—say
such a man as Dr. Rhewold—should love anybody in that devoted,
despairing way, what he would do about it.

When the room was all cleaned and whitened, scoured and
shining, William went about to furnish it with white curtains and a
white drawn-work cover for the table, and stood for a while pondering
on its immaculateness. She went slowly and brought a tall vase, and tall
white lilies from the garden, and, when she had set them on the table in
the middle of the room, said to herself that she could not imagine why
she had done such a thing, and softly shut the door.

All during the summer, as Serena was less able to take exercise,
Evan was in the habit of driving her about the country whenever he
had errands there; and when the properties under his management lay
out in the farming district beyond Rosebank, they would return by the
Caldwells' place to inquire how the old Doctor did, and, if the hour
were suitable, to have a meal there. It was on the last of these drives that
Serena was able to take that the young couple made a discovery most
interesting, and missed making another one nearly as obvious. The day
was warm and fine, but with a tang in it which foreran the autumn
weather. The air was full of the pleasant curative smell of the tarweed;
the far blueness of the hills melted insensibly into aerial softness;
overhead the clear heavens opened upon the door of space.

Lindley's business over, they turned into the lane that emerged
on the country road a mile or two below Rosebank. A close thicket
of willows and Toyon grew by the fence, screening the turn. Here the
horse shied at the rustling of the bushes, and was drawn to a full stop as
the figure of a man rose up from the roadside, with so much an air of
premeditated mischief that it was a moment before the manner fell off
as a disguise assumed, and showed them Jap, the Doctor's man. He had
been sitting hidden by the bushes, and had a thick stem of holly which

he had whittled to the semblance of a club; the litter of his occupation lay on the grass around him.

"I say, Jap, but you gave me a start!" called Lindley. "I thought it was a hold-up."

Jap closed the knife and thrust it in his pocket, letting the stick trail from his hand as he came out into the road.

"I'm sorry I frightened you, Mr. Lindley. I came out for a walk, and was waiting to ride back with Dr. Rhewold. I thought it was his buggy."

"Get in behind if you like," said Lindley; "we stop at the house."

But the Doctor's assistant answered only that he would wait; and as they drove off, looking back from the buggy, they observed him sitting on a fallen tree by the roadside prodding in the earth with his stick, like a man arrested in important business and impatient of delay.

Serena spoke of it to William afterwards as they went up-stairs to lay aside her wraps.

"Yes, I know," said William; "it's always like that now. Whenever dad can spare him, and sometimes when he cannot very well, always going out across lots to ride home with Dr. Rhewold, or sitting up nights to open the gate for him, or riding a bit of the way when he goes out, and always with that curious, tumultuous kind of silence on him that makes you want to ask if he didn't just make a remark, though you know perfectly well he hasn't. And yet to see them about the house you would think Jap couldn't bear the doctor, the way he catches him up about the patients and prescriptions. Jap knows a lot of medicine; you know, he was a student himself once. Dad says perhaps that is the reason he takes so much interest in Dr. Rhewold, the doctor is so much like what he was before his trouble—only not so young, of course."

"What was his trouble? I never heard."

"Oh, some kind of shock and brain-fever. I am not sure I ever heard myself exactly. Somehow I never minded his queerness until lately. But it is good to see how considerate Dr. Rhewold is of him; it is no wonder Jap has taken a fancy to him, though he can't seem to find any way of expressing it but by finding fault and being always in his company."

"And you, William, how do you like Dr. Rhewold?"

"Oh," said William, "I should like anybody who was good to dad. Hadn't you better lie down, Serena, until dinner is ready?"

"Evan," said Mrs. Lindley, in their own room that night, "you know the little room that the Doctor calls William's Heart, and was a laboratory the last time we saw it. Well, William hasn't asked me into it for a long time, so this afternoon, when I was up in her bedroom, I— peeped. I can always tell what William is most interested in by looking into the little room—and she has always asked me before—but, what do you think, Evan, it was all set out in white like a chapel, with white lilies, and her Thomas à Kempis and the Saint Cecilia I gave her for Christmas. Is William going to turn religious, do you suppose?"

"Well," said Lindley, "she is up to most anything." Then, with sudden illumination, "Unless she is in love."

"Oh, Evan, do you suppose it is that? Why, yes, of course; ... that's the way she would feel about it; ... a nice girl always feels like that. Yes, of course, Evan." Serena went up and laid her hands upon his shoulders. "I do believe that's it. But to think you found it out before I did! And you know about Dr. Stairs, too—about the possibility of his making a mistaken marriage, I mean. Everybody says he has done that. There are lots of things you don't know, Evan, about books and ... art ... and all that; but you know *folks*. And, William, ... it's the young doctor, I suppose; ... but I don't see how you found it out."

All that winter Santa Lucia was gloomed with rains that came early and held on wet and cold. Not a day from the first of December until February but had some cloud in it, sagging along the lower line of snows, by day streaming out high and tenuous, falling by night and caught in the leafless tops of trees, tugging and sodden till the morning wind could bear it up; and between such days long intervals of steady rain.

At Rosebank everybody complained of the cold and the wet except William and the young doctor, and that was not wholly because William so seldom complained of anything. In the mist and the damp her cheeks were rosy warm, and her eyes shone from a spirit warmed from within. You found the counterpart of that quiet shining in the eyes of the young doctor if you came upon him unexpectedly, driving tediously in the rain, wrapped in his mackintosh and seeming not to mind it. But in the house he went soberly, played dominoes with the old Doctor, read to him, made good his pretence of not regarding Jap's ungraciousness, and was neither too much nor too little about.

By the end of February the sacred lilies had shrivelled on their stalks; and when the discarded bulbs had lain three days in the corner of the veranda, Mrs. Caldwell, unable to bear the offence to tidiness, pattered out to plant them by the garden walk. In the middle of the morning Mrs. Caldwell had slipped out cautiously while the trees were still adrip, but in a moment William and Jap were down upon her, with Sing clucking and chuckling. But when Jap had persuaded Mrs. Caldwell out of the damp, and gone to put away the spade, the little Celestial's laugh died wheezily in his throat. He sidled towards William, where she bent above the beds searching for tulip crowns.

"Billee," he said, "what you think about Jlap?"

"Think how, Sing?"

"He no more allee same, he difflint."

"Yes, I suppose so." It struck William all at once that for Sing to have noticed it, the change in Jap must be greater than she thought.

"Missee Billee"—he edged nearer, with a certain shuffling air of secrecy, but with a grin still widening above his shagged old teeth— "Missee Billee, I think Jlap no likee young dlocka."

"Dr. Rhewold? Oh, Sing, Jap is very fond of my father; he does not like to see anybody in his place. Dr. Rhewold understands."

The little Chinaman continued to look at her, his head on one side with insinuating intention.

"I think he no likee young dlocka *hard.*" Then, getting no answer: "I think maybe so he kill him."

"Nonsense, Sing, Jap wouldn't hurt a fly. Go and scrub your kitchen, or I shall think you have been hitting the pipe again." But the word stuck in her mind, and chimed with the recollection of that intensity of palpitant brooding thought that had frightened her walking home from town.

"Sing," she questioned, suddenly, "what makes you think Jap dislikes Dr. George?" The Chinaman's narrow eyes inquired of her furtively before he answered:

"All night he no sleep; he walk, walk, sometime he talk, sometime he talk about dlocka." Ah Sing edged nearer with mysterious caution. "Jlap he ketchum big stick; all night he dig in the ground. I think so he want to kill. You come see."

Sing and the Doctor's assistant had rooms in a small building in the rear, Sing's opening towards the kitchen, and Jap's towards the garden. Each had a little stoop by the doorway, where the occupant might take the air. By Jap's door there was a white rose that William had planted years before, beginning to understand childishly that he was in need of kindness. Now, as Sing led the way around the out-dwelling, she observed a deep, smooth hole under the rose-bush, large enough to have buried a cat in, gouged by some blunt instrument. The door was open, and by the bed leaned a heavy stick of holly peeled and trimmed. One end of it was soiled with earth, and the other shiny as with much handling.

"Allee night" said Sing, "he sit by the door, dig, dig. What you thlink?" Hastily William reviewed in her mind as much as she knew of Jap's history, which was as little as was known to everybody, and amounted to the conclusion that he was a little "cracked." It passed through her mind on the instant that "queer" people sometimes went insane in a flash—but Jap, good old Jap!

"I think it is a foolish notion," she said, "and my father must not be troubled about it." Also she resolved in her mind to ask the doctor if he thought Sing could be using opium again.

"Good old Jap," she thought again that evening, when, coming down for a glass of water, after having said good-night, she saw through the crack of her father's door Jap stooping in patient, impersonal devotion over the old Doctor, bent on the relief of his pains.

Seeing the candle passing in the hall, Dr. Rhewold, who had just come in through the office door, called out that he had a packet for her.

"Mrs. McKelvey said you would understand," he said, holding it up across the banister, touching her hand for good-night as she leaned to him a moment.

"Only patterns," smiled William, passing on with the candle to leave the wide hall in darkness, except for the fan of light that rayed out from the crack of her father's door and fell directly upon the spot where she had stood smiling down on the young doctor smiling up at her. Directly opposite Jap bent on above the bed until the patient sank heavily asleep, and, passing to his own room, observed that a steady rain began to fall.

<h1 style="text-align:center">XII</h1>

The rain fell for three days without intermission, and at the end
of that time Dr. Rhewold could no longer delay driving out to a patient
far up on the Toyon grade, though the roads were heavy, and streaked,
steel-gray sheets of rain cut off all view a team's-length on either side.
He was expected back that day, though at Rosebank no surprise was felt
when the dark closed in without him. The household turned in early
to bed, their spirits sodden. William, in her room, tried to read, grew
restless, and ended with standing a long time, forehead pressed to the
window-pane, fixed upon the reflection of her bedroom light and the
vision it evoked. She told herself that since her father's accident she was
nervous about the Toyon road.

There were windows on three sides of William's room—looking
south towards Toyon, looking east across the driveway to the orchards
beyond, looking back above the garden towards the barn. Going at last,
after an hour of fruitless staring, to draw the blinds of these, she was
startled to observe a light moving low and swingingly between the house
and the barn. It passed so quickly that she thought it at first a phantom
of reflection, and drew down the blind behind her to cut off her own
light, pressing against the window to make sure. Now she saw the bulk
of darkness painted with thin streaks of light that glimmered and shifted
to right and left of where the stalls should be. She raised the window

noiselessly, and heard the clink of the harness, muffled and cautious. Dr. Rhewold, she knew, had not driven in, nor had any call come from the neighborhood, yet plainly some one moved with a lantern in the harness-room. The light shifted and broke out again, outlining the wide leaves of the barn-door; the snuffle and snort of the horses broke distinctly through the drum of the rain.

The window opening towards the barn overlooked the back veranda, at the far end of which a vine ran from a stout trellis to a screen of lilacs fencing the hitching space in front of the barn, continuing down the driveway to the gate. If one kept along the hedge it was possible to escape observation from the house or barn, according as one went one side or another of the lilacs. William had discovered this as long ago as an innate boyishness of behavior had made such escapes from the house desirable. The wildness of the night, and under it some prick of apprehension, like the sharp drip of the eaves under the windy gusts of rain, tempted her to try the old adventure. Once the light was out in her room, and the window opened to the night and the storm, her spirit streamed up to meet it. Wrapped in her waterproof, she slipped softly down the stair and into the veranda, feeling for the wet trellis in the dark. Jap, she was sure, was hitching the ranch team, and she would see what it was all about.

By the little light of his lantern, which he showed sparingly, the Doctor's assistant drew out the team and harnessed it to a light buckboard with a covered top. His hand on bit and snaffle was steady, his voice when he spoke to the horses quick and controlled, all his motions homely and accustomed; but to William, watching through the screen of lilacs, full of piercing strangeness, wild and bristling with evil intent. It was not in the wind that drove and lapsed sullenly, nor in the rain pouring furiously or withholden by it, nor in the hour, nor the futile ghostly glimmer of the light—rather in the fearful preoccupation of the man, who made the humor of the night of no account. He neither shook in the wind, nor turned his face in the rain, nor bowed before it, moving steadily to his work. William found herself caught up somehow in the man's secret determination, the urgency of haste, the large disregard of the night and the weather. When he moved, drawing the team cautiously down the driveway, she moved with him behind the leafless lilacs shaken by the wind; when he led them through the wide gate, she slipped behind the bole of the blue-gum that hung above it; when he swung himself to the seat, she sprang on the low body of the buckboard, and drew up against the canvas cover that went over the seat only. The great blast of the wind in the wagging Eucalyptus covered the sound she made.

All this without consideration, naturally as she had stolen a ride before time, childishly, and with a sharp choke of laughter, as if she should presently reach around the canvas curtain and say "*Boo!*" to Jap driving mindlessly in the rain. And then a sudden checking of the pulse, a chill sinking of the heart, as by the steady roar of the creek beside them in the blackness she knew that he followed the Toyon road. She was not afraid; that was old Jap on the seat—Jap the butt, the factotum, the tame cat. She was not afraid, she was not even cold; her waterproof was heavy, and the wind and the rain, roaring down from the mountain, went by so fast they missed her, crouched behind the seat. No, she was not afraid; presently she would put out a hand to old Jap and ask him what he meant by it. Then some emanation reached her from the man's brooding thought, some portent, sharp and disquieting. Reason and apprehension leaped brokenly in her mind, jarred by the leap of the buckboard flying on the heels of the team. Out there on the Toyon road before them was the young doctor swinging towards home. And Jap hated the young doctor. She saw him bend, as she had an hour since, in womanish care above her father's bed—and against that the figure of him as Sing had evoked it, sitting in the dark in the doorway digging a hole in the earth with his club. "I think maybe so he kill him," the cook had said—pawing in the earth as beasts do when the lust of fighting is on them. "Maybe so he kill him"—but why?—why? She missed the clew, and returned upon her track. Good old Jap, to whom the dread of death was an obsession—but Sing had been so sure; and why should they not understand each other, the Chinaman and the half-witted?— no doubt they came nearer together. And this was the Toyon road.

The rain by this time had a way of leaving off suddenly, and the wind and the creek filled up the interval of sound; then the rain began and the wind quieted, the creek droned steadily below the rain. Jap drove too rapidly for the road and the night. Now the horses began to fag, and then to strain as they struck rising ground. The moment she was aware of the change of the grade an intimation of Jap's purpose ran with a chill to William's heart and settled there.

The Toyon road ran up the canon of the creek, and by a sag in the lift of the range into a closed valley beyond. Where the hills began the creek took the whole floor of the canon, forcing the road up and about the steep bosses of its sloping sides. Beyond the little lap of pleasantness where it opened on the valley, Toyon was a lean canon, gaunt bones of the mountains starting through skimp chaparral, cliffs falling almost sheer to the bed of the creek. It was at best a difficult piece of road, narrow, slippery with clay, affording passing only in the small inlets of cross canons. Great teams freighting from the closed high valleys had bells upon them that rang far and echoingly in the straightened rift, but lighter vehicles took their chances, hallooing as they came blindly around the sweeps of hills to warn of their approach. Neglecting such precaution, they had a choice of backing away to the nearest inturn or going over the grade. Over that broken steep teams and drivers had gone such nights as this.

Beginning to chill severely at the greater elevation, and to sicken with apprehension, William still crouched at the back of the buck-board, and saw the moment when she should properly declare herself to Jap receding steadily as they climbed. Supposing his purpose natural and innocent, how should she account for herself, and if sinister, how help? More than all, if Jap's strange ride had to do with Dr. Rhewold, what interpretation must her presence bear to him? And that it had to do with him became clearer. Midway the canon turned sharply to the right; when they had come a team's length from the curve, where the grade was stiffest and the fall of the slope below them steepest, Jap swung the pair across the road, halting them at such an angle as left neither horse nor foot passage between the tail of the buck-board and the falling wall. The noses of the team touched the crumbling clay of the cut on the inner side. The Doctor's assistant must have known at what hour Rhewold would take the road, and planned to meet him here.

The hanging wall of the cut leaned a little above them, and shut off the fury of the storm where it blundered and broke among the peaks. The boom of it along the top of the canon, the crash of unbridled waters far below them, the loud rain, seemed to fall off sensibly before the terrible quietness of Jap, who sat in the midst of it, and held the team so stilly, so much in the attentive patience of the man nurse, that William, reassured for the moment, waited but to steady her hand before she reached out to command him, when faint and strange, as issuing from far behind the hill, came the young doctor's hail. Once, twice it came brokenly on the wind, and the third time nearer, followed by the rattle of his buggy deflected oddly from the opposing hill. All this time Jap had not said a word.

Then the gleam of the doctor's lantern, cutting the mist of the rain like a thin sword, flashed forward over the gulf to point his doom, and drew such a sudden scream from William as though it had entered at her breast. By its light the two men saw her at the same moment out upon the road, throwing up her arms in the faces of the checked team that drew perilously back upon their haunches. The young doctor flung himself forward on the reins, his voice level and urgent, as they slipped and snorted in the wet clay of the grade, and two wheels swung out and poised an instant above the rift and the ravening water. If it had been Jap's purpose to send him there with the buggy crashing above him, he was very near to accomplishing it; but the horses, recognizing their stable-mates, grew tractable, and stood presently in check, with William's hand upon the bit.

"Hey there, confound you! What's the matter with you?" cried the young doctor, getting down at last to turn his lantern towards the invisible blockade. "William!" he cried, aghast. And then: "William! William!" shaken with amazement and sudden fear. William instinctively put up her hand to him, and he covered it with his, holding it against his breast, all his young manhood quick in him at the miracle of her presence. And still Jap had not spoken nor stirred. Now it seemed his silence grew and increased upon him until it over laid the noises of the night. It proceeded from him until the wind sagged before it and parted down the canon like a riven tent; before it the rain receded pattering up the trails. It came from the man, seemed to swell in him so that he was large with it as he got slowly down to face the young doctor holding up the lantern between them.

"Jap!" cried Rhewold, halting uncertainly on the inflection, "is anything—" But he knew without finishing that there was nothing the matter except as concerned them man to man. He took it quietly, turning to set the lantern on a jut of the nearing wall behind, and so to put Jap between him and the edge of the grade. The glass was dimmed by rain, the light shone feebly on the foreheads of the opposing teams, raying out to define the shadow of Jap thrown large against the blackness breaking off in mid-space above the deep well of the canon.

"Dr. Rhewold," said the man nurse—"Dr. Rhewold," and he spat suddenly, as it were upon the title, "you have come to take a place which, if I had not lacked a small matter of a slip of paper with some names upon it, I should have taken and kept with at least as much sureness as you have held it."

"Right you are, Mr. Jasper," said the young doctor. There was so much of intensity in the man's preoccupation with his thought and his purpose to deliver it here and now, so much of wariness in the doctor's attention to it, as seemed to William to put her miles out of their consideration. She stood and shivered by the dripping bridles, not sure if Jap was rightly aware of her presence or if Rhewold had not forgotten her.

"I should have taken and kept it," went on Jap, "with at least as much credit. *At least as much.* You fumbled that last case of pneumonia, Dr. Rhewold, and you have not gripped the minds of our people here or you would not drug them so much." It was Jap's voice: the flaccid, uninflected voice of the man nurse, but with a spark in it, a nuance, a vitality. He came a step nearer, shaking his head with the manner of tossing back his hair, forgetting his hat, and scattering rain from the brim.

"Nor need you look at me with professional attention, Dr. Rhewold." Every repetition of the name was the setting of his heel upon it. "I am not mad. Though I have been thought—though I have been a fool, I am not mad." He stopped here, regarding the young doctor, who gave him his gaze back again with so steady a determination not to be angered by him that the fury of the other increased by leaps and bounds.

"Though I have been a fool," said Jasper, "for not providing myself with that slip of paper which should make us professionally equal, you prove a fool yourself when you neglect to take account of me as a man."

"Since when," said the young doctor, "have I not done so, Mr. Jasper?"

"Since the first hour you came under our roof, Dr. Rhewold."
Here he ground the name to powder and cast it from his hand. "I say
our roof, for since I came to live under it I have been as devoted to its
interests, as much a sharer of its anxieties, as if I had been born there—
so much a part of its labors that I do not think any will deny me the
word."

"Nor do I deny you." Rhewold's voice was steady and courteous.

"By what mark, then," said the man nurse, "do you judge I have
not the sensibilities and the passions of a man not to feel the sting of
your condescension to the poor-witted Doctor's help, nor your studied
tolerance of the antiquated country practitioner? By what right do you
overlook in me a rudeness which you would have proved on the person
of another? But it is not," he went on, in the manner of a man so bent
upon speaking himself out that he loses the sense of his audience—"it
is not for the slighting of my hate that I have called you to account,
but for the slighting of my love." With that the rain began again, as if it
halted upon a purpose too long delayed; as if it drummed that purpose
to the fore, Jap's words came fast and pelting. "Had you shown," he said,
"any sense of the fact that what has grown dear to you in a few months
might have grown inexpressibly dear to me in all these years; had you
shown in the course to which I have seen you set yourself, a perception
that there might be any obstacle to your desire that lay outside yourself,
if you had striven to lessen me with her, had resented my discrediting
of your skill, had you considered me at all, you should not stand here
to-night to answer to me. For though I had seen her take from you
kindness it was my right to pay, though I had seen her turn to you with
the life-long turning that was mine, though I had seen her love you—"

"Stop!" said the young doctor, white and shaking, "you go too
far!"

"Ah, far!" cried the other. "It is far indeed when the mere hint
of danger moving towards you in the night calls her out of sleep and
safety to be your guard." This was the first hint they had of his realizing
her bodily presence, and he spoke now with that touch of wildness for
which the doctor waited. "Ay, too far—too far," he said, "but no farther.
Dr. Rhewold, there is the road by which you came into our lives; take it
now and go out of them, and you go unhurt. Refuse it, and worse will
come to you. Do you take the road?"

Rhewold looked at William where she stood leaning against the horses in the rain, and saw her hand tremble. Something passed in his face like a flash and streamed out in his voice.

"By God, no!" he said.

The horses reared and snorted at the shock of the encounter as the two men closed and panted in the dim arc of the lantern, as they slipped and floundered in the rain-wet clay. The lean arms of Jap bound like wire, the lift of his back was tremendous; they did what the mind purposed. Rhewold cried out to William, warningly, "Stand back, stand back!" and the next instant found himself hanging over the face of the cliff with the creek roaring up at him with a devouring sound. He was over the cliff, but with his arms still tight about the body of the man nurse and his knees digging into the crumbling rock. He was quite clear in his head and little breathed; he felt with his feet for a ledge and found it. Jap's arms were locked under his; the Doctor's assistant had slipped in the clay and lay prone along the road. At any shifting of their positions the two must go over into the gulf together. Jap bent his face to the other, shaking him to and fro in his arms to break his hold.

"Will you go! ... go! ... go! ..." he panted.

Rhewold dug his toes into the cliff and tightened his arms across the other's back.

"William," he cried to her, his voice ashake, "will you marry me?"

"Yes!" she cried to him, and "yes!" again as the wind took her answer and whipped it about in the rain.

"Now," said the young doctor, setting his knees afresh, "do another murder and be hanged for it."

For the moment it seemed that Rhewold would have slipped and plunged downward in the sudden loosening of tension that followed on the word. The arms slacked and fell away from him, the body settled, seemed to give towards the canon. Rhewold crowded it back into the slime of the road. The inert frame was all the purchase he had on life. If he had counted on the revelation of his knowledge to quell the man's fury he counted too far. Thrown back suddenly on the biting estimate of his earlier misadventure, his fire went out of him like a candle in the rain. After a stunned interval, as if he had forgotten what he did there in the mud of the roadway, Jasper made as if to rise.

"For God's sake, man, hold on!" said the young doctor.

"I—I—beg your pardon, sir," and Jap, the tame cat, lay down in the place where Edward K. Jasper had been.

William came crawling out beside him, lying in the mud and inching forward towards the cliff.

"Keep back," the doctor begged.

William dug her elbows in the mud, and slipped out along Jap's lax body until she found the doctor's hand.

"I have the hitching-rope," she said; "there is a slip-noose. It is fast to the buggy." She worked it down one arm to Rhewold's shoulder. They lay still and breathed heavily with the strain. Then slowly, not a word said, Jap slipped it over the doctor's head, and cautiously the other arm was worked through the noose. Dumb, blind in the rain, the three writhed and turned in the roadway, working back along the rope. The sound of their breathing was like the rustle of worms in a heap, the thick clay sucked and sobbed as they dug into it for a hold. But the doctor was his own man again as soon as he felt his feet under him.

"Get in," he said, curtly, to Jap, when he had caught his breath a little and taken the team in hand. Jap climbed fumblingly into the buckboard, falling back once or twice, and reaching blindly for a hold.

"Now, back."

Inch by inch, with Rhewold at their heads, the team was backed away to where the inlet of the hill allowed the turn.

"Home," said the doctor, and stood to hear the buck-board rattle away down the grade. "Now, when he gets there, will he be Edward K. Jasper, or Jap, the Doctor's man, I wonder?" asked the young doctor, as he went up the hill where the lantern glimmered faintly through the rain. William had laid her arms upon the horse's neck and hidden her face in them.

"William," said the young doctor—a little hand came out and stole along Bettina's neck; the doctor took it—"William!" ... Then as William herself came out of the dark, he took her wholly in his arms and kissed her in the rain.

XIII

The night the long rain broke, the old Doctor's bones kept him
awake too much; the hurry of the storm, flying high and wide over
Santa Lucia, troubled what sleep he had. The tread of it was as the
passing of all the feet that had ever come into his life, urgent feet of
men that thudded at the doors, pounding of hoofs that called him
in the night, steady plodding of country funerals, light feet of his
household—those, too, how fast they went! fumbling, luring steps,
faint and receding; noise of wheels and harness, fingerings of the lock,
loitering feet on the stairs, William's feet going by—going by—with a
sense of pain and loss mixed with the ache of his bones that deterred
him—careless feet—young feet—the sound of them and the loss of
them running on into his waking hours when the sun rose clearly on a
wet, shining world. And for the first time since his illness Jap was not at
hand to attend him.

It was agreed between William and the young doctor that nothing
was to be said to her father for a day or two—not until the shock
of danger incurred should be swallowed up in security. In the mean
time Dr. Rhewold was to keep professional watch of Jap for recurrent
symptoms of violence, and to speak, of course, if any appeared. But
it would have been as easy for William to keep back the opening day
as to have withheld her heart from her father. It broke from her rosily

and with laughter, happily and with tears, as soon as she had sight of his white head where it leaned against the cushions of his chair. He had turned away from the door as she came in, looking towards Rhewold to answer some professional inquiry; but when the kind old face was bent upon her, pale from his night's unease, and with a swift strangeness answering through the close-knit sympathies to the change in her, William ran to him, kneeling by his chair, laying her cheek upon his breast, drawing up his fine old hands to fold about her face.

"Oh, dad! Oh, my dear, dear dad!" she said, sobbing there; "never to leave you, never to lack your knee and your arms around me. Though I am so happy, dad, happier than I deserve to be, say I am not to leave you, dear dad—never to leave you, whatever happens."

"What has happened, William?" asked the old Doctor, a little startled, a little sternly, lifting her in his arms and holding her off that he might see her face. But she could not tell him yet, between crying and laughing, and she could not look at him, blushing so rosily, covering her face with her hands, saying only that she was very happy, that he was her dear, dear dad, and that she would never leave him. Then the young doctor very quietly took her wrists, and, gently forcing down her hands, leaning over, kissed her as she lay upon her father's breast. The old Doctor shook at that, sat up, holding her close, rocking her in his bosom.

"Rhewold? Rhewold!" Question and reproach.

"Yes," said the young doctor, youth springing in him to meet it—"yes."

"William?" whispered her father, question and infinite tenderness.

"Yes," whispered William back—"yes, dearest dad."

"I know," Rhewold admitted, "I should have waited—should have spoken first to you, perhaps; I meant to do so. But when you have heard how it came about you will not blame us."

"No, dad, indeed you will not blame us," urged William, with tears. But he would not hear them, put by the young man with a gesture, and bent above his daughter with crooning noises as she had been a child, his lips roving tenderly on her face, her hands, her hair. Quieted at last, he raised her from her knees.

"Go to your mother, child," he said. And then, curtly, to the young doctor, "Now tell me."

"First," said Rhewold, "you must have some brandy, and if Jasper comes to the room before I am done telling, you must send him away."

"Jap!" exclaimed the old Doctor—"Jap! Is it as bad as that?" He took the brandy submissively, and lay back quietly among the cushions. Now and then the old hands twitched or clinched sharply upon the arms of his chair.

"Jap!" he whispered, at last! "Jap. Eleven years he has gone about my house as faithful as a dog ... as trusted as one ... as loved ... and now."

"Now," said the young doctor, standing over him, "you are not to think about Jap any more. You have to think about William ... and me." He blushed. "I ought to tell you that I haven't anything. It is all to make yet ... but I hope—"

Dr. Caldwell put him aside; there would be time for that. He was feeling now that he must be an older man than he had thought, and he wanted his wife to come in and tell him that they should be old in company.

It was well on in the morning before Jap came in and stood by the old Doctor's chair. Dr. Rhewold had gone off to see the Thompson baby. It was not the same baby of the year before, but his brother, already, at the age of two months, addicted to the mysterious habit of straightening right out, sudden, which made a sufficient excuse for the young doctor to be driving out in the shining morning with William beside him. Dr. Caldwell's door stood open to the sun; outside from the wet earth a steam rose and a smell of sap, foreboding spring. Jap had changed his clay-stained clothing of the night before for his best suit, which was black, and lent some dignity to his lean figure; but the mark of the night's work was plain to be seen upon him.

"Well, Jasper?" Jap winced under a name which was not the Doctor's use. "Dr. Rhewold has told you?"

"He has." The tone was level and professional. Jap made way against it with difficulty. "Will you tell me, Dr. Caldwell, how long since I came to you?"

"Ten—no, eleven years—eleven in August." There was a pause as the Doctor's assistant studied the sunlight on the wall, as if he saw the pattern of all the years in its flecked shadows.

"Do you wish to ask why you came?" asked the old Doctor.

"I have recently remembered it." Caldwell abated a little of the professional keenness with which he regarded him. The man was sane, breathed evenly, stood at ease, had quiet eyes.

"You have not always had it in mind, then? Sit down, Jap, and tell me."

"Not at first, I think, but afterwards it came to me as something I might have heard of a man whom I had known. But of late I have recalled it fully, all that it meant to me and what it might mean—to others." The deep, thick blush that spread over the tan to the roots of his bleached hair was the evidence of what it meant to him at that moment. "I have supposed it was known to you—I should not have minded that any more than it should be known to God, I think—but until—last night—I had not thought it could be known elsewhere." If there was any reproach in his manner the Doctor chose not to regard it. Presently Jap himself replied to the silence.

"However it became known, I cannot greatly regret it, since the certainty that it was known saved me from a repetition—a more dreadful repetition—of the first offence."

"It has saved you?" hinted the Doctor—"quite?"

"Quite." He raised his head; the look he gave was clear and serviceable for the exchange of professional information. He smiled. "Have no fear, Doctor, the lesion has passed." Edward K. Jasper knew himself. Insensibly the Doctor settled in his chair.

"At first," went on Jasper, now bringing his own chair to sit beside him, "when I began to realize myself, about … about the time of your accident … it grew out of that, your anxiety to have me take your place, and my regret, my very deep regret, not to be able to do so, and my asking myself why it was I could not … at first I thought it would be impossible to take up my life at the point where it was broken off, because of one thing."

"And that was?" The Doctor's face was turned towards him now with the old kindness, the old understanding.

"The dread of death … not my own, but another's. It was then that I fully realized your own great consideration in having so long spared me what I was so little able to bear … but now … now … " The Doctor's look and lifted hand would have spared him again, but Jasper shook off the kindness, tossing back his hair. "Now that I have come not only to contemplate the death of another, but to think of myself as having a hand in it, the dread is no longer a bar to me."

"Tell me, Jap, tell me, is the consideration of the death of … another … and your own part in it, gone?"

"Gone," said the Doctor's assistant, mournfully but earnestly—"quite gone. Where it came from, by what stress and pressure it was bred in my brain, I do not know, but it is now quite gone. And for her—for whose sake … " tossing back his hair, as if some weakness were tossed off with it, going on with added firmness. "For her, I say, if there were a life to be lived in her service, I should wish to live it, or a man to die in it, or the service of any one she loved, I would be the man. And that not only shall no harm come to her or hers from me, but no wish of harm, nor dream of any, I ask you to believe."

"I do believe you."

"But you can understand—that—that I would not wish to remain at Rosebank."

"What, then, would you do, Jap?"

Jasper got up and looked about the room as if, already on the eve of departure, he would keep its bright, accustomed aspect sealed up in his mind forever. Then, at last:

"When Dr. Furniss was here he saw what I was cut out for, and said then, and afterwards more particularly, that if ever I thought seriously of taking up surgery I was to come to him."

"Good old Furniss," interposed the Doctor.

"I cannot hope," went on the Doctor's assistant, "to become now what I hoped to be before—before this accident befell me. I do not even know if I can be admitted to practice. I shall leave that to Dr. Furniss; but I know that there will be a place for me, and I shall be enabled to visit on others the kindness you have shown to me."

"You must not leave it all to Furniss," Caldwell urged; "anything I can do—"

"When first I came here," said Jap, "there was a question of wages, and *I* remember I said to you then that I wanted none, being satisfied to trust to your kindness. Since then you have two or three times told me that you had kept a sum for me each month."

"It's all there in the bank, Jap," broke in the Doctor. "Mathisen has it. You've only to ask."

"Thank you, then, that will be all that my plans require. I have nothing more to ask except that you will forgive me—if you can—for last night … and I should like to go now," concluded the Doctor's assistant—"now, if you can spare me."

Dr. Caldwell thought to himself he could spare him very ill, but he thought, too, that the man before him could less afford the strain of remaining. Jasper, it appeared, had thought of everything. In the long night he had rummaged and burned and packed, putting behind him the years of his obsession. So with no more to do about it than Mrs. Caldwell crying into his suit-case, and Sing going about with a towel over his shoulder, distracted by a family crisis which had no connection with anything to eat, Jasper had put eleven years of his life behind him before the day was gone another hour. He went out by the Penitentia road, fetlock deep in mud, and the sound of it sucking at the horse's feet came back to the old Doctor like the vanishing tread of his dreams going—going—! But when the Doctor's assistant had passed the road that turned off towards Thompson's, he drew out under the eucalyptus, and remained immovably staring back towards Rosebank until Dr. Rhewold had gone by on the main road in the old Doctor's buggy, with the gleam of William's dress beside him.

XIV

There is rightly a lady in the shield of California, for she is all
woman to the men she draws to serve her, tolerant, full-nurtured, of
ample-bosomed, courtesan charm, permitting to be loved with openness
and acclaim. To one entering it in the eighties or early nineties, the land
was full of a belt-loosening, breath-easing sound as men accommodated
themselves to its largeness. Men of the East, and sons of Easterners,
they were who went about stubbing their toes over business ventures
for the joyous prick of the nerves arousing from sleep. Business villanies
obtained a kind of public sanction if they served her; towns tricked and
decried one another to become the bright particular jewel in her bosom.
There was, around the centres of settlements, a continued ebullition
in affairs of trade, through which bright bubbles of great ventures rose
and broke with a singing sound. Men who went through those years
got a kind of renewal from their very slips and failures, but it was hard
on their women, especially if they were, like Serena, from the East,
and expecting to maintain in Santa Lucia the ideals of Bloombury,
Connecticut.

Serena's son was born in the third winter of her marriage, and
proved the exquisite, unmatched wonder of the world. Emerging from
the feebleness of her first encounter with life, she found all her relations
to her husband suffused with that sentiment which seems to proceed

from its critical functions, to cushion them from the jar of daily living. This was important, since she was so soon to be in need of a new way of estimating him other than the trifling, strained conscientiousness in which she had been bred.

She had been up and about the house for a fortnight when the servant began to be insolent. It transpired that her wages had not been paid, and Lindley had exhibited an unexpected obtuseness to his wife's mortification. Serena took very high grounds about it, conceiving that she owed it to her sacred rights of motherhood to accept nothing less than the best. It was incredible that he should not be able to get the money for a contingency so long foreseen, and amazing that he should respond with so little alacrity to his wife's wounded insistence that the debt be satisfied at once; and this at a juncture when merely to ask for considerate attention argued a dereliction. But somehow Evan did not get the money, and when the baby was eight weeks old the girl left. Serena adjusted herself rather slowly to the idea that she was not to have a successor, for Evan, around whom bubbles were bursting fast, lacked the courage to put the necessity clearly, met it with many slips and evasions. The fact was, he was as untried in the conditions of straightened finance as she, and did not know any better what to do about it, except, being a man, he thought he ought somehow to meet it by himself. His notion of doing this was to keep her as much as possible in ignorance of such particulars of his business as would have given point to her unaccustomed drudgeries. Having so husbandly an intention, he felt himself aggrieved to discover that Serena appeared to herself to be doing housework not so much as her share of a definite achievement of competence, but because he neglectfully failed to provide any other method of getting it done.

In such a case as this the winter dragged by in a sense of bafflement and confusion, and the white and rosy spring had settled on the orchards again without Serena having time to be aware of it, when William came in from Rosebank with a piece of news. She delivered it in snatches over her shoulder, for she had brought great branches of wild plum and almond to stick about the walls making an excuse of the litter she made to do some surreptitious tidying of the room, for with Serena's housekeeping there had come a kind of film over the spick and spanness of her home, as if the faint dinginess of spirit which betrays overworked women, had spread to the furniture. William's news, which she announced with determined cheerfulness, was to the effect that the old Doctor being about again among his patients, Dr. Rhewold was going away.

He had refused her father's proffer of partnership in the Santa Lucia practice, and taken a place which Furniss had found for him in one of the bay towns. He was still in debt to his widowed mother for the money his schooling had cost, and was to learn to stand on his own feet before he could ask William to lean on him. The engagement, therefore, was to be a long one, and Serena gathered that whatever vexation the old Doctor might have experienced in Rhewold's rejection of his generosity was made up for in the satisfaction of having his daughter still to himself.

"And do you remember, Serena," said William, standing up to leave at last, "how you promised, when I asked you, to tell me if marriage is really worth while?"

"Ah, but you said yes without asking," protested Serena. Her back was aching, and the consciousness that the beds up-stairs were still unmade, though it was the middle of the afternoon, perhaps prevented any response to William's insistence that one need not ask to know that she and Evan were perfectly happy.

"And," went on William, with new seriousness, "even if you were not, if you should tell me that it is not worth it, I should know here"— with her hands upon her breast—"within my heart, where I first knew that I cared for George, and what it meant to me. I should know that it is still worth trying; worth it even if you fail."

The baby woke and cried, nozzling for the breast.

"Yes," said Serena, stooping to him, with a sudden lustre in her voice—"yes, even if you fail."

She was sitting still in the glow of this assurance, nursing her child before the open fire when Julia Stairs came in. The two women had thrown themselves into an intimacy with the artificial ardor of those who have every reason for friendliness without the excuse of being interested in each other, though they tried to find a ground for it in the exchange of household recipes and a repudiation of the formalities of visiting.

Outside the wind flapped and scolded to blow up the last of the rains, like a fretful woman working to the point of tears, so when Julia got up to go, at the end of the hour, she insisted upon opening the door for herself—Serena still holding the baby and cautious about draughts—and opened it wide upon two men, who for the suddenness of their appearance might have been blown there by the wind that flung the door backward from her hand—workmen-looking fellows with smears of varnish on their jumpers and faces that wanted dusting. They said, seeing Mrs. Stairs, and mistaking her for the lady of the house, that they had come for the piano; but upon her falling back revealing Serena standing within the room, the long shawl that wrapped the baby trailing from her bosom, they came in over the threshold and said again that Mr. Maskey had sent them for the piano. Out beyond the lawn Serena saw, through the doorway, the moving-van with "Maskey, Pianos," flaring, large-lettered, on its sides, and a torn rag of canvas padding, flung out by the wind, whirling about and beckoning, as if the piano were not to be got out of the house without some urgency. At that moment, Lindley came springing across the lawn and up the veranda three steps at a time.

"Ah! I thought I told you fellows to wait!" sharp annoyance crackling in his voice as he caught sight of Julia, and backing precipitously away from his face to leave it for the moment, vacant.

"That's all right, Mrs. Stairs," he said, in the moment of recovery. "I told Maskey the piano wasn't satisfactory, and I'm sending it back." Then to the men, curtly, "Here, you."

They came forward surlily; one of them was a Maskey himself, and resented the implication.

"We can always tell der piano aindt sadisfactory when der payments is stopped already. Hein?" he grunted. He puffed it out in short stops, as he tugged at the corners of the instrument:

"When der instalments … is stopped … der biano … aindt sadisfactory. Dat was sure, already."

Julia hung between Serena and the door, not knowing what was expected of her. The piano, wheeled out of its accustomed corner, seemed suddenly to swell and crowd her quite out of knowledge.

"Good-bye," she said, uncertainly.

The Lindleys saw her out with steady countenances, but they did not look at each other as she went. The baby began to whimper, and Serena walked up and down to comfort it, with her face in the shawl. It was a long time before the piano was out of the house and into the van. Serena walked up and down, lest in the mere act of sitting she should betray a dreadful inward sinking. She thought at first that Evan would go away without coming back to her when the men drove off, but at last she heard his feet returning on the walk.

"What's the matter with the baby?" he asked, trying to look as if he had not been in the room that afternoon.

Serena turned the child on her arm and patted it.

"You won't need a piano in the house with this youngster to make music for you." He tried for the effect of unconcernedness. Serena sat down. She was still in that state when tears welled readily, and could not trust herself. Lindley blundered on, kicking at the hearth-rug, and trying for a note of justification in his voice.

"I told those confounded fellows to wait until I could come with them." And then, petulantly, "You never played on it—not for months, anyway."

It was impossible for him to understand that to Serena's upbringing the mere condition of indebtedness, the hint of under-breeding in its implication of having lived beyond their means, were of themselves intolerable. As men estimated their means then at what they expected to make, most Santa-Lucians were spending more than they had. To Lindley the piano was simply a venture in which he had failed to make good, inconsiderable among so many others which still gave promise. He had meant, of course, to manage it better. It was unfortunate that Julia Stairs should have been there, but he was really not to blame for it.

"Evan," Serena choked, at last, "was that true about the payments?"

"Yes," he admitted.

"For how long?"

"Almost a year."

"But why … didn't you …?" Serena could get no further.

"I thought you could play," Evan broke in, petulantly. "I didn't count on having to pay for lessons. It wouldn't have mattered if I had

gotten the Bodely business." Suddenly he remembered that there had
not been a word of the criticism bruited in the papers, which had set the
Bodelys against him, that he had not first heard in his own house, and
he whipped about to the defensive. "I could have kept it up if it hadn't
been for the baby, I suppose. I'm sure I tried to please you. You were
always fretting for something to do."

Serena flinched before this unexpected shifting of responsibility,
and the picture of herself in the public mind as the unthinking wife
inciting her husband to extravagance. In the smart of injustice to
herself she lost even a little of the pang of Evan's flippancy in the face
of discrediting circumstance. She felt suddenly that Santa Lucia, the
West, had conspired to entrap her through her noblest meanings into a
situation which she should have been first to disclaim. Her thought flew
to Antrim Stairs … Julia would be telling him …

Evan was standing still in front of the fire, and as she looked at
him with a wounding sense of the loss of esteem which she supposed
must follow on such a lapse, something of her new motherliness awoke
and yearned towards him. She saw how young he was, and the wish
to comfort him and be comforted brought a sudden rush of tears.
Lindley, who was trying over in his mind a way of putting his situation
before her along with the assurance, which was perfectly sincere, that
all he needed was a little time to make it come out right, felt himself
overcome with annoyance. It was so like a woman to cry when a man
wanted to talk business

"Oh, Lord, Serena!" he fretted, "what's the use of trying to tell
you anything?"

He had not told her anything yet, though he had meant to if she
had not made it hard for him. To save himself from visiting upon her a
deserved vexation, he went quickly out of the room and slammed the
door.

It was regrettable that they had not come to a better
understanding, for Serena cried so much after it, not only because of the
mortifying circumstance, but because of what appeared the obliquity
of her husband's attitude, that she made herself ill, and came near
having to wean the baby. In the face of that possibility Evan was very
remorseful, very tender of her, and insisted on her leaving the dinner
dishes until he could wash them for her. But this remorse was all for

her loss of comfort, and Serena wanted him to be sorry for so many other things—for not being fine enough, in the first place, to perceive that the Bodely fountain was impossible; for the lowered standard implied in his willingness to live on other people's money, which was what Serena understood by getting things on credit; and for his own lack of conviction as to his shortcomings in these particulars. As often as she considered the affair of the piano she was able to trace it back to the want of personal ideals such as grew so naturally out of her own life that she supposed none other to obtain among reputable people, and suffered as much as young wives commonly do when their husbands get down from their pedestals and begin to walk about among men.

As was to have been expected, Antrim Stairs had a great many reasons for being interested in all his wife told him of what had passed at the Lindleys that afternoon, and one of them was the regard he had for Serena. He had come to esteem it as one of the felicitations of being married that he had been able to renew his intimacy with her on an advanced footing. To have her coming and going informally about his house, to hear the homely talk of cooking and marketing that went on between his wife and her, the occasional light banter over household shifts and expedients, and the jocular hints which Lindley's awkward and unbounded pride in his son occasioned, had brought him a new and gladsome sense of domestic living. He felt himself awake and sentient on unguessed surfaces. He was not only to be a biologist but a man, and a man fed by profound and secret springs of passion, related to his generation. Fine appreciations of conjugality stirred in him in the offices of neighborliness that he sometimes missed with Julia alone. The impulse which had led him to conceal his engagement from Mrs. Lindley had grown out of the wish not to disturb the wholly satisfactory relation of their first friendship, and the vague touch of estrangement occasioned by his marriage gave to their newer intimacy a pleasing sense of renewal.

Now when he learned of the business of the piano he did not make any mistake about Serena's relation to it. He was aware of how much more mortifying and serious it must seem to her than to Julia, who was rather of Lindley's point of view. Julia was habituated to the method of living up to your expectations; it was annoying, of course, not to be able to keep up the instalments, but so many things might account for it, it was not worth fretting about. There had been a slump in real estate lately, and of course nobody was to blame. Julia liked the young attorney and understood him, and a chivalric impulse saved Stairs from explaining how Mrs. Lindley probably felt about it. What he did say was to the effect that if Lindley failed to manage his own affairs successfully, there would be any number of people willing to say that he could not be expected to do well by the business of the college.

The result of Antrim Stairs thinking so much about Serena and her affairs was a wish to see her. He did not choose to go so soon that his visit should have the appearance of condolence, nor so late that it should seem neglect. He thought it might prove kindlier to have some excuse for it, and found it in the new chapters of his book which he had not read to her. Julia talked a great deal about the book to other people; its success afforded a possibility of his being called to Stanford or Berkeley, a consummation for which Julia was already beginning to scheme, but she talked very little about it to her husband, who, after her two or three attempts, found that he would just as soon she would not. So, with a comfortable assurance of appreciation, he put the manuscript in his pocket, and went to spend the evening with Serena Lindley. He had taken up the *Post-Darwinian Theories* in the elation of happiness, and pushed it vigorously to a close. Already he was beginning to have visions of books and books beyond. He did not know quite what they would be about; he had said to Mrs. Lindley that he felt not exactly inspired but as if he were about to be, and Serena had understood.

XV

Another reason why Dr. Stairs was interested in the fortunes of
the Lindleys was that he had, with his promotion to the head of his
department, succeeded to the faculty committee of affairs, and knew
that the question of assigning the finances to a soberer head than the
young attorney's had more than once been broached among the trustees.
Lindley had been kept on in his father's place chiefly because he
appeared a favorite of the Bodelys, whose patronage since the business
of the fountain had suffered a sensible decline.

Santa Lucia, quick to suit itself to the attitude of prospective
investors, since the fountain was discovered to be in bad taste, freed
themselves from complicity by declaring it absurd. The students, taking
their notes from the town, made a jest of it; one of their New Year's
pranks had consisted in dressing up the figures ridiculously overnight.
All this, which could not quite be kept from the Bodelys, the old people
considered that Evan Lindley had let them in for. They had not yet
conceded the new wing to the college, and there were those who opined
that they never would so long as Lindley held the business management.

That was the time when, throughout the West, the swell of
stable prosperity was met by the returning ebb of riotous enterprise
and whelmed by it in a turgid welter, and all business suffered a check
except the urgency of payments. Everybody had them to get or to make.

Coin travelled through endless instalments to its final pit in the pocket of the man who owed no payments on anything. The college, whose endowment was chiefly in land, suffered along with the Santa-Lucians. Under Lindley's management a portion of it lying contiguous to the town had been cut up for sale, and his fortunate handling of it had been part of the reason for retaining him when the old judge died. But now that the boom had flattened on them like a cold breakfast cake, the trustees were severely put to it to raise the money for the faculty salaries.

Back of Santa Lucia the college owned a vast extent of half-high hills backing away seaward and emerging in windy spaces as round, bald, grassy crowns from thickets of redwood, encinal, and ceanothus. It had been part of the cattle range of the old Spanish Rancho Encinas, and had no other status. During the year past the trustees had been kept from parting with a large part of their hill lands at what seemed a top price for a cattle range by the strenuous opposition of Evan Lindley. The attorney held that the land was potentially more valuable as water-shed, and in fifteen or twenty years should prove the most profitable of the college holdings. Now that merchants were beginning to mark half-dollar goods at forty-nine cents and customers to wait for their change, it was conceded, with a disposition to grumble at the loss of it, nothing so good was likely to come their way again.

So Stairs had what he thought was a good reason besides friendliness for keeping an eye out to the Lindleys' affairs, which went badly. Evan, instead of using the proceeds of his law business to clear the indebtedness occasioned by his marriage, had assumed new and alluring opportunities for turning his money quickly. It was characteristic of most such opportunities that they demanded a constant toll of payments. Since the fiasco of the piano, Serena's way of helping him was to insist on paying cash for everything she bought, and he was often in straits to meet the instalments on the house and furniture, still more—since he persisted in his mannish notion that by not telling her he was sparing her the brunt of his misadventures—to meet his wife's moderate demands for housekeeping money.

Whatever Serena allowed herself of comfort and appeal came from her cousin Kate, whose tentative interest in married problems had acquired a sort of sanction from her having almost had an offer of marriage. The circumstances of its having come to nothing, after all,

were such as made consoling confidences a little less than an offence.
Aunt Luella was right, of course: a chronic lung complaint has no right
to the alleviations of marriage, and the exchange of an excellent position
with a salary for an average man without any had nothing whatever
to recommend it, except that Kate had rather seemed to wish it that
way. Serena tacitly accepted Kate's efforts to lighten her difficulties as a
makeshift for not having any of the same sort for her own.

"If you could only do something to earn the money for a servant
yourself" fretted Kate—"something you liked and knew how to do,
instead of wearing yourself out like this."

"Well, what?" suggested Serena.

Kate had caught her ironing some of the baby's things, and taken
it out of her hands.

"The Lord knows," said Kate, banging the irons about; "you only
know how to teach, and you can't do that because you are married.
More than that, you've got a child of your own, and that is supposed to
disqualify you for the training of other people's."

Serena added nothing to that; her whole body was sore with
the fatigue of the ironing, which she had undertaken because of the
mortification she had experienced in not being able to pay for the last
one. She reflected with bitterness that she could have managed very well
with a salary, and that Kate did not know when she was well off.

Towards the middle of July the hills smoked with heat, the
sidewalks in the new treeless districts gave it back in a blinding glare,
and the unsprinkled roadways clouded heavily behind passing wheels
with stifling dust. Serena's baby, teething in its first summer, ailed, and
Serena demanded to be sent away to the sea-shore. It seemed to her a
reasonable demand. For what else had she done the work of nurse-maid
and cook but to compass their more serious needs. She asked nothing
for herself; she had had no new clothes since before the baby came, but
she would not ask anything for herself. She had been able to meet the
new demands of a family with equal sacrifice; now it was Lindley's turn.
Lindley did not know where in the world he could raise the hundred
dollars or so that his wife needed, and had no resort but to treat her
insistence lightly; he tried to think that women are unduly anxious
about their babies, and that they all cried a great deal when they were
teething, and so beat down the clutch of growing anxiety.

During the hot weather he had been in the habit of closing the office early, getting home to relieve his wife of the care of the child. By four of the afternoon the sun was low enough to take the shutterless dwellings full on the western windows. As he came up the walk to the house he caught the faint, stifling smell of carpets and superheated furniture. He found Serena walking up and down in the darkened room; her dress was open at the throat, and the coil of her hair slipped upon her neck. The room was in disorder, as if some emergency had taken place in it; through the door of the dining-room he could see the table still uncleared. Serena walked up and down, and held the baby out from the heat of her body. The child lay lax and white. She walked and walked. He could see now that the disorder of the furniture was made by her unmindful thrusting of it this way and that, as it impeded her steady pacing. It seemed to have been going on a long time, but she made no motion to stop as Lindley came up to her.

"Serena," he said—"Serena, what is the matter?"

"Oh," she gasped—"oh," as if the heat had dried up her voice, and she shook with the effort to revive it. "Baby was worse directly after lunch, and I sent for Dr. Caldwell, and he said … he said … " She never left off walking, as she whispered, dryly: "He said we must … *I* must get him away … to the sea-shore or the mountains … where it is cooler … or … or … " Her face and throat convulsed with the motions of weeping, but no tears came.

"Let me take him," said Lindley, in shocked concern; "you are ready to drop. Why didn't you 'phone to me?"

"Oh, you!" she said, in contemptuous wonderment. "*You!*—and after he was gone a man came … with that." She pointed to where it lay affixed to the table by its wafer, and Lindley knew without looking that it must be the writ of attachment on the furniture, which had been so much longer delayed than he had any right to expect that he had given himself over to the hope that it might be wholly avoided. He saw now, as he stood looking down at the document, that the attitude that he had persisted in to himself that his successive misadventures were no more than the moves in a game in which, through whatever intermediary failures, he was yet to prove winner, would not answer here. The inward flinching from defeat which he had overborne until now had its way with him for the moment, and made him very sick. He stood staring down at the table without a word.

"So," she said, "it's true, then, that you never paid for it?—that you can't pay for it now? That this table—that the bed I lie on, my baby's bed, is not yours—is some other man's?"

He lifted his head in protest against this view of it, but she did not regard it. He could not know, of course, how much more ominous the unfamiliar document must seem to her inexperience. Even then he thought she was overwrought and hysterical about the child.

"Oh!" she said, and "oh" again, her face and throat working dryly. "Oh, I was so proud of it, and I took such care of it!" looking bitterly about the room, that even in disorder bore the impress of personality; "and it wasn't mine! All the time it wasn't mine, and you knew it and you let me—" She began to walk again, and a breath of air springing up to stir the curtains, the baby, released by it from the heat, fell asleep all at once with the suddenness of a swoon. She moved to put him down softly, all her motions gentle and restrained, which made the fury and distress of her mind more dreadful to see.

"It does not matter just now about the furniture," she said, coming back to him. "That is the sort of thing I've learned to expect from you. You may tell Brainard & Company to take their furniture whenever it's wanted," she said. Evan wondered at the capacity that gentle women have for contemptuousness. She looked about at it for a moment consideringly and smiled. "I've been as careful with it as if it had been my own," she said. "I sha'n't be wanting it, anyway," she went on, "for I am going away. To-night I am going to take the baby to Santa Cruz by the first train; and you've got to get the money."

She came and leaned upon the table opposite him, and spoke with a stifled vehemence keyed to be mindful of the sleeping child.

"I don't care where you get it," she said, "nor how; only get it. You can sell something or pawn something. There is my watch and my things up-stairs. A man like you"—the drop of her voice upon the word, the flicker of her glance across the paper between them, seemed to make it and all his affairs of an amazing opprobriousness—"ought to know how those things are done. It can't be any worse than this." She flicked the writ scornfully with thumb and finger. "But you must get it," she finished, "and get it at once, before I get it myself."

Evan got the money that time. He went out of the house without a word, and at the end of an hour he counted out to her two hundred dollars in bills. She did not ask him where or how he had come by it. Lindley helped her to pack, and saw her off to Santa Cruz by the early morning train. When they stood at the station as the day emerged from filmy mists of night, he said, timidly:

"That's all right about the furniture; I saw Brainard and paid up the instalments."

If he expected her to show any relief or awakened tenderness at this, he was disappointed. She was thinking that since he had gotten the money under urgency he might have gotten it before, and not have allowed matters to come to this pass. She felt that she had been thrown from the balance of dignity the day before, and she would not forgive him.

The morning after he had seen his wife off Lindley went around to the bank to take up a note somewhat overdue. He found Stairs there closeted with Mathisen worrying over college affairs, and said to them both, by-the-way, that though he did not himself think any better of it as a piece of business, if the college still wished to sell Encinas he knew Schweringer was still keen for it. It did not occur to Stairs, then nor after, to connect Lindley's evident disposition towards the sale with the ease of his personal difficulties, which was evident.

The final reasons why Antrim Stairs took an interest in the Lindleys' establishment was because his wife allowed him to take so little interest in his own. If there arose any of the exigencies of homemaking which young people commonly share with so much satisfaction, Julia was always found to have attended to them and tucked the ends under. On such occasions if Stairs volunteered his assistance, she promptly abandoned it to him, and went about something else with the greatest cheerfulness. Julia did not find in her housekeeping matter for sentiment. She considered it quite enough to get it over with without talking about it; there was no denying she did it very well. Stairs, in whom the instincts of generations of homekeeping, handworking people were beginning to stir, found himself indefinably checked by her hard, bright competency; it gave him at times the curious notion that he was boarding with his wife. As the exactions of his studies and the routine of the school closed upon him, he felt more the need to escape into something warm and vivid and human, something that Serena Lindley seemed to express in her way of drawing up chairs for you, of brightening up the fire, and widening her thought to make room for you. Julia never did things like that for one, though she permitted one to do them for her, and Stairs was very glad to be allowed, for she was a very beautiful woman, and he was very much in love with her.

There was no question that Julia was a good wife. She threw herself quite heartily into schemes for her husband's advancement, and disdained for him anything like satisfaction in his situation as it was. She took so for granted the temporary nature of his connection with the college of Santa Lucia that Stairs had often to remind her that the president and faculty were not apprised of its obviousness. It was likely, he told her, that if she made so much of it, the tenure of his chair might become more transitory even than they desired it. Julia's wish was to see him established at the University of California at Berkeley. In view of such a possibility, she took pains to lose none of her social connections in San Francisco, and was studious to extend her acquaintance in Roble Park, where, around the coasts of Santa Lucia, in country estates rendered forever sombre by the summer gloom or oaks or the drip of bared branches on the sodden winter lawns, a factitious gayety went on among the group whose comings and goings, divorcings and dinings-out, furnished the city papers with two columns of small-pica news. This was Julia's world, from which she felt her husband withheld merely by reason of his preoccupations, and took it very much as a matter of course his being bored by Santa Lucia. She was very sweet about it, paid her calls so dutifully, and commiserated him so much on the president's monthly dinners that Stairs was ashamed to admit to her that he quite enjoyed them. And it was precisely for her air of being so at home with the immediate circumstance that he valued his friendship with Serena Lindley.

XVI

But if Antrim Stairs saw no connection between Lindley's affairs
and the sale of the Encinas lands there were Santa-Lucians who did,
for Schweringer was a man distrusted by what was commonly known
as the business interests. Schweringer bought tax titles and overdue
mortgages, and bad bargains of which the proprietors had grown sick,
which invariably were found to discover such possibilities of becoming
good bargains as made the first owners sicker. It was perfectly evident
that if Scherwinger had acquired the Encinas hills at grazing-land prices
he wanted them for some other purpose than grazing. Disquieting
discoveries began to be made about the connection of the city water-
supply and the Encinas water-shed. New interpretations of water rights
and new methods of storing rainfall had come into force with the spread
of settlements; through them the purposes of Schweringer began to
loom portentously, menacing the good of the town.

The *Evening Bulletin,* which made a fetish of the good of the
town, set itself hotfoot on the trail of Schweringer. What the *Bulletin*
discovered and what was done about it has no particular place in this
story, except as it betrayed the fact that Lindley was responsible for
the sale of the lands, and that there were notes of his going about with
Schweringer's name on them. The *Bulletin* was prejudiced against
Lindley for no particular reason, except that newspapers must be down

on somebody, and no man is ever active in the affairs of his town without affording at least one of his local papers the business of being opposed to him.

The *Bulletin* was fair to Lindley according to its light. It notified him that it was about to make a special story of the sale of Encinas, and asked if he had anything to say. It appeared that he had not; he had opposed the sale at first, and afterwards yielded to pressure from the college body; the business between himself and Schweringer was a private matter. Whatever was to be said about that Lindley felt must be said to his wife; but in the three days between the time of his knowing it and the publication of the special issue of the *Bulletin* he had not found the courage for it.

He stood a much better chance with her than he realized, for this was an affair in which he knew himself wrong. He had sinned against his business sense, which was what he respected most of good in himself as he knew it—the sense of the Ultimate Benefit, which in men comes to take the place of orthodox conscientiousness. If the sale had been a moderately good one for the college, if he had known no more of the potentialities of the Encinas hills than the trustees, whose orthodoxy was a part of their qualification, he would have taken such advantage as was to be had of making the sale to Schweringer rather than to any other, as easily as he had taken the prestige which came of being known as the college attorney. He had always felt himself entitled to make what profit he could of its business so long as he prejudiced none of its interests. But in this he had known—that was the perfectest sting of it—he had always known. Tremendous things in the way of water-supply and power and villa streets could be done with the Encinas lands in ten or a dozen years, and he had betrayed them to fat-witted Schweringer. He was not sure even that it was not from talk of his that Schweringer had first a notion of these vague, great enterprises. The college might have made a hundred thousand dollars, and now they would find it out; what could follow in that event but Lindley's resignation?

If the *Bulletin* published its own view of the transaction, Lindley knew his notes would be called and he would be all in; and still he had not found courage or occasion to tell his wife. He meant to do so, remembering how she had taken the affair of the furniture, but the day came and he had not told her. Lindley bought a paper in the evening, and found the Encinas affair written up to all the possibilities of three-inch scare-heads. He understood that its views would be those probably assumed by the college, and felt no inclination to defend himself against it. He was chiefly conscious of a wish to have it all over.

He ate little at dinner, and hoped his wife would ask him the cause of his disquietude, but she did not notice it. He laid the paper under the evening lamp, but she did not take it up. Since the summer before they had fallen into the way of not talking much of their affairs; it led too often to hurts and recriminations. Serena spent the leisure of her evenings reading studious books, chiefly of Antrim Stairs's recommending.

Lindley thought he would begin when they went to their room that night; its intimacies drew them together; Serena with her hair down and soft white ruffles at her throat was somehow a dearer Serena than the lady of the house. She gave him an opening at last by asking if there had been anything of interest in the evening paper, and so finally he told her. He took a long time to it, fumbling and turning back on his trail, and not daring to meet her eye lest what he saw in it should make him fail. He made neither more nor less of his connection with Schweringer than the facts allowed. He had gone to him last summer when the furniture had been attached and they had been so anxious about the baby, and Schweringer had reminded him when he signed the note that it was a courtesy he did not extend to all men, and that he would expect an equal consideration.

"Did you know then," asked Serena, "that he wanted the Encinas land?"

"I was not sure of it. It had been a long time since he had mentioned it. He might have given it up."

"But you thought that he wanted it?"

He knew that the question pointed the way of reprehension, but he did not resist it.

"Yes," he admitted, doggedly, "otherwise I shouldn't have been able to get the money." He went on to tell that there had been other notes after that, and for what amounts. Some of them had gone for household expenses, and others to keep up payments on property that he had already paid too much upon to afford to lose. Serena lay very quiet in the bed; she had put up her arms, as if to screen her eyes from the lamp. Only by the trembling of the ruffles on her sleeve could he tell that she was listening and awake. He made an end at last of all that he thought was likely to happen to his business on account of it, and turned out the light. He was feeling very tired and wanted to go to sleep; the grateful blackness seemed to intervene a little between him and the sickness of defeat. Serena slipped out from the bed and stood in the middle of the floor. Long bands of moonlight crept between the blinds, and showed her remote and inexorable.

"Is it all in the paper?" she wished to know.

"All that I've told you, and a great deal more that isn't so. I wouldn't read it to-night."

"I must see for myself," she insisted. After a long interval, in which he ached for sleep and blamed himself for being able to want it at such a crisis, he went down and found her sitting in her night-dress with the paper on her knees. She was not reading it and she was not crying.

"Come to bed, Serena," he begged; "you will catch your death of cold."

"I am not cold," she answered, as she moved towards the door, evading the arm he held out to her. She slipped before him up the stair and stopped before the guest-room door. "You will sleep better alone," she said, as she passed within and he heard her turn the key.

From that day it seemed to Lindley that the seat of judgment was set up in his house. From the contraptious annoyances and embarrassments set on by the *Bulletin*'s loud knocking, he came home at night to be dragged through the cold inquisition of his wife's legitimate wish to know the whole of his affairs. It was a process prolonged to the point of distraction by the new and incriminating conjunctions which arose chiefly from Serena's not having understood his statements in the first place. He told her everything he could, except the one thing that would have helped him: that he was sorry and ashamed and abashed before himself and shaken in his confidence.

He had never had any sensible appreciation of the pertinence of his wife's point of view to the conduct of his business, but now he was made to see that there was no smallest move of his in the game he played with men but had infinite and unsuspected capabilities of reacting unhappily upon her and the baby. He saw himself thrown from the common masculine assumption of a man's world, revolving about his wife's point of contact with life as the pivot of existence, an escape into independent action contingent only upon the accident of his making a great deal more money than she could use. One by one she possessed herself of his obligations and all his slips and lapses. He saw that she struggled with them to bring them to a head. At first he had attempted to explain to her that many of these would have settled themselves in the natural process, but she put the explanation by, and after awhile he perceived her drift. She had taken the obviousness of his incompetence for granted and assumed the solution. When she had made up her mind what to do about it she would let him know.

One morning at breakfast she asked if he still kept the key to his mother's house. He had, and inquired what she wanted of it.

"To see if there is enough of the furniture left so we can let some of ours go."

"But," he said, astonished, "you are not thinking of living there?"

"Your mother always wanted you to live there, and I don't see how we can afford to live anywhere else."

"But, look here, Serena, things aren't as bad as that. The house is safe, anyway. I've always kept up the payments on that, and it's in your name, so Schweringer can't touch it."

"I dare say you can find a purchaser who will take it for a little less than we have paid," she answered, coldly, and exasperation choked him. It was a day or two later when she told him that she could spare the furniture of the guest-room, most of the parlor things, the refrigerator, and the kitchen range.

"If you begin to let things go," he warned her, "there will be a regular smash-up. I can't keep the others off."

"What can they do to us when we haven't anything left?" she wished to know. Evan fumed with helplessness and vexation.

"I shouldn't think you would want to humiliate me," he fretted. Little flecks of red and white leaped to her face as under a lash.

"Humiliate you!" she said. "Humiliate *you!* Oh, Evan!" He perceived suddenly the defencelessness of the man who has lost to his wife the right to an impeccable moral attitude.

Lindley was fortunate in finding a customer for the house at a figure that enabled him to take up the most pressing of his obligations.

But the relief obtained by this means and the sale of the furniture did not make up for the loss of his home. It stood for that with him. He had never realized how extraneous the new house had always been to his wife, nor how its smartness, which he had worn as the visible sign of his aptness to his time, stood to her as the price of what she most missed in him. It had grown as her marriage had—from the mere exigencies of living rather than from the necessities of life, and the way she let it fall from her was a wounding and an affront to her husband.

There was a room at the head of the back stairs in the old Lindley place which had been Evan's as a boy, and had been left just as it was when he went out of it to be married. Serena had said that he should take it for himself, since the other bedrooms were so small. On the night of the day they had moved into his mother's house it had seemed better at the last moment, on account of its being already in order, for Serena to sleep there with the baby. Lindley went up before her with the lamp, she following with young Evan's head tucked into the hollow of her shoulder, and so fearful of waking him that it was not until she stood up from leaning above the bed that she looked about the room.

"Evan," she said—"Evan, how did those things come here?"

"I brought them."

"But ... but I thought ..."

"Yes," said her husband, mutinously, "you thought you had sold them to Brainard, but I brought them here. Have you any objection?"

"No, of course not. If you had said you wanted them ..." Her gaze travelled slowly about the room in puzzled wonder. The things were from the house on Penitentia Street: a desk that Evan had added to the list of furniture after he had bought all he could afford to, because he wished to buy something exclusively and personally hers, though, manlike, he had neglected to tell her so, and a table at which he had seen her sitting sewing at small white things with the light upon her shed faint and sweet from the little life that neared them daily on so perilous a road.

"But why ... why?" The question trembled and fell away before a vague sense of accusation. Lindley sat down by the little table and laid his arm across it, as if to fend it even from her coldness.

"Look here, Serena," he said, "you are my wife; you may regret it, and I suppose after all that's happened I ought not to be surprised if you do, but still you occupy a certain place in my life, and I can't help having the feelings natural for a man to have. I gave you the best I could in the way of a home, and I am sorry I couldn't keep it for you. I think, perhaps, I might if you had understood a little better. But that's all over and past now, and it's best not talking of it. There is one thing, though, that I didn't know, that I think would have been kinder to have chosen a different time for letting me know, and that is that you hated it."

"But I didn't always—no, never truly *hated* it, until … until I found it wasn't really mine," she protested.

"It was as much yours as I could make it. I don't see what difference it made whether I paid for it with the labor I had done or with what I was yet to do. It was a way of doing things that was common enough among better men; it may not have been a very good way, but it was the best I could do."

"Ah, but Evan," she cried, "that was it. It was the best *you* could do, and I wanted it to be the best we could do together."

"There wasn't much we could do together before we had been married, and you might have trusted me," said the husband, bitterly; "but it's not what I began to say, only now that it is all over you have no right to spoil for me what was the happiest experience of my life."

"I haven't meant to do that, Evan," she protested, taken aback at being found at fault in the finer provinces.

"Don't, then," he said. "You may have cared so little for the home I made you that you are glad to leave it, but I cared. It meant to me all that sort of thing means to any man, and though I have given it up and gone through all this and humiliated myself, because you wanted it, and since I had let you in for it I owed it to you to choose the way out; but there's one thing I won't stand, and that is that you should go on behaving as if I had no more feeling about it than you have."

"Oh, Evan, Evan!"

He had leaned his head upon his hand as he spoke, and now as he turned she saw how his face was drawn with lines of worry and fatigue.

"I am sorry for you, Serena, for what you have been through and for what is still before you. I know how mortified you've been to have me turn out like this; what you've got to remember is that it is easier for you, because you have done nothing wrong; but I have to go through with it, too, and to carry about with me the knowledge that if I have offended you I have also offended against myself."

She was across the room kneeling before him, and the tears were falling on the arm she clasped.

"Oh, Evan, Evan, if you had only told me that you cared!"

"Care," he said—"care! Do you think I can know what you think of me, knowing that it is true, and not care?"

"Oh, my dear!" she said. "Oh, my dear, say that you care, only say it; I can bear it, Evan, I can bear it if you only say you care." She was between his knees, and her head was on his breast.

He leaned his face against hers, and they cried together for shame and pity and tenderness and renewal.

XVII

The old Lindley house, as the Judge's home was called, was a
tall, thin, old-maid kind of house to look at, with a great deal of flat
scrollwork laid on like crochet lace, with prim pillared porticos akimbo
like mittened hands at the sides. The grounds went through from street
to street of the wide block, and the house appeared to have run in
among the sprawly oaks in a fit of shyness, and to peer out skittishly by
its dormer-windows, as if at the slightest provocation it might run on
again. It was the kind of a house that is always alluded to in the country
papers as a residence, and had a great many rooms in it, mostly square
and high with patterned-paper ceilings. Wild lawn spread about the
front under the noble oaks, and the back was given over to a deserted
cow-lot and carriage-house.

It stood on that part of Santa Lucia known as old town,
contiguous to the college grounds. Going out by the carriage-house,
across the street, down half a block, turning in by an alder-bush, across
an open lot, one came to Antrim Stairs's back door, and when one
had gone in so and come out at the front, there was the campus and
the Bodely fountain and the long rows of poplars marching in hollow
squares. By the time the Lindleys had been long enough in the old place
to feel settled—and that was longer than they anticipated—the foot-
trail through the open lots was worn thin and white.

Serena's room overlooked it and the college settlement, and often as she went to draw the curtain for the night, seeing the window lights low among the garden shrubbery, she seemed to look from the billowings of disaster into the port of home. The secure and well-regulated life that went on there, the certain needs and the fixed salaries, the approved and accustomed performance that fenced it from the perplexities incident to her husband's way of life, appeared the more desirable as she believed now she should never attain to them. In the need that women have for deriving judgment from something outside themselves, it was the insuperable disability of Evan's way that it afforded no such touchstone. Serena saw herself forever involved in spiritless evasions of money obligations it was an offence to her foresightedness to incur; for the readjustment of their personal relations had not been succeeded by an equivalence in the means of living. All that the young people got out of the renewal of tenderness was the ease of their private hurts. There were still debts that were only to be discharged by dribbling, hard-won payments. Santa Lucia was far enough from San Francisco to feel the pull of that tide of receding capital that drained the south and left so many enterprises slack and flaccid, and Lindley's business was a long time recovering; a long time for the young man to grow into the knowledge that it did not so much matter what he thought of the thing he did, unless he could make other people think it.

Serena was first to recover a point of contact in the effort to render livable the square, characterless rooms of the old Lindley place. Choked appetencies began to emerge from her in the evidence of wood-stains and denim-covered window-seats. The world-old seduction of creative power exhibiting itself never so meanly in the exigencies of daily living set up in her the process of competency; and Lindley, believing the pleasure assumed for his sake, blessed her for it as far as his pride would admit. Contrivances whereby a dollar might be saved were too freshly a reminder of his inability to get as many dollars as he required, to be relished by him.

There had never been anything in the home place that appealed to Evan Lindley as the exponent of his own attitude, and he rather held it as a failure of appreciation that his wife should have insisted in going back there. The toyon-tree, which his father had never allowed cut, and had consequently grown quite to the second-story window, the low, old oaks leaning above the wild grass, were the flagrant denial of his up-to-dateness. It was not until the following spring that he was restored to any sense of intimacy with it. About the time the tips of the long, maroon boughs of the apricots begin to blow out pink like the lips of children shut upon forbidden laughter, all Santa Lucia was bent on the business of cleaning up. A pleasant, woodsy smell of smoke pervaded the streets, bees mumbled about the dribble of sap from belated prunings; Lindley, for the want of means to hire it done, scratched grudgingly at the oak litter, yielding at last to the obligation of his temperament to make a good job of it. Serena came out with the boy and worked beside him as he dug and raked. The broad, mossy back of a creeping-oak hung a foot above the sward and enticed little Evan.

"Up, dada, up!" he urged, and when Lindley swung him into place he straddled his fat legs and shouted:

"Go it, son," Lindley encouraged, "your daddy has ridden to many a battle on that old steed."

"There wasn't any place for a boy to play at the Penitentia Street house," said Serena, and regretted it instantly, remembering how her husband had taken her want of tenderness to the place; but Lindley was peering up among the oaks.

"There used to be a swing hereabouts," he was saying, reminiscently. "There's the place; there's the scar of the rope. We made a rope-ladder of it when we were too old for a swing. All the kids used to like to play at our house."

He came home with a clumsy bundle that afternoon, and in the hour before dinner Serena heard him whistling among the trees and presently calling her to bring the boy. He was sitting high among the branches of the tallest oak, and wished her to try if the swing hung right for little Evan.

"I'll tell you what, Serena," he said, "we will open up this side of the yard a little, and plant ferns and things—sort of sylvan retreat idea. There will be nothing like it in Santa Lucia; show people what can be done with native shrubs; it will be a great attraction."

He was full of the idea, said they should go out to Toyon for wild roots the very next Sunday. His wife heard him humming cheerfully as he went off to make a seat for the swing. He had become a householder again, and touched contentment. Serena grew happier, seeing he was more at ease; woman-like, she had resented the pain he had brought upon himself.

Being more comfortable, Mrs. Lindley had the more time to give to Antrim Stairs, who needed it. Stairs had completed his book on *Post-Darwinian Theories* in the previous long vacation, and by the middle of the winter two publishers had refused it. The third time it came back he brought it to Serena. There was a long letter with the manuscript, in which it was pointed out that though the book was of undoubted worth, its sale would rest upon the individual reputation of Stairs for scientific performance, and recommended that he get himself connected with some institution a little more in the public eye than Santa Lucia. Now as Dr. Stairs had counted on the fame of his book to provide such a connection, this was disconcerting, the more so for the way Julia took it. She had believed in the book; she had flourished the book before those of her friends who inclined to the belief that she had not made so good a marriage as might have been expected with her looks; she had trimmed her social courses by the book; she had mounted the book, and ridden away in expectation from all the slights and denials of a limited income; and now it appeared there was no book. Julia felt aggrieved, and visited it upon her husband. She had not known anything about the value of *Post-Darwinian Theories;* she had taken his word for it and the word of the college set, among whom there had been quite a stir of expectation. Now they would have to be told; it was all very mortifying. And all this Julia had to suffer because she had believed in her husband. She did not say that he had deceived her, but the inference was in the air, and Stairs accepted it. The first time it had been returned he had read the book over carefully, and, reawakened to his early glow about it, had sent it away again without much misgiving. But the third time it came back he carried it to Mrs. Lindley, and she comforted him. She could do that. All her girlish vision of herself had included something of that sort as proper to her nurture. Here was a man of great and neglected talent to be heartened to the struggle for recognition; even his wife did not believe in him. When they touched upon that, though, they fell instinctively into the assumption that Julia's displeasure was the pang of disappointed wifeliness; poor, dear Julia was to be spared, that was all. Serena lent herself to sustaining Antrim Stairs's efforts at the point of fruitfulness with the more fervor because of Evan's defection from the standards of the college set. She had acquiesced in their finding that he was not to be trusted longer with the management of the college business, but she was anxious to prove herself still of the party that sat in judgment.

After a few days Stairs carried the manuscript home and hid it in a bureau drawer, where he hoped that Julia, in her housewifely peregrinations, might come across it. He supposed that she had done so when he saw by her eyes that she had been crying; she told him, when he asked her, that she was not feeling well, and that she thought she would go to her mother for a few days. He lacked the courage to put his supposition to the truth, and saw her off himself as far as the San Marco Junction. When Julia had been away a fortnight she came home quite unexpectedly, and the very next afternoon went out by the cross-lot path to see Mrs. Lindley. If she had had in mind any purpose of especial intimacy in doing so she must have been disappointed in it, for she found William sitting in the middle of the floor with her mouth full of upholstery tacks.

That William was a great deal with Serena that winter was due to the violent bent of her interests towards housekeeping affairs. She had made a sewing-room of William's Heart, accumulating wonders of hand-made pillow-slips and crooked monograms worked on table linen, and lent herself joyously to Serena's contrivances of denim and Morris chintzes. Serena was glad to have her, since Kate Bixby had carried out her intention of applying for a place in the schools of San Francisco, and had gone the length in her desire for newness and change, of refusing the week-ends at home which the train service to Santa Lucia allowed.

Serena had borne her out in it, so that owing to Mrs. Bixby's not taking it very well, and to her evident disposition to regard Evan's financial fiasco as what might have been expected from one who entertained lax views on the suppression of the liquor traffic, Mrs. Lindley had found herself thrown almost wholly on William for countenance and support; and though both of them would much rather have seen Julia on some other occasion, they warned her cheerfully away from the fresh varnish, and went on with their work. They had found a very good mahogany couch form in the Lindley attic, and were covering it new.

"Ah, don't you hate it," said Julia—"the piecing and contriving, the doing the same thing over again, and never getting anywhere?"

"But I shall get somewhere when I've done this," said Serena, poking excelsior into the hollow places. "I've been wanting a couch for my room for a long time, and now I shall have one for a dollar and thirty-five cents."

"But you keep house so beautifully, Ju," William protested.

"I should hate it a great deal worse if I didn't. I can't bear any kind of mussiness."

Serena flushed at that, for what with excelsior and varnish and furniture gimp, and the newspapers spread about to keep them from the floor, the room had a decided mussiness, rather the more pronounced for proximity to Julia's smooth linen; but she was prevented from replying by the evident preoccupation of Julia's mind with some private worry of her own.

"Have you seen the *Sunday Chronicle?*" she inquired, at last. They had not.

"Well, your aunt, Mrs. Bixby, has," said Julia. "Heavens knows why a woman like that reads the society columns, but she does."

"Well?" questioned Serena.

"She's found about my winnings at Mrs. Whiting's bridge party Saturday."

"Aunt Luella doesn't believe in bridge, of course. The prize was very handsome, I suppose."

"There wasn't any prize."

"But what—"

"We played for money."

"Oh!" said William and Serena, in the same breath. They laid down their work and sat looking at her in growing consternation. And "Oh, Julia!" Serena said again, and then William began to laugh.

"Won't there be a shine in the tents of Kedar! Is the minister going to preach against you, or will they have Dr. Stairs up before the faculty?"

"Nothing so absurd," said Julia, reddening; "but they passed a resolution about bridge at the Ladies' Guild, and the president spoke to Antrim about it. He said it wasn't so, of course; and when he got home and found out it was he didn't like it."

"I should think not," agreed William, in a tone that threw Mrs. Stairs on the defensive.

The two women turned to take up their work again; the movement was slight and unconscious, as if by so doing they had excluded her from the community of their interests. It was not so much the flagrance of Julia's offence against the community standard, but the cheap disloyalty to her husband's bread.

"I didn't know we were to play for money until I got there," Julia explained. "I couldn't refuse then, and I couldn't help winning. Of course, if I'd known that Antrim was going to make a fuss about it, I shouldn't have done it. And I think, Serena, you might speak to your aunt and make her understand how it was."

"Aunt Luella doesn't pay much attention to what I say to her," said Serena, coldly. "You know well enough about the feeling there was at the college; and, anyway, Julia, I don't believe in playing for money myself."

"Oh, if that's the way you feel about it!" Julia forced a laugh as she rose to go. "I wasn't expecting much on my own account, but you were such a friend of Antrim's—" The impertinence, if it amounted to so much, dropped before the cold stiffening of Serena's look and the distraction of her son's small voice crying to her outside by the toyon-tree. He had found strawberries where the Judge's old garden had been, and came to share them with his best-beloved.

"Oh, son, if you have anything nice you must pass it about to the company!" admonished his mother.

"But I bringed it for you," he insisted, trouble welling in the round eyes, so that Serena was obliged to kneel down and have three small sandy berries deposited on her tongue.

"I don't see where you get the patience, Serena," Julia commented. "Isn't he an awful lot of bother?" Some half-wistful wish for contradiction breaking in her voice caused Serena to look up sharply. Julia's splendid color hung at half-mast; there were lines of languor in her handsome, discontented face. Whatever of half-admission and appeal hung between the two women for an instant was cut off by William getting her hat on to go with Julia across lots.

"I should like to know," said Julia, digging her parasol into the soft earth as they walked, "what Serena Lindley has to do with setting standards for other people, seeing what Evan has done?"

"Julia!" William warned her.

"Oh, well, I suppose she can't help that; but it ought to make her easier on other people. But I know one thing: I can't stand any more of this nagging sort of narrowness. If the old women are going to keep on talking about me every time I turn round I shall give them something worth talking about."

"Yes, you can do that, Ju," William admitted, in perfect seriousness—"you can do that. But you won't be happy in it, Ju—you won't be happy at all."

XVIII

Long afterwards, when the Julia Stairs affair had been snipped
and seamed and pulled about at the Ladies' Guild, nibbled delicately
at tea parties, blown upon shamelessly in boudoirs, winnowed by
every guest of talk, it was Mrs. Bixby's habit to insist that it began in
Julia's playing bridge at Mrs. Whiting's and going too much among
the sophisticated, gay country-houses of Roble Park; in fact, the
foundations of it were laid long before that in the austere blood of the
earlier Stairs, in the system that had furnished his mind to the utmost
but afforded no schooling to his passions; and, more than all, in the
social squeamishness that had failed to apprise Julia Maybury that in
marriage, passion is a hard, cold fact to be reckoned with as hunger and
thirst.

When first the largeness of the West had glimmered upon Antrim
Stairs, it had aroused him to that state when to have been humanized
by marriage would have made him secure of the vague precipience that
flashed within his brain. The achieving strain in him had demanded
something which Julia's high color and abundant vitality had seemed to
stand for.

He had looked for the intimacies of marriage to have loosed
upon him the flood by which his soul should have been floated out
forever beyond the straits and shallows of its environment. And the

flood had never come. The source of it lay somewhere locked under his wife's unfluttered compliance, as the little bubble blown upon Julia's imagination by all the talk of his approaching greatness expired soundlessly against the commonplace rim of college life.

Both of them began to be a little contemptuous of his inability to move her. His delicacy, his unaccustomedness, the very profoundness of the effect she produced upon him, making him satisfied with so much less than he should have demanded of her, convicted him of coldness.

There was a time when Stairs had hope that his child might accomplish what he had failed, but the hope died quick and strangled by the still, tearless rage with which his wife admitted her condition. It had come at a time when Julia's social enterprise was beginning to fruit in the shape of inclusions in the leisurely pointless life of the country-side, and was the harder for her to bear as it was so inarticulate to herself. Julia had not reasoned about her life. It was merely the instinct of self-preservation which had made her reach out and cling to all that vitalized her, and made living seem worth while. She had not adjured children, but now that the occasion was upon her, the vase of her spirit overflowed with distaste and cold shudderings of fear.

"Let her alone," Dr. Caldwell cautioned her husband; "they are often so at first. She will come round all right, once she has heard it cry."

"And besides, you know," the women comforted her, "it can't be helped."

"Other people help it," Julia averred.

Stairs was rather relieved that Julia chose to spend so much of her time with Mrs. Maybury in San Francisco. It was natural that she should turn to her mother in such a case. He was able, alone in the house, to think tenderly of his unborn child as being somehow, like himself, outside the pale of its mother's preoccupations. A dream of it began to move beside him with eager hands and soft, condoning eyes for that secret insufficiency which he felt to be the root of his unfulfilment. It bore like a succoring sail towards the desertness of his affections. And then, all at once, there was a call for him, and a hasty journey in the night. There was a time when his wife's life rocked blind and rudderless in the trough of disaster, righted at last, and went on again, slack and feebly, but with no precious cargo to be brought to port—all his dream gone over with her dread. He was too much concerned for Julia's life to think at the time what he had lost, but he found it waiting for him when he returned to his own house. He had no sooner come in at the door than he felt it there, the dream, as he had entertained it, of his child, a living entity, and understood that this was perhaps all he was to know of fatherliness—the sense of the small presence receding, fading from him, voiceless, nameless, not to be spoken of nor to be done for in kindly wise; this, too, he had been unable to hold by and bring to fruition. He shrank suddenly as a man awaking to the amputation of some mortal part of him.

Since everything gets told sooner or later in small communities, and some things are best told quickly, Mrs. Lindley, who had seen him returning from the car and run in hastily to know how Julia did, went over that afternoon to Mrs. Bixby.

"Julia is very sick," she said, "and Dr. Stairs is much concerned about her. It is a great loss to them," covering her friends' affairs with generous loyalty.

"Hm," sniffed Aunt Luella, incredulously, "you needn't tell *me!*" And, indeed, once Mrs. Bixby had formed an opinion there was no use telling her anything. Whatever Julia Stairs did after that she was not to expect any concessions from the A. B. Z's.

Whatever disposition there was in other quarters to cavil at Julia Stairs, was quieted by the ensuing period of ill-health, in which she dragged about, not equal to the tacit resistance which she opposed to the small conventions of the college set. Her husband thought her sobered by regret when she was merely dulled. She saw that he had suffered, and wished to comfort him; but getting no warmth by the process, conceived that she had failed, and at last all efforts ceased. In their early married life his personal attraction and young enthusiasm for her had served at intervals to fill and flood her with its own reflection, but it would not answer now. She did not know what was the trouble, except that since everything was a failure it was fortunate it did not seem to matter much.

She had remained at home in this state a matter of six months or more, and Stairs, noticing how pale she was and the roundness of her figure gone off, insisted that she should go with him south during the short vacation to attend a teacher's institute where he was to lecture. Julia loathed institutes, and was too indifferent for travel; she went instead to her mother, not so much that she cared for being there, but for being away from Santa Lucia. Always before, as she neared it after absences, the city had enticed her—the sights of it, the smells of it, the sunlit, windy hills, the ruddy constellations of lights floating above the bay quickened the renewal of intimacy. As she had moved in it she felt her spirits carried high above the hum and clangor to the note of laughter. Now she perceived that it was a city all very much of one color, and that a dirty one, as if it had worked its way up from the ooze and slime of the water-front, and never gotten quite clear of it—a horned, warty kind of thing that reared its head among the hills, and had its tail still in the formless muddle along the foot of Sansome Street.

She was too listless to go about among her friends. Mrs. Maybury, who, in the process of curing herself of unlimited leisure, had come through all the 'opothies and several 'ists, had now adopted a system which consisted in going about with a fixed smile, and insisting a great many times a day that there was nothing whatever the matter with her, which, as there had never been anything the matter with her, answered very well with Mrs. Maybury, but wore to irritation Julia, whose crying bitterness it was that there *was* nothing the matter to distract her from the aching emptiness of life. She took to walking about a great deal, in the vague notion that if she travelled very far and got herself very tired in the process she might somehow happen upon what she had lost. It was not in the shifty stream of color that clattered to and fro under the lanterned porticoes back of Portsmouth Square. It was not in the full-bodied, well-dressed crowd that poured itself out of matinées of late afternoons, contriving by the sheer heedlessness of its chatty interests to submerge the business of the street momentarily in a holiday aspect. It was not in the lapping bay, nor the hurrying fog, nor the gusty draughts of streets.

One of her habitual walks was out Hyde Street and around Black Point. It had been a favorite one of hers and Jim Halford's of Sunday afternoons, in the days when Jim had been engaged to her and she had not been engaged to Jim. She wondered about him a little dully. His father was dead, she knew, the house let to strangers. After her marriage she had heard that Jim had taken the Pacific Island branch of his firm's business, and it was supposed to be on her account. At the time she had felt it a compliment, but now she began to regret it as a piece of girlish silliness that she had let him go out of her life so easily; they had always been good friends; they might have gone on being so. She tried to reconstruct the sense of his friendliness as she remembered it, failed, and thought that though she had not learned of his death, he might very well be out of the world, she got so little good of his being in it. She asked her mother that night what she knew of Halford, but Mrs. Maybury could tell her nothing except that she was sure he was not in the city, as he always came to see her on such occasions, and he had been away for a long time. Then, by one of those coincidences that happen so often it seems almost a law that the very approach of long-absent friends must set us talking about them, she stumbled upon Jim Halford.

It was such a sloppy day as women choose for shopping because they imagine no one else having the temerity to do so, and Julia had spent a desultory afternoon about the bargain counters. The car was already crowded when she got on at the Emporium and she was urged slowly towards the middle, and at last, torn from the sustaining strap, held on her feet only by the pressure of surrounding bodies, she felt herself grow faint with the motion and the reek of damp, woolly clothing. Rain began and drove in fresh accessions of dripping passengers, and as they trailed heavily through the wet streets the car checked and halted and finally came to a full blockade at the corner of Market and McAllister. As their car stopped suddenly a bare foot behind the forward one, the dense crowd of passengers lurched forward dizzily, righted, and swore softly. Julia, who from fatigue had lost the feeling of her feet under her, staggered and pitched bodily into the arms of the man behind her, whose formal excusings broke off sharply in the middle to call her name. Almost before his hand on her arm had steadied her, she knew him for Halford. When she turned to look at him, he saw how white and sick she was.

"Don't talk," he said, with the readiness she remembered in him. "I must get you out of this." His strong, steady voice clove a way for them as, shielding her by the hollow of his shoulder, they ploughed through the sodden crowd. "Now, can you walk a bit?" he asked. "There's a restaurant close by; you must have a cup of tea, or some brandy, maybe."

He found it presently—a dull little place of dingy table-cloths, where the lights had been burning through the mists of rain since early in the afternoon. They had the place all to themselves, with the exception of three languid waiters who flicked napkins about aimlessly, and tried to look as if they were ready for business, when they were palpably bored by it. They brought her tea in a thick cup, she having refused the brandy; Halford ordered toast for her, and sent it away again because it was scorched, and having tipped one of the languid waiters to have it better done, discovered that he had tipped the wrong one, and had to do it over again. And through all his solicitude of her, through all his readiness, through all the inefficiency of the dull little place and his impatience with it, above the rush of the rain outside and the swish of the gutters, there bloomed the fresh, unassailable fact that they were glad to see each other. They took account of each other by furtive looks like sips of heartening wine, each eye avoiding the other to rove more freely on every well-remembered feature: the breadth of his shoulders, his well-fed color, Julia's long, blue-veined eyelids, the subtle way of the cheek she leaned upon her hand. She found him improved, filled out, assured; a satisfying virility brimmed from the man, a sparkle on it raised by the glow of meeting, as, once she had rallied from her faintness, he ran on lightly accounting for the past four years, as if there had been no bar between them but the natural one of time and space, as if the very crowd that had thrown them together had but surged between them for an interval prolonged beyond expectation, and here he was again telling her how it happened. When at last she was ready for going he insisted she should have a cab.

"Oh," she said, lightly, "wives of college professors don't go about in cabs. They can't afford it." But when they came into the street again, and saw the great lumps of humanity swarmed about a small nucleus of trolley gliding up and down in the wet, she consented. They went along the swimming pavement looking for a cab; the lights behind the fogged windows made dull smears in the cavernness darkness of the shops. The noise of the streets changed rapidly from the dull rumble of afternoon to the high, brisk hum of going home. Halford insisted on buying half a dozen bunches of violets of a street flower-vender adroop in a closed doorway like a rained-on fowl.

"Don't I always buy violets for you?" he urged to Julia's protestation. "I remember you used to make me buy them so the poor chaps could go home out of the wet. I'm coming, too. May I?" he announced, when he had found a cab lurking about the City Hall. "Your mother is always glad to see me."

Well, he was perfectly safe in coming, Julia thought, if he could take it like that; he must have clean gotten over caring in a deliberate, personal way if he could make so perfunctory a matter of her permission to be in her company. Seeing how gay he was, she decided he could never have cared very deeply to have recovered so easily. Without compunction she lent herself to the mood of reminiscence.

"Any children, Ju?" he questioned, with the privilege of old acquaintance.

"No," said Julia, "I—" Suddenly her eyes filled. Halford divined that she had had a loss, and looked upon her commiseratingly. And though Julia had had her own way, she felt for the moment that she had lost immeasurably. She had really wanted children, but the circumstances—her husband had not made it possible. Yes, she had lost ... oh, everything! She felt an impulse to cry out upon it, to be pitied and comforted, and recovered herself with difficulty as Halford went on talking lightly of other things.

Mrs. Maybury was glad to see him. Though she was proud of her son-in-law and a good deal in awe of him, she had always regretted Jim Halford.

"Jim," she was accustomed to say, "would have been so comfortable."

Halford would not stay to dinner, though they asked him, urging a previous engagement. Getting up to leave at last, he insisted that they must both go out to dine with him some evening, and go to the theatre. No, Mrs. Maybury thanked him, there was nothing at all the matter with her—here she remembered to smile in the prescribed fashion, which caused poor Halford the uneasiness of wondering if she were not concealing some gripping, incurable pain from him—she seldom went out, she said, but Julia could go.

"To-morrow?" Halford questioned, promptly. Not to-morrow; there was something else she had to do. This was not strictly true, but Julia did not know how to account for the sudden movement of resistance.

"Wednesday?" Well, perhaps, Wednesday. That was settled, then, and Halford got himself out into the night, which had turned off windy and clear. Julia said to herself, as she went up to bed, that there could not possibly be any harm going out to dinner with Jim, he was such good company, and he had so evidently ceased to care.

XIX

The first thing Halford wished to know when they came out into the clear twilight of the street Wednesday evening was where they should go to dine.

"Oh, it's your party," she reminded him; "you choose."

"Do you remember how we used to stick an umbrella in a crack when we couldn't decide, and go the way it fell?"

"But we haven't any umbrella," she objected; "and, besides, you are grown up now, and ought to know your own mind."

"I have always known my own mind, Ju," Halford declared, soberly, watching the constellations of the signs come out in the little zodiac of the street, "and it has never happened yet that your mind has been the same as mine, so you choose. There's Campi's and the Poodle Dog and that little Mexican joint opposite the Hall of Justice—"

"No, not the *frijole* place," Julia interrupted; I haven't the appetite for queer dishes I once had. And not the Poodle Dog; none of the college people go there—"

"Is it as bad as that?"

"As bad as what?"

"That you can't decide on a place to eat without deferring to the college prejudice?"

"Worse than that," she declared, with mock tragedy. "Do you remember Mrs. Bodely and the custard cups?"

Halford remembered. "What's the old lady up to now?"

"Oh, since Evan Lindley has been dropped she has tucked it under her wing, and a precious lot of prigs she's hatching out of it," Julia told him. And that led to his asking all about the Lindleys, and how William did, so that presently they had come to the corner and the down-town car.

"So it's Campi's, is it?" he asked. "Hurry, then, and we shall have time for a turn about the square."

As they went the long streets blossomed in electrics, and Mrs. Stairs felt the old sensuous allurement of the city come out with them, like an exhalation, as though it were the perfume of those bright night bloomers spread abroad after the sun goes down. The change and flicker of lights began to strike out bright reflections in her spirit.

"Oh," she cried, as they drifted about the Stevenson Monument, "it doesn't seem possible I haven't been here since I was married—not once!"

"I have, often," said Halford, with the soberness she had noticed in him before—"very often; always changing, and yet nothing ever changed. Same old Chinks shuffling in their slippers, and same squad of policemen coming out of the alley yonder like a cuckoo out of a clock."

"And I suppose you come here, too?" she asked, when they were seated at the table in Campi's long upper room and the waiter had taken their orders.

"At least once whenever I am in the city. There's the same old Garibaldi over the window, and the same waiter you used to tease, asking who the old chap was, and what he had done to have a bust, anyway."

How well he remembered, Julia thought, and wondered if his doing so proved that he still cared, or his ready way of mentioning it that he had done caring. Now and then she surprised him in a long, impersonal look at her, a stock-taking kind of look. She flinched inwardly, thinking she must have gone off in her appearance very much for Jim Halford to look at her like that. Her hand hovered above the glass for a moment when Jim held a bottle over it with a gesture of demurrer merging into a laugh.

"College prejudice?" he hinted.

"Well, I am under the ban at present and have to be circumspect." She gave him an amused account of the bridge affair. It had needed just that to put the incident in its proper place; what with Antrim and Serena Lindley and Mrs. Bixby it had been made to assume quite too serious proportions.

"Must be deadly dull," Halford grumbled.

"Oh, I grow used to it. I have fallen so far into line that I am going to have a serviceable silk this winter with two bodices—one for evening and one for afternoon. Commencement is wildly exciting with us, and a dinner at a restuarant with two kinds of wine is almost a dissipation."

"I'll tell you what, Ju," declared Halford, "we'll make a good job of it while I am here. We'll go about and rediscover all the old places where we had our fun together when we weren't grown up and hadn't made up our minds—at least, you hadn't." Some alarmed prick sent a signal flying at Julia's cheek, but Halford was working his way slowly through the dinner with the aim of a man occupied merely with his food, and the signal dropped.

"It would cheer me up a lot," he said, "and I am needing it. It is not so gay, if you must know, selling groceries down in Mindanao."

"You ought to be married, Jim," she assured him, and wished immediately afterwards she hadn't.

"Ah, it's a pity I couldn't have made you believe it five years ago." Halford indulged himself in a tone of mournful reminiscence.

"Well, you can't say I didn't set you an example!" Julia's spirit renewed with this sort of banality, which justified itself in the relieved certainty that Jim had gotten over his attachment, since he could joke about it. On the assumption that it gave him no pain to do so, she was willing to revisit with him the places where they had had good times together in the days when Jim had been engaged to her and she had not been engaged to Jim. They seemed to get a great deal out of it; touching remembered gladness, to find it glow again like pressed flowers from a book, reviving color and perfume in the light and air.

Mrs. Stairs bought her new silk, and it was not serviceable, and she did not take it home to be made up at Santa Lucia, but had it made at once and wore it to the matinée with Jim. It brought back some of the color to her cheeks, but it did not prevent Halford from looking at her still, at times, with scrutinizing intentness that had nothing to do with the becomingness of her new dress. Julia loosened her hair and brought it forward in a pompadour, and began to regard her hat with dissatisfaction. That she must have gone off in her looks a great deal was evident from Halford's wish to return to the girl she had been, to go over old ground with her rather than to establish a new basis for going on. Jim should have been prepared for some change in her after four years of marriage; after all, she had done very well not to marry him if his regard for her rooted no deeper than that. She assayed several times a footing that should prove to him that the new Julia was as much worth his while as the old, but Halford held to the note of the past with an obviousness that began to excite curiosity. And there was something in Julia's own consciousness that implied annoyingly a reversal of their positions. The old sureness of her ascendency over him was gone, and there had come to take the place of it, a certain wistfulness, a readiness to tears, a submissive wish to be dominated and overborne. Whatever their relations in fact, it appeared Julia had lost; she felt suddenly her emotions grown wispy, like the turned silks of the faculty women.

It had been easy to fall into Halford's assumption that the unfulfilled expectation of motherhood had occasioned the mood of pitiableness. It was true that she had really wanted children and great love and abounding light and color, but the stringency of life at Santa Lucia had excluded all that. It was incredible that Antrim would go on in that narrow way. She began to be fevered with the desire to escape into larger possibilities of living. Her soul, hunting forever in its secret fastness, hiding its face from what it pursued, lest to name it was to grow afraid and give over following, perceiving dimly that its satisfaction must be also doom, fled crying in the dark. Then the pang of bodily weakness lingering from her illness surged upon her and filled her heart with tears. Often, as she went about with Halford, she had unaccountable impulses to throw herself upon his tenderness and cry out upon the creeping numbness of her heart. She believed he might have helped her if he cared. That was part of the general unsatisfactoriness of things: that Halford had loved her unnecessarily so many years, and just when she needed most to be loved he had gotten over it. Then quite suddenly it was made plain to her that he had not gotten over it; that it was still going on in him, and would go on to the end of days.

They had been walking in the park, and were sitting now on Strawberry Hill. It was a day full of sunshine shattered and strewn by a cooling wind. Holiday crowds moved on the boulevards, and, drifting towards them and on the winding walks, disappeared down lanes of shrubbery. A silence had fallen between them which Mrs. Stairs broke suddenly, saying she must go home at the end of the week.

"What for?" demanded Halford. "Isn't this good enough for you?" with a gesture inclusive of the day and the company.

"Good enough," she nodded; "but you forget I'm an old married woman and have responsibilities."

He looked at her; he was lying on the grass below her, full and meaningly.

"I've been trying to forget it for ten days," he said.

So that was it. He had ignored the present to hold to the shadow of a past, in which she was almost his.

"But you are good at forgetting," she urged, lightly, seeking his glance and turning away towards the moving crowds.

"Will you tell me, Ju," he said, still with the same deliberateness of meaning, "what, in the last ten days, I've forgotten?"

He had forgotten nothing: about the kind of seat that pleased her best at the theatres, and her not liking to ride inside cars, and the waiter at Campi's. He had not forgotten.

"Two things," she said, lightly getting on her feet: "that the ground is always too damp to sit upon in San Francisco, and that you promised mother to come home to an early dinner, and we haven't seen half yet."

It was true that the ground was always damp and often slippery. As they went down the hill, Halford leading, Julia lost footing once and threw out her hand; it caught at his, where it rested an instant as she slipped and swung against his shoulder. Suddenly at the touch of her his countenance changed, his whole physical aspect altered as if a flame had burst from him, and was caught up again in instant self-recovery. He trembled as at the imminence of a shock avoided. Quick as the flash had passed it caught at the dryness of Julia's heart, kindled and sung in her, made the earth air under her feet as she walked.

If Julia had expected Jim Halford to resist the time of her departure she was disappointed. He made no further reference to it, and only acknowledged it by refraining from making any engagements beyond the day she had mentioned. Julia was a little piqued by it; she was feeling singularly light-hearted since her discovery in the park. It was absurd of old Jim to try to pretend to her; she had always read him like a book. Did he suppose a sober-minded married woman was to forget her dignity merely because an old lover had not been able to forget her. On the contrary, she would be able to give him more inclusive sympathy now that—now that—Julia did not quite know what, but certainly there was reason.

In the five days that remained to them there was a tingling expectancy in their meetings that restored Julia to the ascendency of sex. The last afternoon but one they walked out to Black Point. They had come down the stone steps to the pathway, and leaned upon the rail and watched the flowing jade of the bay awash about the rocks; it turned amber with the lift of choppy waves and flecked white at the top. Black tugs, like mud hens, squattered on the bay, and slow sails of lumber schooners took the light, glinting and fading like the wings of gulls. The Berkeley Hills floated above the molten water like an enchanted coast. Julia stretched out her arms to them.

"Oh, I love it, I love it!" she cried. "I've always said it, I'll say it again, that San Francisco is the only place to live!"

"Why leave it, then?"

"Oh!" Julia felt at a loss in the very obviousness of the reason; then, "You are leaving it."

"Yes, I'm leaving it." Halford mused on the green fronds uncurling in the rocky crevices below them.

"Shall I see you when you come again?" asked Julia.

Halford withdrew himself from his abstraction. "No," he said.

"Dear me," cried Julia, trying for the effect of jocular dismay, "and I thought we'd been having such a nice time!"

"Nice!" said Halford—"nice!" He leaned over and broke off fragments of the crumbling cliff, and began pitching them into the water that choked throatily among the stones. "What hypocrites women are!"

"Ah," Julia answered him, pointedly, "we get lessons in pretending."

Halford laughed shortly, and then turned to her. "Look here, Ju, let's have done with pretending. The last time I talked with you, the month before you were married, when I told you I could never forget you, I suppose you thought I meant no more by it than the other fellows you've turned down, and perhaps I thought so too, but it turned out true. I don't mean to say that I go about wearing the willow for you, or that I haven't taken much of what has come my way; but as for loving and marrying, there has never been anybody but you, Julia, and there never will be."

The moderation of his manner lent conviction to the words. It was as if he had stated soberly that he always expected to have blue eyes and be rather corpulent of body.

"But we can be friends," hinted Julia, timidly.

"No, we can't. I thought so at first; but now, after these two weeks, I know that we can't—at least, I can't—and you have known it ever since the day in the park. Be honest, Ju, and say you know it."

There was a stone seat hollowed out of the cliff behind them, and Julia sat down in it, the finality of the admission leaping upon her.

"Yes," she said, "I know."

"And even," Halford went on, the very roundness of his face, the compactness of his figure, every trait and feature of the man driving home the conviction of his honesty and worth—"even if I had kept you from knowing this time, I should not have tried it again for another reason." He hesitated here, and her lifted face and averted eyes mutely questioned him.

"If I had found you safe and happy, Julia, I might have gone on serving you as I have always done, but now that I see that you are not happy, I know it isn't safe."

"I never said—" began Julia, tumultuously, in denial.

"You haven't needed to," Halford went on, with the same practical calmness, as if he were combating the merits of a particular brand of canned article; "you chose the life you're living now, for whatever reason, God knows; but I don't need to be told that your heart is not in it, that you are bored by it, fagged by it, and very soon you will be at the point of not enduring it."

"Oh!" cried Julia, choked between anger and the sudden betraying sense of pitiableness. "If you think that about me, I should think it would make you want to be kinder to me."

"It does, Julia." He came over and leaned against the rocks, looking down at her. "I'm going to be very kind. I used to regret that I hadn't made any impression on you, but now I am glad of it, because I can say what otherwise would be impossible, what I should despise myself for saying if I had any hope to profit by it; and that is, don't go on with it."

Julia, looking down at her hands in her lap, saw unaccountably that they trembled. Alarms, questions, wild surmises surged and broke upon her, scattering like the spray.

"What do you mean?" she managed.

"Just that; you aren't fit for it, and you won't be able to stand it. You were made for gayety, for change and loveliness and admiration, and after awhile you'll have to have them; at any price, you'll have to have them."

He took off his hat to mop his forehead, and Julia noticed then how nearly bald he was on top, wondered at herself for noticing, and wondered more that it did not make him ridiculous, but it did not. He stood there drying the inside of his derby with his handkerchief like a thoroughly respected representative of the wholesale grocery trade, and went on, steadily:

"You think because you've stood four years of it and nothing has happened that you can stand it always, but you can't. You are a handsome woman, Ju, handsomer than ever; and you aren't safe."

Mrs. Stairs called on all her soul to beat down the swift mortification as she stood up.

"I have my husband to protect me, at any rate."

"No, Ju, don't make that mistake. There is nobody in the world so unprotected as the unhappy married woman, and that is why I say, don't go on with it."

"How dare you talk to me so?" she cried, walking on unsteadily; but he kept even with her.

"Get free of it when you can and how you can. Don't let any habit of doing things or remembered tenderness bind you, or any fear of what may be said. The thing you want you are bound to have. I've seen that in these two weeks, so I say get free while there's time, so you can take freely what comes to you when it comes."

"How dare you—" She was beginning again when they came around the point to a sandy open space, and observed that there were people there, come out, like themselves, to enjoy the rare afternoon. About one group, a man and a woman, there was something vaguely familiar. The man was lying on the sand and the woman reading to him. She spoke with a defiant friendliness:

"How do you do, Mrs. Stairs?"

"How do you do," said Julia, unmindfully stumbling in the sand. The woman watched her out of sight.

"Who was it?" inquired Halford, when they were out of ear-shot.

"I don't know. Somebody from Santa Lucia. Yes, I do. It was Kate Bixby, Mrs. Lindley's cousin. I didn't know she had a beau, though. She's quite an old maid. I suppose now she will go back to Santa Lucia and tell everybody she has seen me."

"Ah, you see!" said Halford.

There were strollers going to and fro on the broad walk, and it was impossible to talk. Julia felt tears of shame and anger welling from a wound.

"Take me to the car," she said. "I want to go home."

XX

The most disconcerting thing that happened to Mrs. Stairs after her return to Santa Lucia was Serena's asking her very directly if she had seen anything of Kate Bixby while she was in the city. There was so evidently an air behind the question of its being pertinent to some anxiety in Serena's mind that Julia was a little put out by it, said no at first, and then yes that she remembered passing her one afternoon, but had not spoken with her. The uneasiness that Julia had lest the attention which Mrs. Lindley gave to it might have something to do with her own matter, caused her to hesitate in a manner of knowing more than the fact said. She saw that Mrs. Lindley had received such an impression, and hastened to cover it.

"I should have stopped," she said, "but she was with a friend—a gentleman. They seemed to be having a good time. I didn't know that she had an admirer."

"Oh," said Serena, with enlightenment, "that accounts for it. What was he like?"

Julia had not noticed particularly, but she was glad to keep the talk pointed away from herself by asking what it accounted for.

"For Kate's not coming home oftener. Aunt Luella is beginning to be quite worried by it. But if there is somebody she is interested in— and I don't know why there shouldn't be, Kate is only thirty-five."

"I shouldn't suppose," said Julia, "that staying away from Santa Lucia needed any accounting for. It is coming back to it that I wonder at."

"Julia," Mrs. Lindley asked, with more hesitation than was usual to her manner of sober frankness, "may I say something to you— something personal?"

"Why, as to that," said Julia, stooping to pick some shreds from the carpet, getting down in front of the grate to poke them behind the bars, and putting up her arm to screen her reddening cheek, "if there is anything personal to be said, I should much rather you said it than any one. What about?"

"About the sort of thing you were saying just now. It isn't liked."

"By Mrs. Bixby and the A. B. Z's, I suppose."

"By anybody. It is thought that since your husband gets his living out of the town you oughtn't to disparage it."

"But I only say that sort of thing to you," objected Julia, lightly, relieved to find no hint of Halford in all this.

"It isn't what you say so much. You spend a great deal of your time in San Francisco."

"With my mother."

"Your mother isn't at Roble Park; and you keep up your calls there better than you do among the faculty houses. And you do all your shopping in the city. There's a feeling, you know, that the money ought to be kept in the town."

"What else do they say?" making the fire to blaze so that the reflection of it flickered and reddened on her face, and using the screen again.

"What should they say?" This was not quite disingenuous, for, in fact, they were saying that Julia not only flouted the town, but thought too lightly of her husband's comfort. "Only Evan thinks it likely to affect Dr. Stairs's standing in the school, unless—unless you could manage to seem a little more interested."

That was just what Julia was trying. The burning mortification of that last afternoon with Halford had driven her back upon her husband with almost a revival of tenderness. He at least thought no ill of her.

"The thing you want you are bound to have," Jim had said. "I've seen that these two weeks past." So that was what he had seen in her kindness to an old friend, in her forlornness, in her trust and turning to him. He had seen that, and had warned her. He had gone as far as that, this man who had used to fetch and carry for her, this common representative of the wholesale grocery trade; and she was Mrs. Antrim Stairs. The wound of her vanity wasted her in the night as she lay awake, and secretly in the day as she went about perfunctorily going through the motions of taking an interest in Santa Lucia. Of the whole implication of Halford's speech she simply did not dare to think; she fled from it, and fled straight into the face of dreary fact that was to drive her back to its fulfilment.

Her husband's position gave her a certain prestige in the college set which her careless behavior had not wholly lost her. She thought it might amuse her now to take it up, and see what she could make of it. She had a propitiatory eagerness to be thought well of. Suppose anybody—suppose Kate Bixby—had taken note of her manner with Halford, and had seen in it what Jim imagined he had seen? Half-instinctively she began to build about herself a wall of good opinion against a possibility which she would not consciously admit.

She was disappointed of part of her plan, which included Serena Lindley, for Serena was then expecting her second child. The time in a practical estimation had not seemed wholly suitable, but, too fine to dishonor it with an unwelcoming thought, she bent her new capability to making the best provision for it. The first had come with trailed glory from a far-off heaven, but she touched earth with this, common ground of the travail of women and the mastery of life.

The Lindleys were very poor still. The necessity for Evan's presenting an unstrained front in his business meant that the ragged edges of their income must be pulled together at home, and there were always little Evan's rapidly growing arms and legs sticking through the thin places; but there had come to the relief of the strain the satisfying sense of reliance on the supplementary competence of the other. The final readjustment of their separate capacities had come, not as it had been her dream to have it with the stir and movement of infinite harmonies, but enforced by the practical necessity of her imperilled health.

The carriage-house at the back of the old place had been substantially built, and had a loft above it for storing hay. Serena thought that with a little labor, most of which Evan could perform out of hours, it could be made into a house, the rent of which would pay for a girl in the kitchen.

Lindley, who was beginning to have a great respect for his wife's capacity for accomplishing things in an unfamiliar medium—he never attempted anything more plastic than town lots himself—came into the plan, as he phrased it, "with both feet," and out of its assured success derived another notion, which in the end provided just the mordant of their mutual interests. A client of his, going East, had left a row of cheap houses to be built, and Evan suggested she should undertake the plans for these—enough to reimburse her for the trouble being added to the contracts which he should let. He took her out in the buggy to see the land, and his facile imagination leaped forward to the largest possibilities to come out of her aptitude for planning, and his skill in disposing of houses after they were built. He brought home books of building plans and carpenters' estimates, and while she sewed, read aloud to her magazine articles on plumbing and ventilation. Such times as these, when the work was done and the fire was covered for the night, Serena would sit upon her husband's knee with her cheek against his, and power came upon them. They felt what they could do together to bear and to rear, hardly and with great pains to themselves, but still to do it. They told each other that they did not know where the money was coming from for the nurse and the doctor, but with the inward assurance that there were some months yet in which they should contrive it together; and being so occupied with their own concerns, saw very little of Julia and Antrim Stairs.

Julia said to herself a great many times that spring that Antrim loved her. She made a little list of the points by which she should have measured its degree had she observed them in another, and spread out her poor heart to be warmed at them with as much success as if she had stretched cold fingers to the reflected fires that danced at night behind the window-pane. She still believed in the possibilities of his greatness, at which she had once kindled her imagination, and tried in some wifely way to reanimate the spirit that had executed the *Post-Darwinian Theories*. Stairs had out the manuscript again, and began to rewrite it in the chill clarity of second thought, losing a little of his present misery in conjecture and winged surmise. But Julia got no renewal from any source, for she knew now what she had lost—the possibilities of passion and self-effacing love. She knew that she was all to her husband that she missed, and felt herself in respect to him thirsty at the dry and crumbling life of a well, hearing the slow wash of its waters out of reach. And Julia had never known before what it was to want without having. All of a sudden, as if they were bubbles blown out to finer radiance by desire, the words of Jim Halford took a new meaning. "What you want you are bound to have," Jim had said. Bound to have, because she had the power to compel it towards her. It had always been said to her as a girl that she could get anybody she wanted, and she had known it was true. She had had no trouble at all getting Antrim Stairs; he had been the biggest man on her horizon, and she had picked him off very naturally—worn him as the ensign of her mastering charm. Now she understood that the desirable thing was to be taken, to be mastered and assumed. This was the point in the game she had missed—to incite men to conquest. Well, if she were to play the game again (the fact of her marriage rose up, an affronting bar); but if she should play that game with Jim Halford—she shut the lid on that thought, and went out to see the president's wife about the annual junior reception, but the thought lay there glowing like a jewel in the dark of its shut case.

In the week after Easter the lock was sprung wide open by her reading in the Santa Lucia *Bulletin* that James A. Halford, San Francisco, had registered at the Monte Vista Hotel the night before. She remained in all that day in turbulent kind of expectation, telling herself, first, that his coming could have nothing to do with her, and then that she did not see what on earth it could have to do with. Nothing happened that day, and the next she persuaded herself that she really needed some things in Santa Lucia, and there was no reason on earth why she shouldn't go and get them; but she saw nothing of Halford, nor did any one mention having seen him. She half looked for his card when she came home, but there was no evidence of him. She began to wonder if she should not have sent Antrim to call upon so old a friend. Really it was ridiculous for Jim to take the attitude that there was anything between them that precluded the ordinary courtesies. This studied avoidance was almost a reflection; she had a good mind to write and tell him so.

Halford, on the afternoon of his arrival, had gone straight to Rosebank, where William was glad to see him, and found him much improved. There was a certain clean commonness about Halford that appealed, as if good grooming and good feeding and sound sleep were somewhere near the root of life, and his never having got very far away from them was not so much a matter of grossness as of simplicity. As he sat with his back to one of the tall old windows in the parlor at Rosebank, his comfortable bulk blocking out the light, he did not look to have broken his heart over Julia Maybury; but William, who was a sentimentalist, when she had told him that her father was well, that Belshazzar had rheumatism, and that she was really going to be married that summer, could not forbear to feel a little tenderly about the edge of old confidences, and was highly gratified at the way Halford played up to it.

He admitted that he should never care for any woman as he had cared for Julia, but that his own feeling had long gotten past any point but the wish to further her happiness, and to rejoice greatly that she was happy. William, honest little soul that she was, not adding anything in confirmation of that, Halford went on to say that there had been a time when he feared that Antrim Stairs was not the man to accomplish that, but now that the marriage had turned out so well—it had turned out well, hadn't it?

Taken so directly, William could only admit her misgiving that Julia was not getting out of marriage what she had expected.

"It is not as if either of them were to blame or could find fault with the other. They just simply don't belong. I suppose," she sighed, "an unsuitable marriage is like a mended tea-cup. It can be put together so it looks well from the outside, but it never holds tea."

"And if you go on trying to make it hold tea?" hinted Jim.

"Then there is a horrid mess at last, and burned fingers for somebody," she added, hastily. "Perhaps I oughtn't to have said so much, but I feel you are truly interested."

They made the usual excuses of people about to discuss their friends' affairs against some pricks of conscious betrayal, and got about by degrees to admit between themselves that marriage seemed to be closing in on Julia and Dr. Stairs like some fearful enginery impossible to be forestalled, and to allow Halford to say at last what he had come

for: that he would be grateful if William could take a message for him to
Mrs. Stairs, whom he might not see again.

"But do see her again, even if only to say goodbye. Such an old
friend—"

"No," said Halford—"no, believe me, it is better not."

Upon which William, very tender of him and very remorseful
with herself for having suggested it, said that she would take the
message. To her simple mind it was natural that Halford, who loved her,
should have the first right to help; but two or three days later, when she
found time for its delivery, she was surprised to find Julia making light
of it.

"I was to conjure you by all that had been between you not to
forget what had passed when you were last together, nor to think that he
would forget it; and that his firm was to establish a branch house there
in the Philippines, and he was to have charge of it, and that he would be
on the coast once or twice more, and then no more forever.

"He said," William had repeated, soberly, "that if ever you were
in trouble, or in fear of trouble coming, if he could help you, you were
only to call, and he would come to you—across whatever lands and
seas, he would come to help you."

Julia laughed. "What an old sentimentalist Jim is, and what
bugaboos he is always conjuring up! I remember, when we were children
and mother sent us off to school together, he used always to be looking
out for mad bulls to rescue me from. Jim never did grow up."

"I thought it very nice of him," said William, a little miffed, for
she was a sentimentalist herself; "and he is going off there where nobody
belongs to him." She told Julia all about the Philippine plan as Jim had
discovered it to her, and though Mrs. Stairs affected not to care a great
deal it did not escape her by a single word. No later than William was
out of the house she wrote him a letter:

"DEAR JIM,— [she began] "What a silly old chap you
are to go sending me mysterious messages by that silly little
William! I should certainly be angry with you if I did not
know by experience it is no use. I am not in any trouble,
nor likely to be in any, unless it comes from old friends
getting notions about me, and not coming to say good-bye

when they go off on long voyages from which they may not return.

"I know that I was not quite myself when I was in the city, but, as I told you, I had been ill, and had suffered a great loss, and had a right to expect the sympathy of my friends without being misunderstood about it.

"It is only because you are such an old friend I am able to forgive you at all. Now do not be silly any more nor go to imagining situations that don't exist, but come to see me when you are on the coast again. Mr. Stairs and myself will always be interested in your welfare, and glad to welcome you at the house of

"Your Oldest Friend,
"JULIA."

She mailed the letter at once, and went about experiencing the relief of having at last got her hand on the situation again. It was unpardonable for Jim to suppose any danger in the renewal of their friendship. She was not afraid; she had proved she was not afraid by writing that letter; she would see Jim when he came again, and prove to him that there was no reason for anybody being afraid.

XXI

The Beauty of Glazenwood was past the time of its bloom and ready to shed its petals bright and soft as blessings by the time William was ready to be married under it. There was something so suitable in the notion of William's being married out-of-doors that on second thought it did not appear she could be properly married anywhere else. To begin with, no house could have been large enough to hold all the people who had a right of interest in seeing William married. There was always an air about the Rosebank gardens as if they pertained more to the business of living than other lawns and roses. From the end of rains to the beginning of rains there were always steamer-chairs and tea-tables under the pine tree, hammocks among the shrubbery, and rugs across the grass, as if the abounding cheer and vitality of the house had flowered out of it in the summer's heat and spread abroad upon the grounds. And, besides, William herself had declared that she could never be married happily except she could see Toyon winking at her between the bridge and the willows, and hear it singing as it ran.

"That," said William, "is without doubt 'the Voice that breathed o'er Eden' much better than any church choir could render it." And whatever William said in regard to that wedding was considered settled. There had such a long time gone to prepare for it, and so much loving consideration to making the occasion a happy one, that at last it went off very quietly for every one except Lew Sing. For as much as a month before, there had been the sound of a fruit-chopper going day and night in the kitchen, and for as much as a month afterwards a smell of citron and spice hanging about all the rooms. There was a particular friend of his, with a particularly green tassel at the end of his queue, come down from San Francisco to help at the last, and a great deal of rushing to and from the express-office for a box of colored-sugar ornaments for the wedding-cake, which another particular friend of his was supposed to have created expressly for this occasion, and altogether such a sliding about of pots and kettles and banging of oven doors as indicated that Sing was having the time of his life.

William's boxes with the hemstitched pillowcases and the embroidered table-linen were all packed the week before, and the room called William's Heart cleared for the wedding-presents, conspicuous among which was a great bronze pagoda with bells all over it, which had been imported from China by a particular friend of Lew Sing's for this purpose many weeks in advance of it, much too large and magnificent an ornament for such a house as the young doctor's wife could afford and was wholly satisfied in having. The young doctor's mother had come down some days before, and had been taken in by the Lindleys for fear she would feel lonely at the hotel; the young doctor came; Jap—that is to say, Dr. Edward K. Jasper—got in on the evening train, and Dr. Furniss had sent word that he would be there on the 11.20 next morning if it took a leg to do it. Serena had driven out, though she was scarcely able, to claim her privilege of laying out William's white dress in the spare chamber, and the little white slippers with the bows on them, and the white gloves and the veil which William decided at the last moment not to wear, because it was "too millinery," and so, everything being in tune for it, William was to be married.

The day before the *Day* the young doctor had had a short talk with William in the morning among the roses, and a long one with the old Doctor, walking up and down beside Toyon.

"It is not for me to tell you," said the old Doctor, "who have lived in my house, and know what my daughter is to her mother and me, what it means to have her go from us even to her own home, and with one who is in every way what we would wish a son of our bodies, if we had been so fortunate as to have one, should be."

"It is very good of you to say so," said the young doctor, "and I will try to deserve it."

"When first," went on the old Doctor, following his thought, "you refused my offer of a partnership in my practice and my home, I felt hardly towards you, that you were setting up your young egotism in the face of my daughter's comfort, and taking her out of her safe home to endure the slips and chances of your inexperience, in order that you might be all to her, and cause her to forget what her parents have been. But when I made that offer I was still not quite past the weakness of recent illness, and I have realized since that I was myself selfishly trying to keep your young strength and her young spirits to prop my sinking and broken body. And, now that I am stronger, I know that I am not ready to surrender the reins to you as I should have had to do to give you the chance to stand upon your own judgment, as is the right and necessity of every young pair to do. And it has become the most comforting assurance that we have, Mrs. Caldwell and I, in this separation, that you had the wisdom to see this and the strength to resist us even in that time of yielding and tenderness, after"—the Doctor's voice broke here, as it always did when it dwelt upon that incident of the Toyon road—"after that dreadful time that brought us all together. For I hold that it is not so much passion nor the community of taste, nor yet the means to ward off the ills of poverty, that makes for a happy marriage, but to know that in every situation wherein men and women come together there is a rightness and a truth; and to have the sureness to know and to seize upon it and hold fast by it is to have the mastery of life; and to see that sureness in you is the best witness to me that I do right in trusting you with my daughter."

"I am very glad that you find it so," said George Rhewold, a flush coming in his noble, homely countenance.

"But though it is best now," said William's father, "that you live to yourselves awhile, for I have ten good years in me yet, the time will come when I must resign myself to sit by the fire and nurse my children's children on my knee; and since all I have must go to them, I should like to think that this home, as I have made it, should be to them as it has been to my daughter.

"From what you have told me, Rhewold, of your natural bent, I perceive that in time, no very long time either, you must work towards the city and the hospitals, and I should like you to keep in mind when that time comes that there is a country home for your wife and children, already steeped in associations of loving kindness and right living. For it is my belief"—Dr. Caldwell paused in his walk to tap the emphasis of his thought upon the ground—"it is my belief that here in the West, perhaps in all America, we do not take enough account of the power of our inanimate surroundings to take on the spiritual quality of the life that is lived in them, and give it off again like an exhalation, and not pains enough, when we have made such a place, to preserve it for those who come after from generation to generation; and I could, to my notion, leave my daughter no better legacy than a place so hallowed to bring up her children in. I should be greatly obliged to you, Rhewold, if you could keep that in mind—I should be greatly obliged."

"It shall be borne in mind, Doctor."

"And now, George, my boy, for I suppose I must call you that," said the old man, with his hand on the other's shoulder and a misty twinkle in his eyes, "business being over, there is a little matter of sentiment which must be between us two, and is not to be discussed with our women until a proper occasion."

"Not to be discussed with our women," reassured the young doctor, as if the phrase warmed him.

"You have been told, of course," went on Caldwell, "how, in lieu of any male issue to bear the name, William was so called for a brother of mine who died at Antietam; but you do not know, for I do not find myself able to speak freely of it even yet, how much that brother meant to me of all that was heroic, romantic, and nobly minded, beside whom I seemed always a poor, plodding sort of fellow." He paused a moment to wipe the mist of recollection from his eyes, and went on:

"It was to hold the memory of his brave, bright spirit I gave the name to my daughter to keep until she could give it to her son. But now that she has borne it these twenty-odd years, and borne it as gallantly, as you will believe, there has grown up around it an association of so much that is sweet and gay and tender that the figure of the dashing young soldier has grown quite dim beside it, and I own I should not like to have this newer sentiment about it displaced by any other."

"It is so I should feel about it," answered Rhewold, with great earnestness.

"Then you will agree with me, George, my boy"—the old Doctor covered his own seriousness with a thin veil of laughter—"that if a proper occasion should arise, as God please it may, that we are to stand by it, and not be beaten out of it, that William is a girl's name forever in our family."

"A girl's name forever in our family," repeated the young doctor, putting his own hand over the one that slipped along his arm. Then the two men shook hands, but, being men, did not look at each other, and went back to the house for what, her father declared, was positively the last appearance of Miss William Caldwell. They were very gay about it, and one of the Sterling girls, who was to be bridesmaid, put Rhewold through his paces—how he was to come down the stairs, where he was to turn, and where the minister was to stand—and at last the old Doctor sent them all away, and the house was quiet; quiet, but very cheerful still, all set about with flowers and the smell of fresh baking arising from the kitchen. They were persistently cheerful together, so that no shadow of separation should spoil the day. After supper William came and sat on her father's knee, Belshazzar purring contentedly on the other one, made her last joke with him, and had her cheeks pinched quite as if nothing were about to happen, and Mrs. Caldwell smiled at them in her Dresden-china placidity; but the shadow was there, and tracked out behind William as she went up the stairs with her candle at last; and nothing disturbed the soft summer night but the singing of Toyon, running low and small in the season's heat.

The shadow was there, and William woke to the knowledge of it at the beginning of the morning shine of the waters. She got up and found an old flowered dressing-gown left over from the day when the little room at the head of the stairs was a studio, and a pair of loose slippers of the same period, for all her newer things were packed, and looking, except for the curl papers, very much as she had before her father had been carried home from Toyon, and Dr. Rhewold had come in at the door with the wet instrument-cases and his hand up to ward off the sudden light, she crept down to her mother's room. They were awake within, for the shadow lay heavily on them, and William crept into her mother's bed, as she had used to do before ever she had grown up and thought to be married, and cried as if her heart would break.

"Oh, my dears, my dears!" she sobbed, with her arms about them; "let me lie here where I used to lie and feel so safe and happy, and hear you say that you love me—in spite of my being so ungrateful and selfish as to go and leave you—that you will always love me!" And they assured her that it was so.

"When I think," said William, "how just and patient you have been with me, my dear dad, and how loving and gentle you always are, dearest ma, and how wilful and careless I have been, and how poorly I have repaid you, I cannot bear it."

So they told her, crying, that she had been none of those things, but their dear, dear daughter, and William cried the more, and said that they must promise, when she was gone, never to think of the time when she had tried their patience and their love, but only how fond she had been, and they made no difficulty about that promise, you may be sure.

"For I always did love you," said William; "and there were times, dear ma, when it seemed more to me that I made more of a point of loving dad, and was more open about it, and I was afraid you might think I loved you less, though it was not true; and I could not understand why you never minded it. But I think I understand now, that if I should have a daughter I should want her to love—I should want her to feel that way about her father, for it would only be another way of my loving him through her. And is that why you never minded it, ma?"

"Yes, that was why," said her mother, kissing her.

"And, oh dear dad," sobbed William, "when I used to hear people say it was a pity you had no son, and I was glad it was so because there was no one to divide your love with me, you understood, did you not, dearest dad, it was because I loved you so very, very much, and not because I was a mean, selfish girl?"

"Yes, I understood," said the old Doctor. And then William cried harder than ever, and said since she was so poor a daughter as to think only of her own happiness she was afraid she would never be a good wife to George. But they left her in no doubt as to what they thought about that; and so, at last, kissed and petted, she grew quieter and fell into a little doze as if it had been a very long time ago and she had waked out of a bad dream and been taken in between them to be comforted; so they slipped away and left her.

It seemed almost no time after that it was nine o'clock, and they were bringing her breakfast in on a tray, and William was to sit up and eat it in her rosy-flowered dressing-gown in her mother's bed, for all the world, said William, as if she were just getting over the measles or the chicken-pox. Belshazzar came, leaping lightly, and purred against her shoulder. And almost before breakfast was over there was the Doctor poking his head in at the door to say that the Schallaber boy was hitching up to go for the minister, and William must really get up and dress, if she expected to be married that day.

Then there was another interlude of skurry and bustle of arriving guests and excited bridesmaids, and a great diversion, created at the last moment, by Dr. Furniss driving up wildly in a grocer's wagon, because so many people had driven out in their best clothes to see William married that there was not another conveyance to be hired in Santa Lucia.

Finally, just at noon, the crowd of guests fluttered back from the doorway and settled themselves on the lawn, when William and the young doctor, very quiet and shining-eyed, came down the pathway from the house and stood up under the rose-tree between her father and her mother. The crowd fell into silence under the bright boughs and the blossom drift, the Toyon lifted up its voice and sang joyously to the willows in the interval, and the minister began.

It was such a gay wedding, so many guests, and everybody with so much to say about it, and nobody happier in it than the slight gentleman with the professional manner and the white lock falling over his forehead to give him quite a distinguished appearance, whom everybody called "Ja—Dr. Jasper," until in a very short time he must have believed it was really his right name, that it was quite two o'clock before Lindley got around to his wife, who was sitting in a corner with a footstool, and whispered to her to come around to Jap's room as soon as she could without attracting attention, as he had something to say to her there.

She had hardly been there a minute before him when he came in with Dr. Jasper, both of them looking as if they had with difficulty detached themselves from the festivity for a business that merited some concern.

"It is nothing for you to worry about, Serena," Lindley assured her, at once; "it is only that we wanted your advice about something. Show it to her, Jap."

Dr. Jasper drew from his inner pocket a folded copy of the San Francisco *Chatterer,* and opened the page for her. The *Chatterer* was a weekly journal which throve upon the propensity for taking pleasure in believing that one is not quite so bad as one's neighbors. Consequently, if it got hold of anything about the neighbors, especially those who were rich or notable, or in any case to put it over one a little, it was printed joyously; and if there was anything at all that could be made to look bad by a way of stating it, the *Chatterer* could be counted so to state it that whatever went in gray or a little speckled came out a fast black. The Santa-Lucians were always more or less interested in the *Chatterer,* because, though they were seldom socially worth the spatterings of its envenomed ink, they had a quasi relation to the large estates that spread through the rolling oak lands about their borders, that gave a fillip to the *Chatterer's* exploitations of whatever reprobation was among them. Serena paled a little when Jap spread the page before her—the tang of that old mortification about her husband's connection with the Encinas lands still clung to any personal mention in the newspapers and clutched at her throat a little as her eyes trailed slowly down the printed column.

"Dr. Furniss bought to-day's copy on the train as he came down," said Jasper, "and called my attention to it. He thought I might know the parties. I asked him to let me have the papers, as William—Mrs. Rhewold—was a friend of the lady, and it might cast a cloud over her wedding day to know that this had gotten about here."

"The papers wouldn't get to the news-stands until noon," said Lindley. "I sent the Schallaber boy to buy every copy; that was all I could think of; but it is bound to get out sooner or later."

Serena sat startled, looking down at the page as she would have looked at some foul, slimy thing that had gotten into her friend's house and could in no wise be gotten out again, and suddenly they heard a voice calling her.

"Serena—oh,—Serena they are leaving for the station, and William is asking for you!"

The voice was followed by the figure of Julia Stairs blocking the doorway.

"What is it?" she asked, checked by Serena's face—by the startled, conscious faces of all of them. "Am I intruding? What is the matter, Serena? Is it about me? Why do you look at me so? What is in that paper? Why are you hiding it?"

She came boldly into the room, handsome and commanding. The two men looked at each other and made a movement towards the door. Julia never minded them.

"There is something in that paper about me," she insisted, towering over Serena, who was sitting on the bed. "Give it to me!"

Lindley and Jasper got themselves out of the room; it was, after all, a woman's affair; there was nothing for it now but to let her have her way. Serena gave up the paper.

"Of course, Julia, nobody will believe—" she was beginning, but Mrs. Stairs did not hear her. She read the column quite through to the end.

"Oh!" cried Julia—"oh, oh, oh!" in a kind of dry torment wrenching the paper in her hands. "Who," she cried— "who—" Then breaking out angrily: "It was that Kate Bixby—the spiteful old thing! I told Jim she would make mischief—" She bit her lip and stopped, her color coming and going with the shudderings of her chest.

Mrs. Lindley stood up quite white and shocked.

"Then it's true?" she said. "I never thought—"

"True!" cried Julia, beating her hands together, as if the occasion had taken her unawares and she was trying to beat up the proper feeling for it. "True!" The implication of the tone was denial, but the feeling, whatever it was, that should have weighted it with conviction would not come. All uncommanded, a signal of exaltation rose up and fluttered in her face. She recovered herself stiffly.

"I was sent to tell you," she said, "that William wanted you."

Serena left without a word.

XXII

From some far seaward cisterns of the air billows of fog poured down over the city of San Francisco; rebounding like smoke from the summer-heated fronts of hills, they settled in shady hollows and caught wispily at rows of trees. In the park, among the tall plantations of pine and eucalyptus they thickened in pools and shadows, overflowing into the cleared spaces and thinning luminously at touch of the sun. In such a moving mist of thought, dispelled by the warmth of passion, chilling and glooming where it touched the unsunned reality of her life, Julia Stairs took the car for the McAllister Street entrance, looking from left to right with those hasty half glances that betray the latest arrival at a point of meeting, and lost herself to view in the thick shrubbery that masked its paths. She had gone but a little way when Halford joined her; they moved on side by side without speaking.

"Let us sit here," said Halford at last, when they had come to a bench set deep in a thicket. As they sat down Julia's hand lay for a moment on the seat between them, and Halford touched it with his own.

"I was a little late," she said; "some people called."

"It does not matter. I should not have gone without seeing you."

"You had something particular to say to me?"

"Very particular." But he did not begin at once. Julia had put up her veil, and his eye roved tenderly over her face, her hands, her hair. She was looking a little wasted, but very beautiful. A fluctuant color played upon her cheek, there was a veiled brilliance in her eyes, a flamelike quality in her movements that was now a little dulled by bodily weariness. Whatever it was had made the change in her had been plainly not without loss.

"Julia," said Halford, abruptly, "why did you wear a veil to-day?" The color flooded up to her eyes.

"I," she began, confusedly—"I often wear a veil."

"The sun is not shining, nor the wind blowing, yet you wear a heavy veil."

"Has that anything to do with what you have to say to me?"

"Everything." He paused to collect himself, and began: "When you wrote me enclosing that clipping from the *Chatterer,* I wrote you in return that if your husband was seriously disturbed by it, I would see him and do whatever was demanded, but since he was not—"

"He never believed a word of it," interpolated Julia.

"—Then the best thing was to let it die a natural death. But when I saw you again at your mother's, and you told me that the thing was very much talked about in Santa Lucia, and you were made unhappy by it, I did not find myself able to undertake the measures you proposed for your relief."

"All I wished for was for you to come to the house sometimes, and to go about with us a little," protested Julia. "I thought if you could be seen there as a friend of the family, and if it could be shown that you and Antrim were on good terms, appearing not to mind what was said, then others would not mind it so much."

"I know that was what you thought you thought, Julia, and under some circumstances it would have been the best thing to do. But, as the fact was, you were asking me to sit at the table and appear as the friend of the man whose wife I loved. You would have had me there as a sort of tame cat, wholly devoted to you, touching your hand sometimes, looking into your eyes, sharing with you a sentiment and an understanding from which your husband was excluded.

"And even," Halford went on, letting the words fall slowly, "if I had found myself equal to it, it would have failed—failed," he repeated, "because every word of that infernal *Chatterer* was true."

"Oh! how can you say such things?" cried Julia, anger struggling with her hurt. "How can you say such things?"

"What did the paper say," pursued Halford, steadily, "except what you have always known: that I have always loved you, that I still love you, that we have been seen together; and to hint at what I now know to be true: that you love me. Oh, I know it was said, vulgarly, with the vilest implication, but the facts in the case were not misstated. I suppose to those who saw us going about, it was as plain as it was to us that the man we saw with Kate Bixby was an admirer of hers, though we had never seen them before, and only for an instant then. They had, at least, as long to look at us—Julia, why did you wear a veil to-day?"

"You sent for me yourself," she began, defensively. "There has been so much talk." She put the veil down now to hide the gathering tears. "I think you are very cruel to me," she said.

"No; but we must get this matter straight," he insisted, gently. "I sent for you to-day to say to you what I was afraid I should be interrupted in saying in your mother's house: that since these things are so, there is only one condition on which I can see you again, and that is that you separate yourself from your husband and marry me."

He could feel the shock with which she received this, though she made no motion and not any sound. "For though you are a good woman, Julia, and may not have given away your heart wholly, we know now ... do we not ... that I am the only man you ought to have married ... it is so ... is it not, Julia? Be honest with me, Ju, you owe me that; say that it is so."

She turned towards him, perhaps with the impulse of denial or extenuation; she raised her eyes to his, and they fell before him. A sudden flood of weakness swamped her utterly; she felt herself borne out upon it beyond the help of speech. She put out her hand, and Halford's closed over it firmly. They sat so for a moment and trembled with the shock of acknowledgment. Halford was the first to speak, soberly.

"Since that is settled," he said, "we have only to think how it can be best arranged. I shall have to be in the Philippines again soon for two or three months, but that is better for some reasons. You must see

Dr. Stairs and tell him, and then go to your mother at once. Lindley will be best to advise you about—about legal matters, unless you prefer a stranger. And as soon as it is over, I shall take you away to the Philippines, where you can forget all about it." He spoke constrainedly and slow, like a man trying to be practical in the face of a great distraction. It had a hard, ready-made sound to Julia.

"Oh," she expostulated, "it isn't as easy as that! I must have time. I must think."

"Time to be unhappy in? Time to think of the wound and dread the knife? Time to let things happen that must taint it forever for us both? Best have it over with, Ju. It isn't a pleasant situation. God knows I feel like a cad talking this way to another man's wife, but it's what I have to pay, I suppose, for being such a fool as to let you go in the first place. I feel that I have let you in for this by not understanding you better, and enforcing my claims on you. I am doing the best I can to set it right; don't make it any harder for us both."

Julia was not attending closely. Halford's business-like statement of the way to go about it had set her shocked, disordered thought face to face with the situation at Santa Lucia, with imponderable difficulties that Halford could not estimate.

"He wouldn't understand," she whispered. "He would never consent."

"I can hardly imagine that," said Halford; "but he must have the opportunity."

"He would think it wrong—wicked," she said, her mind busy with Antrim Stairs. She stood up. "I must have time to think. I must see you again."

"Of course, if you wish it, but you are taking great risks, Ju," he warned her. "We can hardly see each other without its being known. It would take very little stirring to make a nasty scandal. It is hardly possible for us to come through without something sticking to us. You owe it to me, to our future, Julia, to make the risk the least possible." He saw at once what an advantage it gave him to take this tone towards her, and pursued it steadily. Julia was not used to having her behavior impeached.

"You haven't always been discreet, Ju, and as for me, if you allow me to come, I own I haven't strength to keep away. If it is to be done at all, it had best be done quickly."

"If I could be sure you cared," whispered Julia, her breath coming short.

"Cared?" he said. "Cared!" He came close to her and looked full upon her, his face suffused with passion. He bit his lower lip to keep back what trembled on it. He ought not, he knew very well for both their sakes. He ought not to kiss her, but as he looked upon her soft cheek wasted a little by thought of him, as he saw the yielding of her figure acknowledging the power of his bodily presence he was very near the verge. They swung upon it dizzily for a moment, and Julia started back.

"Oh no; no, *no!*" she cried, and dropping her veil began to walk rapidly away from him down the path.

Mrs. Stairs had been quite right in saying to Jim Halford that her husband would not understand. He had never understood. Early in their courtship, friends had attempted to point out the probable nature of Julia's attachment to him, but his manner of receiving it had been such that soon all attempts ceased. Julia's explanation of her relation to Halford as a boy-and-girl affair, had entirely satisfied him, and he was too far sunk in the convictions of his class to entertain serious consideration of rivalry in a representative of the wholesale grocery business. Of all the circles in the world, the profession of learning, perhaps, allows the least interpenetration of extraneous life, and grounds itself most firmly on the tradition of its superior inviolateness.

Stairs had loved his wife too passionately to have any inkling how flavorless to her their marriage had become, had humbly assumed a lack in himself for any dereliction of hers, and had come to have towards her dissatisfaction a manner at once eager and propitiatory, snatching at Julia's slightest acquiescence in his interests as the evidence of their true relation, though often enough they sprang from sheer good-nature on Julia's part, and an unwillingness to wound him; and excusing her petulance and indifference as arising in disturbances of health, or a wifely sense of his situation being less than his deserts.

He had been concerned over the *Chatterer's* vulgar screed, chiefly because of his wife's annoyance. He had consulted with Grenning about it, and Grenning had assured him that the only dignified thing to do was to do nothing; the reputation of the *Chatterer* was such that merely for a statement to be printed in it was an excellent evidence that it wasn't so. Lindley's prompt action in buying up the issue had prevented most people from knowing just what had been said. But the fact of her having got into the paper at all gave a vantage for sundry small pricks and snubs which, it was considered in the college set, Julia's open indifference to its standards had deserved.

On the whole, Stairs had not regretted the incident of the *Chatterer;* it had driven Julia back into the sense of his protection; she had needed a great deal of comforting and assurance that he wholly believed in her, and would stand for her before the world, all of which had been very sweet to give. The confused and broken state of Julia's mind had made her very humble and appreciative of his generous loyalty, so that she found herself at the very moment of renewing her relations with Halford, in a position of more tender dependence upon her husband than she had ever known.

It was when she had returned from the visit to San Francisco, in which the last interview had occurred, that Mrs. Stairs realized the full difficulty of her situation. Her explanation of the circumstance, which had given rise to the *Chatterer*'s account, had been so far disingenuous that her husband was still unaware of the extent of Halford's former interest in her and his continuance in it, for she had allowed him to think that the occasion when Kate Bixby had seen them at Black Point had been the only one of their being together. She saw herself now under the necessity of initiating an irrevocable break with a man who had done her no offence but the unforgivable one of not being able to make her love him.

On the evening of her going home, Antrim had asked her, pleasantly, whom she had seen in the city. She named over their mutual acquaintances, and finally Halford.

"Do you think that was wise, Julia, just now?"

Julia caught at the occasion for resentment. "Am I to drop all the old friends I care for, just because you have brought me to live among a lot of prurient-minded old women?"

Stairs had been sitting at his writing-table adjusting his eye-shade; he got up now with it still across his forehead, and came to stand behind her chair leaning over it.

"It isn't the old women who write the personal items in newspapers," he reminded her. He took up her hand and beat it lightly between his own. "Such a handsome woman as you are, Julia—and Mr. Halford was once in love with you—"

"Was?" slipped from her, sharply. "Is." She caught her breath for a moment, but the shot had gone wide.

"Well, so am I," he admitted. He bent as if to kiss her. Julia jerked away her hand impatiently.

"Do take that thing off your eyes, Antrim, it gives you such a color. And don't tease me tonight. I can't bear it."

He took it off with the propitiatory haste of one diverting a child about to work itself up to the point of tears, and blinked at her anxiously.

"What can't you bear, Julia?"

"You, *you!*" was the thought that leaped in her, but she controlled it. "Everything," she said, "everybody—here! The things people talk about, the things they do, the narrowness, the self-righteousness. Oh!"—she stood up and stretched her arms—"I have said it all so many times. I hate it so—I hate it so! It seems as if you will never understand." Indeed, it seemed he never would. He picked up his eye-shade and went back to his writing.

"You are tired, Julia," he said; "you had better go to bed."

Always, after any outburst of his wife's dissatisfaction, Stairs renewed the attention and tenderness that was so much more difficult to be borne, as she felt it rendered a real understanding between them more impossible, and augmented her want of respect for him, as it gave definiteness to the impression that he did not sufficiently feel the seriousness of their inharmony. But, in fact, he felt it all too deeply; the only way in which Antrim Stairs could bear the things his wife said to him was to suppose that she did not mean them. Accordingly, he persuaded her to take a nerve tonic and to have help in the kitchen. There were days when, removed from the sustaining power of Halford's presence and wearied of her own struggles, Julia conceived herself beyond caring what became of the rest of her life, and yielded to her husband's solicitations with a gentleness that spun a fine web of tender obligation needing to be broken again thread by thread. There were times when, under the influence of a meeting or a letter from Jim, she flamed secretly with a force that gathered up all the tattered garment of her attraction for him and made it whole again. The truth was that Julia lacked the courage to accept the responsibility of her situation between her lover and her husband, and was merely trying to beat up such a storm as should carry her clear of its harassments and throw her into Halford's arms in such a case as that she should seem to herself not able to help it.

She saw Halford for the last time just before he sailed, and tried him to the utmost with all the charm she knew so well how to use with him, to get such assurance of his love as justified her to herself, without finding the strength to accept his suggestion that she should take her mother into her confidence, definitely concluding her relation to her husband by letter.

"I shall be back in three or four months for the last time," he advised her. "If you manage it right, you can be free by that time, and I can take you with me." That was before the law of the interlocutory decree, and neither of them anticipated then, or at any other time, the thing that would happen. They spoke softly, for all the stir of grief and passion that was between them, not to disturb Mrs. Maybury, who was up-stairs nursing a cold she had got by a practical demonstration of the truth, that draughts would not hurt her if she only insisted upon it sufficiently.

"I should have liked to have managed it differently for both our sakes," he said; "but I cannot leave you here to endure the talk and the annoyance. Have some consideration for me, Julia. God! do you think it is pleasant for me to think of your going back to be that man's wife even for a day? I don't see how you stand it."

"Oh, I can't! I can't!" cried Julia, with a rush of tears. "You don't understand! You don't understand!" Indeed, there was no way in which she could make him understand the pull of home ties, the obligation of her husband's generosity, the pitiful wish to be thought well of, which, in the beginning, had betrayed her into this marriage, all the entanglement of temperament and habit from which she had no skill to free herself; beyond all, the feeling she had that since her love for Halford involved the best there was of her, that she ought somehow to come into it rid of the sense of blame which must follow upon the violent rupture of her marriage.

"Oh, I wish we could just go away together, Jim, and that be the end of it!"

"I wish we could, darling, but I would be more of a beast and a cad than I think myself now if I let you do that. Come, promise me, Julia, and say good-bye." But the promise was slow in coming, and he did not wait for it. He swept her to him in a gust of tenderness, and left her kissed and stunned.

Once Halford was away, Julia let her matters drag on for a month or six weeks; but as the opening of the fall semester approached she felt that whatever was to be done should be done before the closing in of the college life centred attention upon herself again. She found her opportunity at last in the question as to whether, for several reasons, they had not better move to a larger house which had been offered them.

"You don't seem to take any interest, Julia. I wish you would make up your mind," suggested Stairs.

Julia perceived that here was an opening, and took her courage with both hands.

"I have made up my mind," she said. "I shall go to my mother's this winter."

They were sitting, after dinner, in the dusk of their tiny porch. In the room behind, a lamp burned dimly under its green shade. She could see her husband's correct profile against the block of light, and the thin shoulders with the slight professional stoop.

"But only—" he began, and checked himself as if he felt the imponderable quality of disaster coming upon him through the dark. "Do you mean to leave me?"

"Nothing could be worse than going on as we are," she said—and felt. Than the unhappy wish to rule by the personal quality rather than reasonableness, the necessity of her temperament to be justified by her emotions, rising insatiable in her—

"Oh, Antrim, Antrim, let me go! It is all a mistake; it has always been a mistake! I have tried, and the more I try the more I see how mistaken it is. Let me go! Let me go, and I will bless you for it."

She could see the slight clutching of her husband's throat against the dim-lit window, as if he swallowed down her speech with difficulty.

"But I don't understand," he managed, at last. "What do you wish?"

"My freedom. Just to go free of it all and forget it." She could see plainly the alteration in his face even in silhouette, and hardened herself against a wish to comfort him.

"Let me go," she urged, "and after awhile we can get a divorce, and each of us marry somebody more suitable."

"Julia, Julia!" burst from Stairs. He got upon his feet unsteadily. She could feel him staring down at her. "A divorce … I do not believe in it! You are my wife, nothing could make you not that. How could you think I would wish to marry any other woman?"

"Ah," she interjected, bitterly, "you never think I may wish to marry another man!"

He stiffened; she heard him fumbling at the back of the chair as if for support.

"And do you?" he asked, at last.

"Yes," she admitted.

"Who?" After another inconsequent interval the question broke thinly with scarce breath to carry it from his lips. "Tell me who it is."

"Jim Halford." It was out now, and she must stand by it. A stinging excitement ran in all her veins. Some one crossing the campus whistled a light, incongruous air; the tune and the smell of the damp mignonette from the garden beds remained forever after charged with the power to suspend the breath for an instant's heart sinking. Julia, on the step below, clasped her arms about her knees awaiting judgment. It came coldly at last, and digged a pit into which her hopes dropped with dizzying sickness.

"If you cannot manage to live with me, Julia, I suppose you must leave me; but a divorce … no … I will never help you to it."

XXIII

Santa Lucia invariably spoke of itself as a Christian community
as against East Santa Lucia, where the Church and College influence
gave way a little to a less complex worldliness. If Julia and Antrim Stairs
had lived in Santa Lucia, and had been connected with a newspaper
or the banking business, they might have come through with their
difficulties with something less of disaster. Letting alone the alleviations
of distraction in a freer social living, they might have talked over the
difficulties with their friends, and got such aid as society ought to afford
to a social adjustment.

In East Santa Lucia there was the beginning of the perception
of marriage as the living spring of social well-being, whose waters
must purify themselves or pollute the stream of life. In Santa Lucia
proper, marriage was the holy state of matrimony, as if there resided
in the words pronounced over it some mysterious quality as of blessed
oils, or of Ganges water, to sanctify the union of man and woman
whatever unsuitability of mind or temperament or cold indulgence
or mean subservience went to it. It was, therefore, not to be talked of
openly, especially if it were unhappy, but to be shied at, to be relegated
to conversational holes and cupboards, where it acquired a flavor of
uncleanness from want of air; and as if the mere weight of such misery
were not enough to be borne, the odium of it was made to be felt more

keenly by the unhappy couple who were caught with it on their hands.
It is evident that something like this must occur in every community
devoting itself to sectarian instruction. The college of Santa Lucia
provided no course of lectures in successful living, but it would have
been chary of exhibiting in its Professor of Biology an instance of the
failure to maintain his marriage, which is, perhaps, as near as most
schools get to admitting that the study of biology ought to make for
successful living, even though it does not.

So islanded by the sense of their community that whatever was
the matter with their marriage, nothing must be said about it, Julia and
Antrim Stairs were no more able to solve their difficulties by themselves
than are most people; but few confidences as they were able to give,
the stir of their unhappiness made itself apparent under an outward
conformity like the bubbling of an infernal essence in a crystal vase.
A presage of the construction that might be put upon what she had
in mind to do, set up in Julia an attitude of defiance to the accepted
convention of the place that drew around her a ring of edged comment.

Serena's had been the only intimacy of Julia's life in Santa Lucia,
but she was kept from confidences not only by Serena's condition,
which seemed to exempt her from complicity in her friend's anxieties,
but by the certainty, which she had entertained without jealousy, of the
closer parallel between husband's ideals and tastes and Mrs. Linaiey's,
whose progress from young ladyism had been too slow, her new freedom
of practical adjustment yet too much weighted by bodily frailty and
insufficient means, for her not to regard the salaried confines of Julia's
life as a safe and comfortable groove in which to fulfil her function of
living. But Serena had come to be so far superior to her antipathies,
and so near to discovering that behind Evan's utilitarian view, that
had gloomed across her early married life as the shadow of an essential
offensiveness, there was a perception of the ultimate benefit much larger
than lay in any observance of traditional sanctity, that when he was first
to declare that the only possible solution of the Stairs's marriage lay in
divorce, she did not dispute it, but merely asked him why.

"Because it isn't effective as it is," he declared, "and nobody is
so stupid as to maintain any other kind of partnership when it isn't.
Marriage is a sort of partnership for the business of living, and this
one isn't doing business, so to speak. It is hindering Stairs in his work

and making him miserable, and if you look at it that it's her part of the business to make him happy and have children, it isn't enabling her to do that."

"But if she did it, anyway—had children, and made him as happy as she could—wouldn't that settle it?"

"No; for if she did she would have a right to expect something back, and whatever it is Julia wants to make her happiness, it is perfectly evident she isn't getting it. I haven't a doubt that if one of the parties to an unhappy marriage could make an everlasting martyr of herself, the other one could be kept ecstatic; the devil of it is that they can't make up their minds which one. But nobody has any right to pretend that such a one-sided arrangement is anything more than a means of keeping the marriage going rather than a justification of it."

"But for the sake of society—"

"Well, if you can see any good of society in the Stairs's marriage, except of its being good for a mighty lot of gossip, I wish you'd put your finger on it. You said yourself that you could not take any pleasure in going there any more, for all they're so polite. It's too much like picnicking on top of a volcano. They are not the kind to throw plates about; they're too well bred; but at least if they did that, you could see 'em coming and dodge 'em. As it is now, you can scarcely make the most innocent remark there without seeming to put your foot in it."

All of which sounded so sensible that Serena did not quite know how to answer it, and was not yet convinced, not being entirely free from the traditional notion that marriage, however wisely you might consider it beforehand, once it was accomplished was not a thing to be sensible about. She felt cautiously back along the thread of her own experience.

"But, Evan, when we were first married we didn't always agree about things."

"Ah, but that's different," he insisted, beaming upon her; "we had to get acquainted, of course, but we belong."

Did they? She remembered a time when she had believed despairingly that they never would, when she had thought her husband excluded from a vast block of her aspiration and ideals, those ideals which she shared with Antrim Stairs, and their only chance of happiness lay in her capacity to shear away the best part of her. Certainly she belonged to this new epoch of practical sufficiency to the exigencies of living, but now was the time to show him that her success in it was grounded in an idealism which, though the habit of esteeming it inestimably finer than anything Evan had yet offered her, stayed with her, seemed suddenly to become tenuous and eluded her grasp. To save herself a sudden sense of check and floundering, she turned the talk upon the point of wondering how much Jim Halford had to do with Julia's unhappiness, or whether he had anything to do with it.

"I hope so," said her husband, cheerfully; "if Julia can escape into a happy marriage—if they both could—it would save them from the feeling that they had marred each another's lives. As it is, they are spoiling two good marriages in the effort to patch up a bad one."

That such an effort would not be a success Julia was more convinced every day. Stairs could not be brought to admit a divorce, could not so much as admit its being discussed between them. A failure of imagination, perhaps, prevented his understanding from her meagre statement, what Halford was to her, and by no reach of hers could she understand how the mere word cried upon him with a hundred tongues of noisy vulgarity and hissing shame. She supposed she would have to deal only with his fondness, and instead she had put her hand on generations of stiff-necked Presbyterianism and the stubborn male resistance to the public acknowledgment of his failure to hold her allegiance.

She had written to Halford and heard once from him, but the letters crossed in mid-ocean, and as the days went by with no sustaining word from the outside, she sank into a kind of lassitude of mind, the reaction from the emotional struggle, which Stairs mistook for submission. He acknowledged it by an accession of husbandly attention which redoubled in her a desperation of effortless desire for escape.

Often her misery would expend itself in long attacks of heavy tearless sobbing, from which he would seek to draw her by caresses until, in very weariness, she yielded to his comforting—a yielding which he invariably mistook for the renewal of his ascendency over her, leading to a resumption of their marital relations. Stairs thought the hope of a child might resolve their difficulties, and could not understand why Julia set her mind against it. But though she understood at last that she might undergo even that for a man if she loved him, it was beyond her, in the absence of a justifying passion, to have suffered it for any other sake. It was the chief of her bitterness that while she reached out for the inestimable treasure of life, she must seem only to flee its obligations. In one of these moments of utter abandonment to the misery of her situation, she found among some chemicals in her husband's study a vial labelled poison, and was taken with its subtle suggestion of relief. She hid the bottle among her own things and immediately forgot it, though the consciousness of it at the back of her mind, or of the possibilities of instant release it opened for her, created a suspension of despair that lightened almost like hope.

She had heard nothing from Halford since her letter, and had determined nothing about him in her mind, except that she would see him. When she found in the papers notice that the steamer upon which he was to return from the Philippines was expected in, she told Antrim simply that she must go up to town. She watched him covertly, and saw that he did not once in her presence turn to the page of shipping news, nor exhibit any knowledge of Halford's whereabouts, though he gave evidence of relief when she went without her trunk and no preparations for being away more than a few days.

Mrs. Maybury, by the way of a long series of imaginary ailments, had sunk at last into a gentle, enjoyable decline, of which the chief interest was the taking of her temperature, and had floated out of the storm of her daughter's life into a backwater of ineffectualness which made any appeal to her an absurdity. Besides, Julia had made up her mind not to commit herself to anything until she had seen Halford. He had received her letter, and knew how matters stood between her and her husband, but he did not understand.

"I have felt like a cad," he protested, "plotting to take you away from him, but I am not mean enough to understand how he can wish to keep you whether or no."

Julia felt herself obliged to enter a defence.

"It isn't meanness, it's righteousness. He thinks divorce a sin, he has thought so for generations. He would have to get the divorce himself. I haven't any grounds, and he simply won't do it."

"How much have you told him, Ju?" Halford insisted on knowing, suspecting her weakness.

"Everything." She laughed shortly and bitterly. "He isn't jealous; it isn't in his constitution. And he is so sure the things he wants are intrinsically better than the things I want. He thinks I will come back to him if only he is kind and patient with me." And, after a pause, she added: "I suppose I will."

"Julia!"

"Yes," she affirmed, drearily, "that's what I wanted to say to you. I love you as I never have, never could love anybody else; but since I can't have you, it doesn't seem worth while to tear my life up by the roots; and you do take root in five years of married life. Antrim is kind, deadly kind. The whole atmosphere of the place takes hold on me like a creeping numbness. There's no facing a real situation: what you have to face is a standard of behavior; everything that doesn't come up to it is kept dark. There's nobody speaks out, nobody *feels* out; after a little I shall be like myself, and then it won't matter."

Nothing could shake her out of that attitude in their first interview; she cried a little in deprecation of Jim's vehemence, but she could not be persuaded to try any other point of view. And then the moment the door was closed on him she experienced the accession of tenderness which a woman has for a man she is interested in, immediately on parting from him, and wrote him a little note which brought him back the next day in a mood of rebellion.

"You don't understand," she kept on insisting, in regard to her husband's attitude. "It isn't only me he would lose, he would lose standing. Maybe in the big schools it isn't so bad, but in a church school a divorce ... wouldn't be acceptable."

Halford sat opposite her, tracing the pattern of the carpet with his stick, looking down doggedly.

"There's one cause, I suppose—"

"Yes," she admitted, at last.

"Then give him the cause," Halford dared.

"We wouldn't care for our happiness if we had to take it that way!" she cried, instantly retreating from a position she was not prepared to hold. "You said yourself we shouldn't care for it that way— not that way, Jim." She raised her face to his as he bent above her, leaned her head upon his breast, and cried very bitterly.

The more Julia protested that since she could not have her freedom honorably she must go back to Santa Lucia and make the best, or the worst, of what she found there, the more Halford promised himself that at whatever cost he must get her away from a situation that crippled her faculties and seemed likely to unseat all that he found in her desirable. He justified himself in Stairs's selfish binding of her unwilling soul, but in truth his passion had reached a point where it needed no justification to himself. He had come up from the islands hungering for her as his wife, and when that sort of hunger reaches a certain stage in a man he will not reckon with the means of satisfying it. Secure that she loved him, he was yet able to understand that Julia's weakness was not to be able to free herself alone from the dread of wagging tongues and the odium of divorce. Well, it should be his part to assume that weakness with the rest. He had no definite plan as yet, but asked merely that since this was all he was ever to have of her, he might have as much as the time allowed. He knew enough of women, though his knowledge had never served him with Julia before, to understand that she was never so near yielding as at the point of protesting she would not yield.

On the morning after her formal and passionate renunciation of him, Halford had asked Mrs. Stairs to drive in the park with him. It was a lowering day, broken and freshened by a sea wind. Vagrant showers loitered about the bay like urchins spitting and quarrelling in the street; whenever the sun thrust a long-rayed arm among them they scattered and ran. The park, except for some draggled custodians, was deserted. The landscape swam in the deep blueness of wet shadows, the cloud-wrack seemed to move and make a little isolation for them. Now and then it opened, and the vista of Tamalpais and the bay seemed to wink upon them like a solemn eye. Sitting beside Halford, Julia was quiet and comforted. She tucked her hand under his arm, and he pressed it to him; their eyes met with the lingering confident tenderness of a married pair. They said, how lovely it was, to have this quiet hour together for the last—at least, Julia said it was, and Jim did not contradict her.

"It's only your saying so that makes it a last time," he reminded her.

"Don't, Jim!" she begged, her lips pitiful; she made a little indefinable movement half nestling, half appealing. Halford shut his teeth and drove straight westward until the wind had a strong tang of the sea. About a quarter of an hour after, they ran into a fringe of a shower, which closed about them as they turned. He drove rapidly a few moments, and suddenly brought the team about.

"No use trying to get out of it," said Halford. "There's a place here where I can take you." A little later they came out of the park entrance, where a staring, vulgar bill-board announced "The Casino." Julia made a movement of protest.

"Not there, Jim, not there!"

"Nonsense, you will get wet through in five minutes. Oh, it's not a place for the Santa-Lucians, I suppose, but I know men who take their wives there. Put down your veil if you're afraid. There will be nobody there in a day like this."

They had to bend their heads before the shower, and run to make the shelter of the house. As Halford had said, there was nobody about. A swollen, brute-faced man came out to take the horses; nothing stirred within. The place looked to be a second-rate café in morning disarray; a vast expanse of window opened on the blank, leaden mist, barred by drip of the rain from unguttered eaves. Julia shivered with the cold and nervous apprehension. They heard the laughter of another party driven up without, seeking shelter. The noise evoked a pale, flaccid attendant, who asked them what they wished.

"A room with a fire," demanded Halford.

His peremptory movement and the irruption of the gay party drove Julia forward. Halford interposed his heavy shoulders behind as they went up the stair, shouldering her into a room that had a window opening seaward, now curtained darkly by the storm. Julia remained standing with her veil on until the attendant had lighted the cheap gas grate and brought a drink which Halford ordered. As the firelight glinted on the gilt and varnish one by one the features of the room—the tawdry paper, the florid pictures, the bed against the wall—leaped out of the gloom, and the significance of them pricked themselves on Julia's numbed sense.

"Why have you brought me here?" she demanded.

"What do you care where you are so long as I am with you?" Halford answered, boyishly, irradiant with suppressed excitement. "Drink this; you will be having a chill."

Julia drank mechanically. Indeed, the chill was upon her so that she could scarce command herself to speak. Halford caught her hand as she gave back the glass.

"How cold you are!" he cried, shocked. He took the damp outer wrap from her and turned up the fire. A sense of mastery seemed to emanate from him and fill the room; it was part of the warmth of the grate and the revivifying wine. Somewhere in the house a piano banged, and a voice rose impudently in a lively song. Outside the wind veered suddenly and flung the rain with a sharp splash against the pane; it struck against Julia's spirit, sick and empty with the passion of denial. She started at the sound and broke piteously into tears. Halford came comfortingly and drew her down upon his knee.

XXIV

On October 3d Antrim Stairs was to lecture before the Ladies'
Club at Dos Palos. It was fifteen miles by the county road, so that he set
out to drive there early in the morning, meaning when the lecture was
over to drive on to a certain orchard where a new sort of scale insect was
making ravages, and when he had looked into it to get home at the end
of the following day.

He was feeling rather cheerful over the expedition, and would
have liked to have Julia go with him, though he did not feel equal to
urging her, once he had asked and she refused. She had seemed so much
more tractable and at ease since her return from her mother's two weeks
before, that he dreaded any renewal of the storm and the stress of the
summer. Knowing nothing of Halford's movements, and not being in
a position either to seek or to hear news of him, he did not know even
of his having come up from the Philippines, nor of his intended return
there on the very day of driving out to Dos Palos. Julia had been half
right in saying to Halford that he was not jealous, and wholly wrong in
naming the reason for it, which lay chiefly in his poverty of the stuff of
human passions. All that region in which his wife and Halford walked
amid thorns and tears was an unexploited country to him, and a kind of
male pride not to admit defeat stood to strangle back his instincts. He

found it easier to ascribe the errancy of his wife's fancy to nerves rather than to inquire too closely of them what it might mean.

There was a phrase risen somewhere in the exigencies of school life, and become the usage of student slang, that exactly described his state: Antrim Stairs had not "come through." Neither his mind nor his figure had filled out to its expectation. The whole personality of the man remained forever screened and dim behind the insulating formality of his professional attitude. The blind struggle of humanness and ideality in him brought to the surface nothing but the rooted determination to keep his wife and hold by her. He thought it a conviction of righteousness, and it might have been. Nevertheless, he was feeling inspirited by the day and the circumstances of Julia's new quiescence as he drove out to Dos Palos. There was a rich smell of apples in the county road that suited very well with the turquoise sky and the yellowing orchards underneath. There was a winey tang to the cool morning that raised his spirit to the point of whistling softly as he drove. At the ranch house of Mira Monte they told him that the Marysville bridge, which crossed a steep barranca ahead of him, had been burned two days before, and that the best way to reach Dos Palos was to return and take the local train to Marysville, driving out from there with no more than half an hour's loss of time. Accordingly, he set back on the road, arriving at Santa Lucia a little after noon. He thought to have lunch at his own house and telephone to the ladies at Dos Palos the cause of his delay. If there was anything abroad in the clear splendor of the noon to warn him of what he was to find as he drew towards his own door, he did not meet it. The incident of his turning back upon the road was charged with no new and unusual meaning to Antrim Stairs.

It was just when she was feeling strongest, directly after luncheon, that Mrs. Lindley chose to walk out in the golden flood that poured on all the world and take the new baby to see Julia. Serena had not been so far from home since it came. She walked bareheaded, and felt her strength given back from the elastic earth. She raised her face to the pale vault lifted so high above the world by the wondrous clarity of air, and the gilded leaves of the poplar whirled down through it and touched her cheek. She walked on, pleasantly conscious of the weight of the soft body and the cuddling of the small head in the blessed hollow of her shoulder.

Serena found the back of the house closed, and went around to the front, remembering that Dr. Stairs was to have been away, and surmising too late that Julia might have gone out for the day. The house presented that appearance, with the blinds all drawn, but the front door was a little ajar. Serena called, "Julia, Julia!" There was no answer, but a stir within that encouraged her to push the door wide open, and to see Dr. Stairs seated at his desk in the room which opened directly off the entrance hall. She came forward quickly, and asked him where Julia was and what was amiss.

"Gone," he said; "left me." He spoke slowly, with great care, as though he felt himself at a distance from her and endeavored to make himself plain. "The bridge was burned. I came back ... and there was her letter." He held it in his hand as though reading from it, but his eyes went beyond it. Gone where? With whom? Serena did not know whether she had asked the questions or if it was to the leaping thought he answered: "Halford. They leave for the Philippines to-day. She has been gone an hour."

It was evident he had found the note immediately on entering, and had been sitting so ever since; his driving-gloves were still in his hand.

"I saw the bus for the San Marco local drive up," murmured Serena, vaguely. "I wondered—" The trivial circumstance seemed to be so little to the point that it trailed off, and then her lively instinct leaped to the conclusion. "She went out on the 11.45 to meet the Monterey Express at San Marco," she said. "It isn't due until two, even if it is on time, and it generally isn't. You can get to her in time if you drive out to the Roble Park trolley. Oh, it's not too late!" She put down her baby and came up to him, her eyes widened with the horror of the offence. "Do you understand? She is still at San Marco. You can save her."

Stairs looked at her, blank frustration in his gaze.

"I think she loves him," he said, as if he thought that might have something to do with the case, though what he did not quite know.

"All the more reason," Serena insisted, "why you should not let her throw away her chance of happiness. If she must go to him, at least let it not be with shame and disgrace. Ah, what have you done to her to drive her to a thing like this?" Her quick sympathies had run from his apathy to the woman.

"You, too!" said Stairs.

"Oh, go to her!" urged Serena. "Julia is a good woman. I know she is! She must have been crazy with misery and hopelessness to think of such a thing."

"She has left me for another man. She wanted a divorce, and I refused it to her. Would a divorce make it any better now?"

Serena wrung her hands. "If you wait to argue about it now it will be too late to consider."

"It will not make it any better now," insisted Stairs, like a man determined to have it out with himself, "because it was all wrong from the first. She said I did not love her or I would wish her to go where she was happiest, and that was true. I have been sitting here with this letter, knowing what I feel, and despising myself for it, and I know that it is true. She says here"—with every reference to the letter he shook it before him, as though it were the warrant for what he was about to do—"here, that I never cared for what she really was, but only for what I tried to get her to be, and that is true. I was infatuated with the shell of her, but the soul that I insisted on reading into her and the mind that I wished to arouse in her were the mind and soul of you."

He made this extraordinary statement without passion, more as if he drove it home to a slow and unwilling intelligence.

"Why was it, when I fancied myself most in love with her, I carried my work to you, if it was not true?" he went on, working it out steadily. "Why, when I moved into this house and established my married life, did I regard it as a fault in her and a disappointment to myself for her to like what she liked and be what she naturally was, except that all my thought and interest were centred in another ideal which was personified in you?"

Serena's baby whimpered, and she quieted it with little caressing pats and crooning noises, but her gaze never left Stairs; one might have supposed, to look at her, that the quieting gesture and comforting sounds were for him.

"Why was it," the man persisted, as being sure of her assent if she would only hear him out, "when my wife told me that she wished to marry Halford, that I endured to hear it and still held to her, except that I never cared for the soul of her, and was satisfied with the shell. And why have I never experienced the natural jealousy of a husband until now, when he has put out his hand to take the body of her who has so long held her heart? Let her go," he said, the natural heat of a man rising in him and getting him on his feet at last. "Let her go! Damn him!"

"Dr. Stairs! Dr. Stairs!"—alarmed at him, and only bent upon her point—"you do not know what you say, or if you do it is all the more reason why you should go at once and save her from what you are in part to blame for." Serena stood before him, holding the baby against her breast, as though it were a buckler against whatever was aimed at it. "If it is true," she panted, "that I—that any of us remotely or unconsciously are to blame for this dreadful thing, you owe it to us to save her from it."

"For what shall I save her—for Halford?" He laughed shortly.

"Yes," said Serena, stoutly, "if he loves her best." She was instantly afraid when she saw him blanch under it, but in a moment she began again: "Listen to me. She is there at San Marco. There is still time. If you let her go in this way nothing you can do will ever make it right again. There will be bitterness and remorse come of it. There will be scandal and disgrace reflected on her, and you, and your work. You must bring her home and settle it between you in a quieter way. Now go, or it will be too late." From whatever source the instinct for action had sprung she convinced herself. He moved before her urgency, and she pressed upon him, shut the doors, and hung the key in the accustomed place.

"And, Dr. Stairs," she interjected, "I wouldn't say anything to Julia about my knowing—at least, not right away." She was not sure he heard her or that he really meant to go to San Marco; she was not sure of anything, except that he drove away in the right direction.

When Mrs. Lindley reached home she was taken with so violent a fit of trembling that the maid was alarmed, and would have sent for Lindley had she been allowed. The shock that had galvanized Antrim Stairs into a live perception of his situation had served, like the cannons fired to bring up the bodies of the drowned, to float to the surface of her own consciousness secret defections she would rather not have looked upon. If it was true what Stairs had protested of his failure to adjust, was her earlier married unhappiness in any better case? Had she not passed over what her husband inherently was, denying him the right to be just that, because of her preoccupation with an ideal prefigured dimly in the personality of Antrim Stairs? In the flash struck out by the crash of his disaster she saw the swimming mote of her own priggishness that made of her adaption to Evan's point of view a condescension and an abandonment. In the drowned, flaccid body of her young sufficiency she perceived the odor of offence.

Lindley found his wife hysterical when he reached home that evening, readily accounted for by all that had occurred in the afternoon. It was a great relief to her to know that her husband approved of what she had rather imposed than suggested for Stairs.

"Of course," he said, "it ought to be done respectably; if it can be," he added. "Halford is a decent chap—though men who elope with other men's wives don't usually marry them. Stairs must have made an awful mess of it to bring it to such a pass."

Now that the crying need of doing something was past, Serena had the impulse of the untempted woman to blame Julia. The very nearness of the offence gave her a sense of implication. She felt she should never be able to meet Mrs. Stairs without the wish to do or to say something to clear her skirts, but having committed herself to Julia's return, she was palpitatingly anxious to have it accomplished.

The shadow of their neighbor's tragedy hung over the household as the night closed. They clung together, gave and demanded renewed assurance of confidence, spoke and moved softly as those who have been brought suddenly to contemplate the separations of death not their own. By unspoken assent they spent the evening in their own room, which overlooked the Stairs's. About six there was a smoke rising in the cottage, but it told little. Had Stairs been in time for the train, had Julia made a scene, or had Stairs known how to control a quiet compliance? Lindley thought so.

"Women like Julia aren't so much afraid of doing things that are thought wrong, but they are mighty afraid of being found out in them."

They saw the light at last in the cottage, low and reddened by the lamp, but it spelled no news. Serena walked to and fro in her room, and could not be quieted; Lindley, fearing she would get no sleep in her anxious state, went out to reconnoitre. At the end of half an hour he came back blinking, and drenched with dew.

"She's there," he announced; "the blind was up, and I could see her sitting by the fire. I couldn't see her face—only her skirts, and her hands clinched on the arms of the chair, and Stairs sitting by the lamp. There they sat, each on his own side of the fire, and neither spoke nor stirred. You would have thought there was something dead in the house and they were sitting up with it."

"I'd give a lot," he added, as they went to bed, "to know what happened at the station."

"Oh, I wouldn't," said Serena, fervently—"I wouldn't know for worlds! I never want to know any more of it than I know now." She did not tell him then, she never told him, what had escaped Stairs in the moment of his unseating; the quality of that deprecation was too elusive to be freed in speech. He thought her distress very natural and womanly, and loved her for it.

XXV

There was very little time in which anything could happen when Stairs arrived at San Marco Junction, for the train was within a moment of arriving. Even as he passed through the waiting-room in his search for his wife it drew up stertorously, and the crowd of East-going passengers debouched upon the platform, obliterating the movements of half a dozen departing Santa-Lucians. Mrs. Stairs, anxious not to be engaged in talk with the between-train loiterers, had walked far out along the track, and had just reached the edge of the platform again when the train came in. Stairs saw her in time to cut in between her and the rear car, and as the impact of the crowd threw them together the shock of surprise deprived her of all wit. She halted, went white, choked, threw out her hands as the strangled do; he drew her arm through his and deflected her course towards the station; a group of chatting Santa-Lucians, come up from their summer cottages at Pacific Grove and Santa Cruz, closed about them. Mrs. Mathisen poked at her with her parasol over Antrim's shoulder.

"Drive back with me in the surrey," she urged. "I've been wanting to see you about my musicale on Wednesday."

Julia's self-possession was coming back to her, and her color with it. "I am leaving for San Francisco—" she began; but Stairs had had a longer time to prepare for it.

"Mrs. Stairs was going to her mother," he put in, politely, "but she has just learned that it is unnecessary."

"Oh! Is your mother worse? I hadn't heard." Mrs. Mathisen was not without perception. She melted back into the crowd that swarmed upon itself and produced Mrs. Murry-Felton. This lady, falling upon her dear Dr. Stairs in the interest of the Saturday Morning Club, swept them to the edge of the platform in a gush of enthusiasm. Julia struggled to free her arm from her husband's, and swayed against his shoulder.

"What is the matter with Mrs. Stairs? Is she going to faint?" Mrs. Murry-Felton's high-keyed exclamation arrested a ring of concerned friendly faces. The departing crowd streamed from them like tide from a rock, and left Julia stranded in their midst. Through the reeling of her sense slid the black phantom of the outgoing train.

"We'll miss the trolley," declared Mrs. Murry-Felton; "they are waving us to come on. Help, Henry." Mr. Murry-Felton's shoulder being thus brought into requisition, Julia was half lifted to a seat in the crowded car. She had not said a word since her husband had cut her off so neatly; only by the fluctuation of her color could he discover how she flung from wave to wave of anger, mortification, and despair. It was quite four o'clock when they came to their own house, and she had not spoken. At the edge of their porch Julia drew back.

"I can't—"she began. Stairs was just in time to catch her. She came out of her swoon at last in her own room, and as the familiar objects swam out of the mist of obliviousness to advise her of failure, they pricked her like the pangs of the resuscitating drowned. Late in the afternoon the bar of the westering sun striking through the window aroused her. She sat up and assayed to arrange the disorder of her dress.

"I must send a message," she said.

"I cannot leave you." All this time Stairs sat by the bed, and tried not to think what to do. "There is the telephone." It stood upon his writing-table, and, not to seem to spy upon her, Stairs went into the other room when she sat down before it. Though the door was closed between them, he could hear that she did not call for the Western Union, as he had expected, but asked instead for Long Distance. After a little he heard her asking for San Francisco, the Palace Hotel; then a shorter interval and Halford's name; then a smothered ejaculation or two, and the click of the receiver dropping into place. She sat still before it a long hour, but nothing reached her over the vibrant wire. Stairs prepared food for her, but she did not eat. He built a fire in the grate, for the nights were falling cool, and brought a shawl for her shoulders, but she let it slip mindlessly to the floor.

"Do lie down, Julia," he begged; "I will call you if you're wanted."

She answered only with an inarticulate murmur of negation. Her head sank back against the chair for weariness, but her hands clinched strongly at its arms. It grew dark without, and the noises of the neighborhood died; still Julia sat there in the attitude of expectation, and still no sound came out of the mysterious black cylinder. Her eyes closed at times, but Stairs could see that it was merely a tenser way of waiting, and if any movement of his or any distraction from without drew off her attention for an instant, she looked hurriedly back at the 'phone, as if fearful lest the message had come and gone in the instant of her wandering. Stairs sat down in the chair opposite, and felt his soul drawn with the tension of her anxiety. Why had Halford not resorted to it himself upon discovering Julia's non-arrival, or had he done so while they were still on their way from San Marco? Stairs had an impression, almost as vivid as a sense perception, of the alarmed and urgent ringing of the bell through the empty house. It seemed as if the thing must have occurred to Julia at the same instant by the sudden heaving of her bosom and the convulsive clutching of her hands. He had not known at what hour Halford's steamer was to clear; he was not sure that Julia knew, and hesitated to ask. They waited. So intent were the thoughts of both upon the same matter it seemed to create a visible presence in the room: first the hotel, with its cavernous galleries of stale air and stairways ascending from the open court like the spirals of a shell, and the roar of the city without, made faint and hollow, like the sound of the sea in a shell; then the steamer, swinging at the dock, the roll of the bay in the flat light of evening, the looming of the Heads; then the black water, shot with pointed, bright reflections of the steamer lights. Nine o'clock came, ten—there was no sound but the dropping of the ashes on the hearth—eleven; at the sound of its striking, suddenly Julia's strength gave way, her head went down with a gasping shudder on the table before her.

"You'll hear nothing to-night, Julia," said Stairs, not unkindly. "You had better go to bed." With a little broken cry she went.

Whatever Julia had hoped for in the morning, all that she found was a notice of the departure of the steamer *Imogen* for Manila, and Halford's name among the passengers. Stairs divined that she would be looking for a letter, and was careful to leave the mail untouched until she had handled it. None came. Julia wore through three days in taut expectancy. Every household exigency—the vegetable man at the back porch, the flapping of a curtain in the wind—provided an interval of cover in which a messenger boy might have stepped to the door with a yellow envelope; eating and dressing and sleeping were means of getting through the time between mails; but nothing came.

Whatever Stairs had meant to do, once his wife had come home again he found he had still to reckon with his feeling as a man. He could not bring himself to question her as to her relations with Halford, nor to offer the relief which had been part of his purpose in preventing her elopement. He waited, thankful, man-fashion, for a cessation of active miseries. Julia herself did not know what she should do until she heard from Halford, or until, by not hearing, she had discovered his attitude towards her. She could not think of leaving her husband's house where a message might reach her, nor did she wish to expose the torment of her bosom to her mother's innocuous platitudes, and there was somehow in the familiar furniture of her own house a support to the terrible sense of loss and sinking.

On the third day, unable by any other means to obliterate the dragging afternoon, Julia dressed and went out to the president's house to a meeting of her section of the woman's club. She had it in mind to resign her place on the committee of entertainment, for she was in that state in which the wounded tear at their bandages, and felt any form of opposition or disruption a relief to strained anxiety. The maid let her into the hall, and as she paused an instant before the thick portière of the drawing-room she distinctly heard Mrs. Murry-Felton's high, artificial voice saying, "Why, he positively had to drag her away from the station; and it is my belief—" All Julia's outward sense was so numbed with anguish that the nature of Mrs. Murry-Felton's belief did not get home to her, but the silence that ensued on her lifting up the portière, and the hasty friendliness with which her hostess came forward to cover it, apprised her of a grave discomfiture.

It turned out, as the meeting progressed, that the president of the section had also entertained a belief of some sort in regard to Mrs. Stairs, for she had already asked Miss Radcliffe, of the Mathematics, to serve in Mrs. Stairs's place, though she experienced some embarrassment in giving Julia to understand why she had done so without waiting for her formal notification.

"We understood—I was told—that your mother required your presence so constantly that it might be a relief to you—" the president began.

"My mother is quite well." Mrs. Stairs cut her short. She had had a glimpse of the postman out of the window, and was calculating that if he had a letter from Halford how long it would be before she could get to it. There was no letter when she came home, and it was a long time before she could face about from the growing conviction that there never would be any, and began to take account of the incidents of the afternoon.

She was sitting by the fire after dinner when the meaning of this began to sink in and work a subtle poison in her blood. She sat, biting her full underlip, tapping the carpet with one foot, clinching and unclinching her hands as the poison quickened in her and apprehension grew. Julia understood that she was being "talked about," and she knew what that would mean in a Christian community. She thought she would go and consult Serena as to the state of the community knowledge, when suddenly it flashed into her mind that she had not seen Mrs. Lindley for several days.

"It is strange," she said to her husband, "that Serena has not been here yet. I know that she goes about everywhere by this time."

Stairs was sitting at his desk leaning his head upon his hand; his work was spread out before him, but he was not working. So he might have sat waiting till one came and told him that his wife was dead.

"She was here Monday," he admitted, unguardedly, and then recalled in consternation that he had been told not to confess so much.

"When?" Julia insisted on knowing, and there was nothing to fend behind; his wife had it all out of him, and her wrath was loosed; it seemed the pent-up bitterness of all her married life needed but this one point of contact to discharge upon him. It was all perfectly clear in Julia's mind. Antrim had betrayed her to Mrs. Lindley, and Serena had cast it forth upon the town.

In fact, Mrs. Lindley went out too little to know what was afloat in the way of gossip, and only waited at home to collect a frame of mind in which she could go and meet Julia without making subconscious admissions. She hoped Julia would run in, as she had been doing every day or two since the baby came, but Saturday afternoon arrived, and there had not been a visit exchanged between the two houses.

"It's no use, Vene," Serena said to him. "You will have to go, too. I simply can't face it alone the first time, and if we put it off any longer it will begin to look pointed. Come home early, and let us do it this afternoon."

Accordingly they went about by the front street in the late slant light, over the fallen leaves, Lindley pushing the baby carriage in the most casual manner, loitering past the Stairs's yard. It was the time of year when anybody who owned the smallest scrap of lawn was out raking leaves from it, and they found Stairs so employed. Julia was tying up a rose over the front porch; she looked up as they approached, gave them a stiff little nod, and went on tying. Stairs leaned upon his rake, and Lindley put his elbows on the fence. Serena began to say how well the crysanthemums looked, and Julia, having done with her tying, gathered up her gloves and shears and went into the house. They heard her making obvious noises in the kitchen after a little, but she did not come out again. Stairs reddened slowly, and his remarks about the prospect of early rains lost their cogency. Lindley felt his wife's hand tremble on his arm, and took her away before the tears gathering in her eyes should fall.

"How unhappy she must be," she whispered, "to behave like that! Oh, Evan, isn't there anything we can do to help?"

"I'm afraid not, honey. When things like that can be helped they don't happen."

When they came to their own house again Serena cried upon her husband's shoulder and was comforted. But there was, in fact, no help for Julia Stairs; it was evident now that Halford had accepted her desertion as final, and gone away without a word.

It would seem as if society needed nothing so much as a bureau of unhappy affairs, for though Julia and Antrim Stairs were not able to help themselves, they were not past being helped. Had there been some large and kindly power to accept the responsibility of their separation, to communicate to Halford the purely accidental nature of Julia's defection, their sick and shaken souls might yet have been nursed into something not unlike satisfaction. No such remedy forthcoming, they reached the end very quickly.

Cut off so instantly and hopelessly from Halford's vigorous mastery of the situation, Julia drowned the emptiness of her days in an infinitude of blame. Lacking the solace of affection, she grappled with her husband in resentment, as if the fresh contact of his wound was an ease to hers, and threw herself from wave to wave of hysteric pain for the short purchase of oblivion in bodily exhaustion. Yet in a little time even this failed her, for there is a limit to a man's capacity to react from the stimulus of misery.

It was the tenth day after the frustration of the elopement, and Stairs, who had very little sleep and was still under the necessity of meeting his classes in the usual way, began to exhibit the callousness of profound fatigue. When she perceived she could no longer move him with recriminations, Julia pulled down the props of the house she had betrayed. When she saw him being borne from her by deeps of indifference more impassable than the waste of waters that divided her from her lover, she told him very clearly and without prolixity what that one had been to her and she to him.

It was the last mistake but one that Julia was to make, grown out of that vague hope of women that happiness is somehow to be taken by assault, the instinctive motion by resistance to provoke this man to the mastery of her, that, with all his advantage of being married to her, he had not won. Even then, while the truth leaped from her, swift and stinging like a flight of arrows, if he had come upon her strongly, stopped her mouth, overborne her—she saw instead that he drew himself together injured, astounded, for at last he understood. A kind of cold ecstasy of cruelty sustained her through the devastation of that hour, though she was a little sorry when she saw his face at breakfast and understood what she had done. She was relieved and yet stirred to new

resentments when she observed that he could breakfast, and experienced
a shock when he said, upon the point of leaving:

"I did you a wrong, Julia, when you asked me for your freedom
and I refused you; now you wrong me more by staying. I will make any
provision for you that you wish, in the place where you shall go; only
go, and go quickly."

At noon he left a little heap of money by her plate, and she
understood that it was a provision for her immediate departure. Well,
she would go, since he wished it. He had spoiled her life, and now he
was done with her. He would have stopped her when she had a strong
arm to go to; when she would have gone out of his house to love and
happiness he held her back, and now—but she would go. She did not
know just where. It did not particularly matter; the game was played
out. She would go before another night.

She began a desultory packing that afternoon, but she had
neither the strength nor the mind for it; she sat in the midst of disorder
and brooded on despair. In the process of packing she had pulled her
wedding-dress out of a closet; it lay, a shimmering heap, on the floor;
beside it, folded in a square of silk, were some little things that had been
sent her when it was known among her friends that she had hopes of a
child; as her glance lighted on them it touched the springs of self-pity,
but she had so emptied herself of grief of late that no tears came. She
heard her husband come into the house and go directly to his study, as
though she were already out of the house. Oh, she would go, she would
go at once! She shook out the folds of her wedding-gown, and there fell
from it the crystals of poison in the vial; she had pulled it down with
the dress from the shelf where she had once hidden it. It appealed to her
now as the thing she had always meant to do. She was to go out of her
husband's house and life. Well, here was a way of going that provided
her with the last word, that should dissolve whatever of blame was
directed against her in poignant regret. She desired nothing so much
as to be quit of the whole affair, yet as she poured the crystals into
her palm the possibility they afforded of the vague relief of one more
emotional encounter with her husband intrigued her, and she shook
out half the crystals from her hand before swallowing them. She did not
know much about the nature of the poison except that death by it was
said to be painless; she was glad of that, for she was very tired.

She found her husband sitting at his desk, leaning his head upon his hand. The window behind him was open, and the smell of the late roses, steeped in the afternoon sun, was like a sweet flavor to the winey tang of the autumnal air. The world outside swam in a mist of dreams with the hills behind the town adoze under the checkered pattern of the farms that slipped across their knees.

"Antrim," she said, and the sound of her voice seemed to herself to reach her from far across a void. She saw his shoulders settle at the sound as one who said, "The rack is about to begin again." Then the fear of darkness was upon her, and the love of life woke and cried in her, and with the first pang of the poison the vision of what their life together might have been had she the wit to make it. She sank beside his chair crying terribly upon his name. "Antrim! Antrim! Antrim!" And while he bent to the grayness of her face, almost before she whispered to him the thing she had done, the words broke chokingly, and she died between his knees.

XXVI

Julia's last word had served with Santa Lucia insomuch as it was
the last word; once she had assumed the dignity of death they did
not deny her any of its privileges. Nobody went to the funeral from
pushing curiosity, nor avoided it from despite. Mrs. Murry-Felton sent
flowers. If there was a disposition among the Santa Lucians to felicitate
themselves on the evidence of decent behavior in keeping all but the fact
of the death out of the city papers, there was this regnant sign of their
Westernness, that they did not batten on the dead. They had not been
able to make livable terms with her; but once Julia Stairs was done with,
there was no exhuming either of her faults or her misfortunes.

As for Stairs, the want of readiness in his emotions, which had
kept him lagging out of touch with Julia's leaping passions, gave him
the appearance of supporting her loss with great dignity, and to the
relief of his immediate distress came that curious sense of nearness and
profounder intimacy with the dead which follows soon upon their
taking off, as if in the spiritual clarity after dissolution they smiled back
upon us made all wise and tender.

It came to arrest the corroding last admissions that else had
eaten away the tenderness of his early illusory passion, and before the
reawakened glow had spent itself he had gone clean out of the life of
Santa Lucia. About a month after his wife's death his book was accepted,

and some business of the proofs demanding his presence in the East, he seized upon it as a pretext for breaking off his connection with the college at the end of the fall semester. Two days before Christmas he came in unexpectedly to bid Mrs. Lindley good-bye. She received him in the dining-room, standing before the open fire, for she had been busy in the parlor with young Evan's first Christmas-tree, and shut the door very quickly upon such of her preparations as she feared might remind him of his loneliness and loss; but as she stood there leaning against the low mantel set with holiday branches of scarlet-berried toyon, she was the witness of all he had never had. As he stood looking down at her, mechanically warming his hands at the blaze, and explaining why he had come, his gaze went tenderly from the soft disorder of her hair to the slight matronliness of her figure, the curves of her drooping mouth, and the condoning, steady eyes. And at the thought of parting from her he had a sense of loss as intimate, as personal, as in the violent severing from his wife, for Serena had known how to put life before him fruitfully; and of himself he understood inarticulately only that he was so lean a soul as not even his sorrows could have nourished.

He made a short call, and did not once sit down during it, going on to say that he was leaving the house to be rented as it stood, probably to his successor, but that there were some things of his wife's still there which he wished Mrs. Lindley to collect and send to her mother.

He moved over to the window when he had done enumerating them, and finished with his face averted.

"And if," he said, "there should be any one who knew her well and cared for her, who should ask you for a remembrance of her, I have brought you this." He held a packet towards her, not looking back. "She wore it often. I should like it to go to any one who cared—any one," he repeated, after a slight interval. And it came into Serena's mind that he must mean Halford.

She looked at the packet, and saw that it contained a little turquoise ornament that Julia had owned before her marriage. She thought, then, that perhaps Jim might have given it to her.

"It shall be attended to," she promised.

"And the grave where she … lies …"

"I shall see to that, too," Serena assured him. "I thought only to-day that I should take something from her garden to plant there—"

"If you think she would want it … She did not care much … for … that … sort of thing."

"I am sure she would." Serena's eyes filled. "It would be like a sign to her that … that you only remembered her as she would wish to be remembered."

"The white rose, then, by the east window," consented Stairs. "She often wore it in her hair."

"She was very beautiful," said Serena, simply. She had taken that note with him, falling into the commonplaces of consolation, as if Julia's end had not been otherwise than the natural way of things; and nothing more presenting itself to be said on either side, she gave him both her hands, and said good-bye to him out of the goodness of her heart.

She saw, as he went between the oaks, that he stooped as he walked, and though she could not see very well for the dimness of her eyes, her heart was dry; though she said to herself that she should never see him again, she knew in the moment of saying it that she would not miss him much.

Lindley found her in a mood of springing tears when he came at night—not unhappy, but in want of tenderness.

"I told him good-bye," she said, when she had recounted the incident of the visit, "and he looked so forlorn, Evan, so *unbelonging*, and I was so sorry for him—I—kissed him, Evan. You don't mind, do you?"

"No, of course I don't mind," he said, heartily.

But she thought he did mind, perhaps, for he took her in his arms and kissed her strongly himself.

"Do you know," he said, "I've a notion Stairs was always a little sweet on you? You were the sort for him, the only sort he had the ghost of a chance of understanding. There are men like that who naturally suppose all women the same sort, but with different trimmings; and I've a notion the whole trouble grew out of his trying to make Julia be that sort."

So he had known all along; he had seen that, and gone on being busy about the practice of law and good government and city water-supply, as if they and not the delicate and critical adjustment of personality were the proper concern of men.

"And did you think—" Suddenly a deep red flamed outward from her thought.

"I didn't think you knew ... or that it would have made any difference if you did." He caught her to him, laughing at the quick suffusion, the lovely feminine confusion of her face. "As long as I can make you color like that, I am not afraid of anybody," he said, and she colored yet more deeply at the implication of his embrace.

Evan Lindley went out again, after dinner, with Grenning to see Stairs to his train, as the last office of neighborliness, and after that to the Chamber of Commerce, where the affair of the Encinas water-shed was to come up in a new connection.

It had turned out, after Schweringer's plan became known, that he had found himself confronted with so many conflicting claims that, in view of the local depression of values, he was persuaded to part with all rights and titles at a reasonable figure to the municipality. And as the project gained upon the public mind, it was discovered that credible information in regard to Encinas was to be had from Evan Lindley. When he found himself sought on this business he had hesitated to name it to his wife, listening always for the revival of the whisper of self-interest which the report of his former dealings with Schweringer had waked; but that very punctiliousness of economy forced upon him by his wife's attitude, which he had fretted against as putting him out of touch with his time, was a veil before his earlier slips. In the estimate of Santa Lucia, Lindley was a man who paid down, and knew all about the water-shed of Encinas. As for that college business—well, they had a chance at both Lindley and the land; served 'em good and right for not seeing farther than the end of their noses. Get busy now, and have Lindley appointed on the Board of Public Works. Being so reidentified with the good of the town, Lindley saw Stairs off with no sharper regret than the shamefaced one of not being able to regret it more.

After he left the house, Serena sat in a muse of thought, half sad, but pricked through with intimations of larger understanding. She moved in it, half aware, through the routine of the house: saw the children asleep and the lamp set for Evan's return, and, drawn at last by the association of her brooding thought, stood long at the window staring down at the block of darkness that was the unlit house of Antrim Stairs.

An arm's-length outside the pane the reflection of her lamp on the fogged atmosphere painted her a vanishing picture of Stairs rushing eastward, going fast out of her life. She had never loved him; she knew that, though she had been drawn by his semblance to her young ideal. The surfaces of life set in motion by the slight circumstance of environment had turned towards all he seemed to stand for, but underneath the primal tides drove fast; she saw herself and all women moving on them by the way of colorless, unimpassioned marriages, by fatigues and homely contrivances, by childbirth and sorrow and denial—oh, a common story! She thought of William, upon whom happiness descended from the skies, ushered by wild risks, long thunder, and the drumming rain, and brought on her own face a rain of tears as she knew herself, with so many women, untouched by any color of romance. Then she thought of Julia, flaming with tormenting passions as she drifted to disaster; she threw up the sash, and at the quieting touch of the night and the drifting film of the fog the pang of unfulfilment passed in the sense of saving commonness.

A line of swinging lights ran from the town towards the hills, and drew her thought where she knew her husband's to be—busy with things to be done. She understood at last his wish to be one with the current interest of his time, as the relish for life, the undaunted male attitude which begot great achievement on the West. She felt herself shamed by its largeness forever out of the complicated futility of her moral conventions.

Far down the block she heard the quick, nervous step that announced him, but before she ran to let him in she leaned from the sill to gather a late chilled rose that bloomed hardily on a climbing vine. She kissed it once and threw it far from her; it was her greeting to life and the land. So, smiling, she turned and drew the blind.

The End

About the Author

Mary Hunter Austin is one of the most prolific and eclectic writers of the American West. She was born Mary Hunter in Carlinville, Illinois, in 1868. Her beloved father and younger sister both died while Mary was still young. Mary graduated from Blackburn College in 1888 before her mother moved the family to California because her bother wanted to homestead there. In the west Mary Austin created herself as an author and, after initial success in 1903 with the publication of the *The Land of Little Rain*, became an acclaimed writer. Austin wrote thirty-five books and 250 articles in magazines, both fiction and nonfiction, including short essays, drama, poetry, and novels. She won the Pulitzer Prize for the play *The Arrow Maker*. She alternated between living in New York and Carmel, and she traveled extensively in Italy, England and across the United States. Ultimately, the Southwest attracted Austin, and she moved to Santa Fe and built an adobe home she called "Casa Querida" or "Beloved House." She lived there near other artists and writers until her death in 1934.